The *Dirty* Divorce Part 4

A novel by

MISS KP

Life Changing Books in conjunction with Power Play Media
Published by Life Changing Books
P.O. Box 423 Brandywine, MD 20613

Library of Congress Cataloging-in-Publication Data;

www.lifechangingbooks.net
13 Digit: 9781934230626
10 Digit: 1934230626

Dedication

You mean more to me than you know-Kameron, Mateo, Lil Rodney, Jordan, Sydni, Javone, Ashley, and Wynter.

Acknowledgements

First I would like to thank God for not only this opportunity, but giving me this gift to share my crazy imagination with the world. I am thankful for having a devoted husband, Rodney, amazing children, Kameron, Mateo, Jordan, and Lil Rodney, thank you for your patience through this process and putting up with my mood swings LOL. Love you guys dearly. Khaleel, Ashley and Wynter, you guys hold a special place in my heart. I love you!

Many thanks to my supportive family, my mother Lita Gray (EB) I love you so much! Daddy I love you! To my sisters, Jawaun (Jai), Mia (Brent/ Sydni), and my brothers Cornell and Harold (Helen), thanks for putting up with me. Books and Babes and all my cousins, love you! Mema, Pop-Pop, Eve, and Jaron love you! To my West and Thomas Family, love you.

To my friends that support me through it all, Pam (Gill/Demi), Toyia, Tiffany, Toni, Shana, Peta Gaye, Sharawn, Shelrese, Jermaine, DK, April, Kiana, Deon, Ranata, Latrese, Letitia, Darb, Rob, Detrick, Renee, thanks for putting up with me. Much love to my Mt Pleasant, 1-4, and 640 fam. Love you Joy, Karla, Ro, Matt, Kara, Sue, Kelly, Raquel, Neil, and Curtis, you guys are special…hashtag…you know the rest!

To the promoters that hold me down, Eric Taylor (EVIPlist), Mike Walker (Pure Lounge), Dominique Moxcey (Jetsetdc.com), Terrance Brooks and Lonye Nicole, Frank, Taz,and Arlene (Suite 202), Big Akil, Big Troy Miller, Suave (NYC), Troy, Tarik Wallace, and Dorian (Philly).

Marcus H, Maurice K., KRB, Musa, Gerald Thompkins, John (Whitey), Lorenzo, Salah Benson, Tuffy; I'm wishing you the best during these hard times.

To my three muskateers, Tam, Leslie (Bean), and Tressa. I could never verbally explain how much your friendships mean to me. I love you guys so much and appreciate your support!

Eyonne, Kwan, T.Styles, Nikki Turner, and JM Benjamin; thank you for welcoming me into this business with open arms. Ella Curry thanks for being a great partner. You are greatly appreciated.

To my LCB family I love you all, but I would like to give a special shout out to Kendall Banks, Nicole Cannon, C Flores, Chris Renee, and Winter Ramos; best of luck on your new projects and thanks for supporting me. Azarel, now I go in business mode lol…Thanks for being the best publisher and mentor a girl could ask for. Tonya Ridley and Tiphani Montgomery, my road dogs for life, luv you! Many thanks to my support team; Aschandria,Virginia and Necole. Kelli, you know that book cover is fire! Muah!

To my readers, I appreciate you so much and thanks for supporting me. You asked for it, so here it is-Dirty Divorce PT 4. Fasten your seatbelts Dirty Divorce Lovers for more Sanchez chaos. And now the drama continues…

Much luv and hugz, Miss KP
Instagram @therealmisskp
Facebook/Twitter @misskpdc @lcbooks

Chapter 1
Juan

"Juan, what time are you coming?" Peaches asked in a low seductive tone.

"Man, I'll be there when I get there. You know I can't spend the night though," I said, thinking back to the last time I fell asleep over Peaches' house. My girl went postal on me. These days I needed to keep the peace in my household.

"Boy, please. I just want you to break me off, give me some stacks, and then you can go home to your bamma ass girl."

"Watch your trap, Peaches. Anyway, I just put 10 g's in your account not even a month ago. What the fuck do you think I am? A bank?"

"So what? It costs to be the side bitch. Anywho, can you bring me some pills?" she asked, sounding geeked out as usual.

"Yeah man. See you in a lil' bit."

I dismissed her quickly, wanting to get off the phone, and then shook my head. I figured that trick was addicted to E-pills and Molly now. Peaches knew I kept a stash just for her. Her head game was sick, especially when she was on that shit. I couldn't wait to be in the back of her throat.

"Juan, don't play. I've been a good girl, waiting just for you, Big Daddy. You know I miss you so much. Shit, I can feel your dick on my tonsils through the phone."

"Girl, you trippin'." I laughed.

"I'll be waiting, wet and all."

After hanging up the phone, I looked at my Hublot black diamond watch and was pleased. It was just past midnight and I was finally done for the night. Today had been a good day. Life was treating me real good, so good, that I was thinkin' about coppin' me that private plane I looked at last week. It was a whopping two mil, but I didn't give a fuck. That kind of money meant nothing to me.

The cash I'd made in the last few months was definitely an indication that things would only get bigger, and better. It felt like the first of the month. For it to be the middle of November, business was pumpin'. It didn't hurt that I had the best supply in the Mid-Atlantic region. My coke was the new blue magic. Thanks to me comin' across my 'supposed to be aunt', Marisol's stash house, it was my come up. Who would've ever thought I'd be bigger than Marisol or Rich had been. Maybe it was meant to be. I definitely wouldn't be a millionaire still down South. My sister Denie's bullshit with her dudes in Florida landed us back in the DMV, but I'm a strong believer that everything happens for a reason.

Gettin' off of I-495 onto the Branch Avenue exit, I was ready to drop off the work I'd left at the stash spot out Clinton, Maryland. There was no way I was riding dirty, with cocaine on me in Potomac, my white neighborhood, so I was gonna make sure to get that shit out of my car.

I had a meeting with my father's old friend, Grady, but he never showed, so I figured I'd drop the dope off. Grady owed me money anyway, so it was a good thing that I didn't see him. The nigga turned into a charity case. Dude used to be paid, but ever since Marisol died, he'd fallen off. Without Rich and Marisol, Grady had no connect for gettin' major paper. That was the reason he got a pass. As of late, it felt as though he had started to take my kindness for weakness. Shit, I even bought the nigga a house, paid for it straight cash, three hundred thousand, since his last spot went into foreclosure. I mean damn, how much more did the nigga expect? I told myself this was gonna be his last favor. Tryin' to call his phone again before I pulled up to the house, he still didn't answer. Too bad. No more Mister Nice Guy, I thought to myself as I made the last left to the stash house.

Most of the time, I came to the house after midnight to keep the nosey neighbors out of my business. The neighborhood was middle-class, mostly black families, and was very quiet. Usually there was no one out unless it was daytime. Now I see why Marisol had this house to begin with. It was out of the way and now *my* best-kept secret. Turnin' down Piscataway Drive, I drove towards the brick, single family home. As soon as the house came into view, I pumped my brakes. I had to make sure it was my house where the activity was taking place.

All of a sudden, a black mid-size car came screeching out of my driveway in a hurry. It backed up so swiftly I barely got a good look at the driver. It looked like a woman, but I couldn't even make out a face before the car whizzed right past me. I thought about whipping my shit around and going after it, but decided against it when I looked back at my house. My heart sunk as soon as I saw that the door was partially open.

Crazy thoughts invaded my mind as I slowly pulled in the driveway, noticing the light was on.

What the fuck? Who the hell had just left my house? Was someone still inside? I asked myself. No one knew about this spot. Not even my business partner, Julio. So I could've been the only person to fuck up and leave the door open. Then my mind switched gears.

"Hell no," I shouted out loud. This spot was what got me on top of the game so I couldn't have been that careless to risk losing all my fortune, by forgettin' to lock the door. A part of me grew too nervous so I backed out of the driveway quickly with my lights off, and pulled the car down the block a bit. Gettin' out of the car with my 9mm at my waist, I crept up to the left side of the house quietly. It was really dark out so all I had was the moonlight to help guide me. My instinct told me to go through the back, just in case someone was still in there, so I trusted that was the best idea. Pullin' my gun from my waist, I cocked it back, just in case I needed it.

Suddenly, the back door swung open causing me to freeze. I could see someone well over six feet tall stacking two, black suitcases on the back porch. It was hard for me to make out who it was so as soon as he went back in the house, I hurried into position on the blind side of the door ready for war. Just as the tall figure came back out with another suitcase, I cocked my hand back and hit him in the back of the head as hard as I could with my gun. Instantly, he fell to the ground.

"Nigga, turn the fuck around," I barked with authority as I watched the black-hooded guy lay still. Waiting for any movement, I stepped back slightly, ready to blast off. He seemed to be knocked out cold but I wasn't takin' any chances. I kicked at his body a few times, until I knew for sure he was out. Although it was a struggle, I decided to drag his body back into the house as fast as I could. I wasn't tryna wake up any neighbors and bring heat to my spot. If the police got a whiff of my stash house, and all the drugs I kept inside, I was goin' away for life.

As soon as I made it in the house, I turned over the body on the kitchen floor. I couldn't believe what lay before me. My heart sunk to my knees.

"Grady? How could you?" I said to myself in shock. All I did for this nigga and he was tryna rob me? As I stood over him with my gun aimed at his chest, he finally came to. I cocked my gun back, and stared him in the eye. I made sure my silencer was in tact.

"What the fuck are you doin' Grady?" I asked as I pointed my gun, ready to pop his head off his body.

"Tryna come up, fuck you think?"

"Who the hell just pulled off?"

"I work alone shawty," he said sarcastically as he rubbed the back of his head.

The more Grady talked the angrier I became. "Nigga, all the shit I've done for your punk ass and you gonna try and rob me. Nigga, I bought your fuckin' wife and kids a house, and you do me like this? You betta tell me who you workin' wit' before I bust yo' ass."

I lunged and smacked Grady across his face with my pistol. Instantly, blood gushed from his nose and mouth and splattered across my fresh butter Tims. That took me to the next level. My Superman syndrome was back. My chest inflated then deflated over and over again.

"Nigga, you got your blood all on my boots! I should kill you for that alone!"

"You a tough guy now, huh? You think you the shit, wit' all your diamonds and fast cars. You think the Porsche, the Maserati, the Escalade, the Audi, makes you invincible. You a mark, Lil Shawty. You made it easy. I've been peelin' from your stash for a year, and your faggot ass didn't even notice," he instigated, with a sarcastic laugh.

I knew I wasn't supposed to care at all, but Grady's betrayal hurt. The fact that he'd been stealing from me and I really didn't know meant I needed to step my business skills up.

Man, I should kill yo' ass. Grady, you got one more time to answer me. Who was here with you?" I asked as I lifted my gun for a better aim. He should've known from my tone I wasn't fuckin' around.

"My damn self, nigga. Who else would I need to rob your punk ass? Man, you made it easy for me. Who the fuck would use their dead daddy's birth date as their alarm code?" He laughed again then licked the blood from his lips.

Even though Grady wasn't on my level, his laugh did something to my insides. It bothered me more than I should've allowed. But I needed answers. Glancin' over at the bundles of money over on the floor, my heart stopped. I always kept my money bundled in thousands. Looking on the floor, I counted 16 g's scattered across the hardwood.

"Grady, why my money all over the floor? Where's the rest of it?"

"I don't know, Mister Sanchez," he laughed, trying to throw salt to my injury.

I knew what he was thinking. He thought I would keep him alive to get answers. He was wrong. He had to go. Keeping my gun on Grady, I walked backwards over to the painting in the hallway. The huge painting of Marisol hid my safe. Just like I thought, it was open. Skimmin' through, there was at least 30 g's missin'. I was pissed. Closing the safe back, I walked back over to Grady and kicked him straight in his mouth.

"What the fuck, man!" Grady yelled as he held his bloody mouth.

I knew I'd knocked a couple of teeth loose.

"How you know about this place, Grady? Huh? Who put you on to me and who got the rest of my money?"

"Juan, you'd be surprised about who wants to get a piece of your action. Lil' shawty, you'd really be surprised. Real OG's built this street business up. Now you youngins think y'all gonna eat meals, while we nibble on crumbs? I've been in this joint a couple of times. So thirty grand may be gone this time, but trust and believe I've been eating."

"Fuck you, Grady!" I kicked him in the side with more force than I knew I had. He still continued to talk shit though.

"I used to fuck Marisol all up and down this joint in the good ole days. When shit was real good." After seeing the shocking look in my eyes, he continued. "That's right, your Uncle Carlos never knew I was banging that whore. Your Auntie Marisol's daughter, Carmen, probably mine. Haha, my mama keep saying she look just like me. Anyway, outta all the spots you own, why yo' dumb ass keep yo' shit here. You made it so easy."

Grady fell into a wild snorting sorta laugh thinking his jokes were getting to me until I fired the first shot right in his knee. Something told me his ass was lying.

"Aigghhh, you shot me!" he groaned loudly. "You wanna be yo daddy so bad. Lil' homie, you ain't ever gonna be Rich!" he belted, grabbing his leg. "As much as I hated that nigga, he was real. You knew what you was gettin' wit' him. You, lil' homie, you a wanna-be…" he said, as he squirmed on the floor.

Before he could say another word, I shot him again, this time in his stomach. Grady had found a way to get me where it hurt.

"D-a-m-n, aigghhhhhh s-h-i-t. Fuckkkkkkk!" he squealed. Barely able to talk, he managed to get out his last words, "See shawty that's the difference between y-o-u and y-o-u-r p-o-p-s." He breathed heavily before gaining the strength to talk halfway normal again. "If I had taken anything from Rich, he wouldn't be doin' all this talkin' like your punk ass."

Grady spit blood from his mouth.

"You know what, Grady? You right," I agreed as I stood over him and released two bullets straight into his head.

"I guess I'm more like my father than you thought, huh?" I whispered as I watched Grady's brains ooze from his head. Saliva started to fill my mouth. Suddenly, I started sweating like a pig. I got dizzy and in an instant a migraine filled my head. The sight of Grady's brain matter had me disgusted. I couldn't believe I'd blasted my father's good friend. I decided to deal with Grady's body later. Quickly, I grabbed the first blanket I saw from the closet in the living room and wrapped his body up.

I rushed out to my car and brought the shit I'd been riding with back into the house. Then I grabbed the coke Grady had moved to the back porch into the house, too. I gathered all the drugs and all of my money, and headed down to the basement. My adrenaline pumped like crazy just thinking about all that had taken place. There was no way I'd allow myself to be robbed again in my own spot. There was a wine cellar behind the wall that I was certain no one knew about. I had it built just to hold my new shit that would be coming in soon, so even if someone came by thinking about a repeat, they'd find nothing. Of course I changed the alarm code.

After I locked up the house, watching my back, I ran to my Porsche in a panic. Gettin' in my car, watching my back, I drove away frantically, gettin' the hell outta Clinton. I made my way to the beltway and hit Baltimore Washington Parkway. My mind was in disbelief. I couldn't believe I killed Grady. He watched me grow up. He was supposed to be cool with my father and was betrayin' me right under my nose. Times like this I wish I could call Rich and he'd come to the rescue. While I missed my dad daily, I was now responsible for killin' somebody else's father.

"Trust no man," my father's voice rang through my head.

Once again, Rich was right. No need to feel remorse, I tried to convince myself. Grady was a snake and had to go, but whom he was workin' with was the bigger problem. Somebody was still out there, after me, lurkin'.

I had to get at them before they could get me.

Chapter 2
Juan

My music blasted while my Pirelli tires hit the pavement at 120 mph. I grabbed my phone, knowing I needed someone with a level head to calm me down. That person was my man, Julio. He was the only real friend I had. Rich had taught me not to trust anyone, but Julio was that dude. We met through Star, a dude I used to do business with from Cali. Once Star got killed last year, Julio and me linked up and took over the East Coast.

Originally from Cali, he moved to Philly last year, allowing us to explode in the streets. We'd even been on a couple trips together out of the country. I even spent Thanksgiving with him last year over his chick's house in Philly. Julio was my main man, so he needed to know what was going on, just in case somebody tried to get at him, too.

"Yo, Julio," I roared as soon as he picked up. "Mannnnnnn, somebody tried to rob one of my spots!"

"My nigga, stop playin'. How bad is it?"

I knew I couldn't tell him what I wanted to over the phone, so I sighed before speaking. "I'll fill you in when I see you. But it's bad."

"Man, be safe down there. I'll tie up some loose ends here in Philly, then I'll be down there in the next couple of days."

"A'ight."

Turning up my music, I hoped the words to the song would drown away my guilt.

The motivation for me is them tellin' me what I could not be, oh well…

Every time Jay Z's song, "So Ambitious", blasted through the Burmester speakers of my Panamera Porsche, I thought about Rich. What would he have done with this whole Grady situation? I thought to myself. Who the fuck was fucking with my shit? I wished like crazy Rich was alive to help me through the bullshit. Pushin' the pedal to the metal, I slowed down just a bit. No other cars roamed the BW Parkway, so my chances of gettin' pulled over increased.

Instantly my mind drifted off to another place as I thought about my father even more. Shit, anytime I heard some old school Jay-Z or Biggie, I reminisced and wondered how my life would've been if I had just stayed in Rich's shadow, and just let him lead. Me as lieutenant would've been a lot easier. Being captain came with a high price tag. The bread is all good, but constantly watching your back, and not knowing who was really on your team, wrecked my nerves.

'The streets is always watching,' was the motto my father lived by. Who would've ever thought that I would've missed Rich as much as I did? It had been three years since he'd passed and it felt like just yesterday. Was it normal to miss arguing with my self-absorbed father? Damn, I even missed the adrenaline I got proving Mr. Know-It-All wrong. If I could've just talked to him one last time before he died, just to let him know that I really did love him. It would've made me feel so much better. I turned the corner thinking, Rich would be proud of me right now.

Being on top had always been my plan. Finally, I was here. Laundering my bread through different investments like clubs, rental properties, and Denie's new boutique, they all seemed to work out. Things were lookin' good. The only downfall, I wasn't building my credit. I paid cash for everything. Soon, I hoped to build some credit, and make things on the business end right. Then I could leave the streets alone, this time for good.

I was here, but being on top was scary and lonely. Hell, this was nothing like I thought it was gonna be, but fuck it. I'm here now and I'm a fuckin' Sanchez, hoping my father was lookin' down on me saying, 'That's my boy'.

I knew he had to be proud of me. Taking out Marisol for killing him still keeps me up sometimes, but I did it for Rich and for my mother. That whore ruined our family. She left Denie on our doorstep never giving us a fighting chance at being normal. I ain't no killer for real, but that lion was in me. What she did to me and my family was unforgiveable. She was the one who insisted on me going to Cali, and no matter how she pleaded, I knew that bitch set me up with Uncle Renzo, causing me to be sodomized. That's why no guilt existed when I killed her. Now she was six feet deep where she belonged.

The more I thought about it, I felt me and Rich could've taken over the world together if Marisol hadn't fucked us all. We could've been just like him and my Uncle Los was before everything went wrong. Breaking me from my deep thought my phone started ringing again.

"What, girl!" I yelled, irritated that Peaches had called me back.

"Juan, when the fuck you plan on getting over here? My pink panther is dripping wet and I need to feel that big muscle all up in it!"

"Peaches, I told you I'd be there. I'm like fifteen minutes away. I'mma give you this pole, be patient," I said, as I turned off the parkway onto her exit. Before I could hang up on her ass she kept going in.

"Well, I wanted to make sure your ass wasn't bullshittin' like you did last night. You know my baby daddy in town. Hell, I could've gave him some for all that!" Peaches said, being extra, popping those juicy ass lips of hers.

No lie, I couldn't wait to have her lips wrapped around my piece like a blow pop. I had a lot of tension I needed to release.

"Man, I told you my girl was trippin' the other night. You knew what you signed up for when I started fuckin' you. I can't have a whinin' ass side chick. That shit won't work. See you in a minute."

I hung up on her freaky ass, thinking, damn, I had become more like Rich than I wanted to admit. I was a sucker for a phat ass. In the hood, Peaches was a dime. She was that chick that every dude around the way wanted to hit, but knew if their money wasn't right, they would barely get a hello. That red bone had a long, blonde weave that fell to the crack of her ass, with a set of double D's her baby daddy, Slicc, bought her when he got his record deal.

Peaches was hood rich. And being the top stripper at Norma Jean's, she stayed kept. She drove a Cayenne Porsche truck and always rocked the latest bags and shoes. Some of her come up was because of me and all the bread I tossed her way but she was definitely a grinder. A bad bitch to some, but to me, she was just a fuck. There was no way I'd wife a bitch like her. Being a man, I'd slipped up a couple of times to feel that wet, warm pocket. But she would never be more than a trick that got hit from time to time, especially when I wanted adventure in the bedroom, which was one area my girlfriend Mecca lacked in.

When I pulled up to Peaches' townhouse, I parked in the driveway like I owned the place. The light was on in the living room, which meant her badass kids were still up. Them bastards made me sick. Why the hell they were up this time of night didn't make any sense. She birthed three ratchet motherfuckers. A grown ass eight year-old girl and a set of thirteen-year-old twin boys. One acted like a faggot sashaying around playing in heels, while the other one was a fake thug. His wanna-be thug ass was always mean muggin' on me and shit when I came around.

I banged on the door loudly like the police was out front.

"Who the fuck is at the door?" Peaches' son, Lil' Man yelled.

"It ain't your punk ass Daddy," I shouted, just to push his buttons.

"Ma, come open the door for your own damn company!"

"Lil' Man, open the damn door!" I heard Peaches yell.

I could hear the door unlock and that was it. As soon as I pushed the door open, the little nigga started muggin' like he was tough, looking just like his ugly, black-ass father. Her other son, JR, was my instant entertainment. He was in front of the TV with some ruffled socks on and high heels dancing hard as shit to 'Twerk It' by Busta Rhymes and Nicki Minaj. I couldn't help but to burst out laughin'.

"Juan, what you mad cuz you can't twerk like me?" he asked, sounding like a lil' bitch. His hot red mohawk made him even funnier to me.

"Naw homie, do your thang. Gangstas don't twerk, we get money," I said as I pulled out a stack of twenties bounded by a rubber band and threw it at him.

"And gangstas from the Eastside take niggas from D.C. money," Lil' Man chimed in.

He got up, grabbed the stack from the floor, and threw the wad of cash back at me.

"We don't need your short stack. My fatha' taking good care of us. Believe that."

"Boy-Boy," I began with bass in my voice. "Let me tell your punk ass something. If you had any sense you would sit back and learn some shit, instead of…"

"Juan, what's taking you so long to come upstairs?" Peaches interrupted.

I mean mugged the fake gangsta and started walking toward the steps. "We'll finish this conversation at a later date. I need to handle some business upstairs, partner. Mama needs this gangsta to come help her fix a couple of things in her bedroom," I said, continuin' to get under his skin.

"Bitch ass nigga," he mumbled under his breath.

"Ha, ha! Peaches, you ready for me baby!" I said, runnin' up the steps.

Before Peaches could answer, my cell went off. It was Mecca again but of course I didn't answer, Peaches' pussy was waiting. When I made it to the bedroom, candles had been lit all over the place. One thing I could say about Peaches, she kept her house in order. She had an obsession with anything pink. The whole house was decorated with damn near every shade. Maybe that's why JR was so damn fruity.

"Candles, really? Tryin' to burn the house down?" I laughed at her romantic efforts. There was no need for romance. I was tryna bang. I wasted no time with more words. I began unbuckling my belt.

"No, I'm tryin' to make you want this every morning and every night. You know I'm betta than your girl. She can't give it to you like me. Just admit it."

"Peaches, stop runnin' your mouth before I put something in it."

"Admit it. What's her name, Mecca?" she asked, walking closer to me. "You know her bougie ass ain't rocking you like I do."

"Hey trick, don't speak her name." My facial expression tightened and frowned into a knot. "Man, I'm 'bout to roll," I snapped, while bucklin' my Gucci belt back up. I had no time for BS.

"Boy, bring your fine ass over here, with that fuckin' wavy ass head of yours. You know I like making you mad so you can fuck me hard and stuff. Anyway, where my pills at?" she asked, rubbing her hands slowly between her legs.

I pulled a bag from my back pocket and tossed it to her. Like a lion ripping into its prey, she ripped open the small plastic baggie, then threw the pills to the back of her mouth, geeked out.

"Want one?" She laughed wildly.

"Hell no. You know I don't do that shit. Don't ever disrespect me again like that. I don't put that poison in my body!" I said, instantly thinkin' back to my mother, Lisa.

"But you can sell poison, huh?" She laughed even more, then continued, "Well, I already popped mine and I want you bad as shit, so let's go."

That drug shit wasn't my thing after I watched it destroy my mother, but if it made Peaches sex me better, so be it. She wasn't my main chick. Anyway, how could I resist her with that sexy ass lace, pink bodysuit she was wearing? All of a sudden, Ciara's song 'Body Party' came on and it was time for me to pull out my cash.

As I sat back in the hot pink, chaise lounge in her room, Peaches gyrated to the music. Suddenly my man was at attention. Mecca kept calling my phone so I had to dead that and turn it off. There was nothing stopping me from getting inside this freak chick. As I watched her sing and move slowly to the music she rubbed her silver nails up and down her curvy, thick thighs. Instantly, I unbuckled my pants and took my pulsating man out. Finally, her big melons released from her bodysuit and sprung open as if they were waiting just for me.

The next thing I knew she'd sprawled her body across the floor and maneuvered the bodysuit off. Finally, she was completely naked and was on all fours, ass high in the air. As soon as I heard 'Bust it Open' blast through her Bose system, I knew it was money time. She was ready to earn this stack. Watching that phat ass jiggle and vibrate made me horny as shit.

"You like that?" she asked, lookin' back at me as I watched her silver nails play peek-a-boo, going in and out of her wetness. The hell with makin' it rain, I made it hurricane on that ass. Money was flying everywhere.

"That's what I'm talkin' bout, Juan Sanchez. Pop them bands on this ass baby!"

Poppin' bands was nothing, especially for a chick like Peaches who knew how to put it down. Don't get me wrong, Mecca was my first priority, but being a millionaire made it easy to throw a couple of g's out. I'd thrown at least two grand out to Peaches after five minutes of dancing.

After Peaches teased me a bit longer, I could no longer take it…out came the Magnum.

"Damn Juan, bring that fine ass over here and put that colossal wood up in me. Why you putting that on?" Peaches asked, pouting, still rubbing herself, laying back on the bed.

"Because you probably still lettin' Slice hit it. Ain't no tellin' where that fake, wanna-be rapper's shit been." I walked right up to the bed and took all my shit off. Ass naked, I stood confidently while my man grew rapidly.

"I told you before, you the only dude I been with in a long time. Anyway, why is it a problem now when you just fucked me raw last month? It's so much better like that Juan. Pleaseeee…" she begged.

That shit sounded tempting, but I knew better. I stood my ground as I continued to open the wrapper. No matter how that shit was nice and wet without the condom, I couldn't keep disrespecting Mecca like that. Before I could put the condom on, Peaches was already on her knees with my piece in her mouth damn near swallowin' all nine inches.

"Peaches, damn that shit feel good."

"You like it, baby? Cum in my mouth, Juan. I want to drink all your babies."

The shit felt so good, I couldn't even respond. "Aaaaaaaaahhhhhh," was all I could moan. As she slurped up and down on my dick and moved her hand up and down my shaft, I thought I'd died and became king. Peaches had my dick in a zone. Just when I was about to nut she stopped.

"How bad you wanna cum, Juan? Huh?" she teased.

The bitch kept lookin' at me with those chinky eyes that made me weak. "I wanna cum bad," I told her unassertively.

"Well, put that dick in this pussy. Don't you wanna feel it?"

"Hell yeah, I wanna feel it."

As she took my hand and rubbed it around the circumference of her wetness, I had to get in it. She had me by the balls and I wanted her bad. Finally, and it was on. I hopped on the bed, flat on my back.

"You want me to sit on it?" she teased.

"Yeah, sit on this dick. Sit on it, Peaches."

I watched her slowly straddle me, then strategically place my pole inside of her, squeezing the lips of her pussy around my dick. Peaches started grindin', forcefully bouncing up and down on my dick and balls. She started making some wild, outrageous sound that I couldn't make out. Then the oooohs and aaaaahhhhhs followed.

"Damn, you got some good dick, Juan!"

I lifted my body and held on to her whirling hips, thrusting into her as hard as I could. I thought I'd died and gone to heaven. Her shit felt so good, I'd forgotten about my guilt of not puttin'on a condom.

"Am I better?" she moaned as I watched her double D's bounce up and down as she rode my dick like a prize bull rider at a rodeo.

"Yeah, Peaches, yeah. You better," I muttered with my eyes damn near rolling up in my head.

"Tell me, Juan. Tell me I make love to you better than Mecca."

"You better Peaches, way better."

"That's right, big daddy."

Mind over matter. Trying to control my nut was an art, and I was good at it. I felt the blood rushing to my dick but I wasn't ready to explode. I needed some head to change it up so I wouldn't bust.

"Peaches, suck it for me."

Just like a pro, she hopped off of me and started wrapping those juicy lips around my dick. Fuckin' was easy for me but for some reason after being sodomized, thanks to my Uncle Renzo, lovemaking was hard. That's probably what kept me cheating with hoes like Peaches all the time. Even though it had been a couple of years it was still a struggle.

The music was on point as she sucked me off until that Twerk song came on and all I could think of was that little faggot ass son of hers and his ruffled bobby socks dancin'. My man instantly went soft.

"What's wrong, Juan? You don't want me?" Peaches asked, looking up at me as she slurped my shit like a slurpee from the 7-Eleven. Nothing she could do at this point aroused me.

"Hold up, I know what will do the trick. Lay back," she said, hopping up. She headed to her freak drawer. That trick had all types of lotions and freak shit up in that chest.

"Just lay back and relax," she instructed, massaging my six-pack.

"Turn that fuckin' song off, man!" I yelled. My mood was blown.

She did as she was told and put on some old school R. Kelly.

"What you know about that youngsta?" Peaches asked, while grinning. Her tits were standing at attention.

"Your freak ass only got me by a few years, Peaches. You only 27? We know your ass started fuckin' early."

"So what? It made me into the good pussy chick I am today. As long as these skills get me coins, I'm good. Now lay back while I show you how real bitches take care of their man."

'Bump N' Grind' blazed through her speakers as I reared back and tried to focus. I needed to bust bad. As Peaches put my legs up so she could get the right angle, my balls were in her mouth. She sucked and gargled them like they were covered in Listerine. Peaches jerked and slurped on my dick until we were back in business.

"Alright get back on top. Ride it from the back!" I told her frantically.

She got back on top and started poppin' that ass on me, so I thrust into her, viciously. We went hard. My dick rapidly pounded her insides until, I accidentally bust all in her.

"Get up bitch! Get up!" I shouted, scurrying across the bed.

I pushed her ass off me, but she lunged back on me like a lion, sucking the rest of the cum out my dick like a flavored milkshake. Even with my resistance, she still didn't stop. I turned on my side and let her do what she do. All of a sudden, I felt a hard thrush. Something was tryna penetrate my ass.

I jumped up! "Bitch, what the fuck are you doin'!"

I realized Peaches had some of her sex toys nearby.

"It's just a dildo. You ain't stopping me. You must like it," she said with a devious look in her eyes.

Instantly, I blacked out and slapped the shit out of her. As her body flew off the bed to the floor something came over me. I flashed back to that night in California when Uncle Renzo's partner Pablo violated me. He took my ass. No longer was she Peaches, she was Pablo as I punched her in her face again and again. It was like I was looking at Pablo. He took my ass under Uncle Renzo's orders and I vowed it would never happen again.

"Stop it, Juan! Stop it!"

I couldn't stop beating her.

"What the fuck are you doing! Get the fuck off of me," she wailed.

Her screams were a non-factor as blood flew all across her pink sheets. As she grabbed my face and dug her nails in my eyes to try and stop me the door to her bedroom flew open.

Nothing could stop me from beatin' the shit out of that hoe but a round of bullets.

Blop! Blop! Blop! Shots rang out as I dove on the floor.

Chapter 3
Denie

It felt good to be down to just one pill a day, I thought to myself as I threw my Reyataz pill to the back of my throat, and washed it down with some freshly squeezed orange juice. Even though I was HIV positive, I didn't let my disease get the best of me. I was still a bad bitch. As I glanced in the eight-foot gold, foiled mirror, I looked myself up and down, instantly impressed. My gold Herve Leger dress hugged my curves in all the right places. Going for a more sophisticated look, my hair was in a high messy bun for the day. I was being interviewed by one of the top bloggers on the East Coast later in the day, so everything had to be perfect. The countdown was approaching to the grand opening of *Rich Threadz*, my new boutique that Juan made possible for me.

Rich Threadz was a queen's palace and any relevant chick in the DMV was gonna break down the doors to shop here. The dé cor was reminiscent of royalty with rich, black velvet and gold trimmings. Black chandeliers hung from the ceilings as the best of the best threads filled the boutique. There was only high end pricing. My target customer was the girl who made major moves, or had a dude with long paper. All of my employees had to be dressed to the nines, so I supplied them all with clothing allowances even though the store hadn't opened yet. They had to be beat, but not more than me, of course. So far, I'd hired two college girls from Howard, Kiara and Linda, as well as a gay guy named Chaz who I adored. He had style and class and was gonna make me a lot of coins. We were all working around the clock to prepare for the upcoming grand opening.

"I'm done," Milton said, extending his head around the corner. Even though my maintenance guy invaded my privacy without knocking, I couldn't get upset. He'd made my place into a palace, fit for a queen.

"Thanks Milton, eight thousand, right?" I confirmed, as I pulled two stacks from my custom two-toned Celine bag.

"That'll do it, pretty lady."

Milton's old ass grinned from ear to ear, eyeing my twenty-six inch waist and thirty-four inch hips. I gave him the evil eye but decided not to blast him because he'd installed all the new light fixtures, and my camera system for the boutique. Usually I dealt with street dudes to get work done, since Juan always gave me large amounts of cash. But I didn't need the feds all up in my business, so I hired Milton, a licensed contractor. I had so much sneaky shit brewing there was no telling whom I could trust.

"Call me if you need anything else," he told me, as I led him to the door, locking it when he left.

That pervert had a look that told me he might double back for some unauthorized ass. Sashaying back through my new palace, my cell phone rang from a blocked number.

"Hello," I answered through my Bluetooth, hoping it was my boo.

"What's up, babe? Ducking my calls, huh?"

"Allen, what do you want? I'm kinda busy right now," I said, annoyed that I even answered the phone.

"I miss you. You know you got the juiciest shit I ever felt. How you gonna hold back on me like that? I ain't had that good stuff in over a year," he said in a low tone attempting to whisper.

"Excuse me. I didn't hear what you said. Speak up a little so I can hear you," I said sarcastically. I wanted his chick to hear him.

"When you gonna let me come up there and show you what you been missing?"

"Allen, how's your money flow? Because, last time I checked you was on the injured list on MLB.com. By the way, I heard the Marlins were thinking about cutting you. Something about you and your personal trainer getting busted for steroids," I said chuckling. "Is it true? Because if so, you know there's nothing you can do for me. No money, no honey."

"Oh, it's like that?" he asked, sounding like he was in his feelings.

I knew I'd hit a nerve. Maybe he'd stop calling if I kept the conversation going in that direction. Just when I was about to go in on him, I could hear a female in the background.

"It's just Denie," he told her as if he wasn't just trying to make his way to D.C., to get some of my good loving.

"Boy, give me the phone. Hello." Cheri's squeaky, proper voice came through my Bluetooth.

"Hey girl," I said, playing it off.

"What's up, trick? Long time no hear from! You done moved back to D.C. and forgot about your girl. I see how you do," Cheri said all hyped up.

"What's up, boo? I'm at my boutique getting ready for my grand opening in a couple of months."

"How's it going?" Cheri asked.

"Girl, it's upscale and fly as shit. I'm so happy that it's all coming together. You know me, I keep a couple of side hustles. It's all good."

"I know your little sister, Carmen, is happy that you moved back to D.C.. How old is she now?"

"She's almost nine years old. Look, I'm not gonna lie, Carmen is such a cute little girl, hair to her ass, deep dimples, caramel complexion…"

"Sounds like she looks like you."

"Yeah right, anyway, I just can't fuck with her. Even though she's my sister, she reminds me of her mother, Marisol, my egg donor." After all these years I still couldn't get over the fact that Rich and Marisol were my real parents. Both were dead and gone leaving me with Juan's bitch ass. I blacked out for a minute until Cheri's voice brought me back.

"Denie, you can't be like that. You're all she has."

"She got Maria, my nanny. I didn't sign up for this shit. I got a child of my own. The good thing is, she's not around all the time. She's always with Maria at her house. My mother bought them a spot not far from mine. She's definitely more comfortable with Maria since that was my mother's nanny and all."

I shocked myself by referring to Marisol as my mother. That wasn't often, since I hated her so much.

"How's Ariel? I know she's gorgeous as ever."

"Girl, Allen is obsessed with my daughter. She's getting big. Allen just potty trained her."

"I guess he's grown to be quite the hands-on dad."

"Girl, it works for me, so I can get things done without toting around a two year old."

"Thank God for nannies," I laughed. If it wasn't for Maria, or having money, I would be raising my son with no help at all, since his faggot-ass daddy, Javier, was six feet deep.

"And how is Juan? You know he don't answer my calls no more."

"Can you blame him?" I shot back quickly. "Girl, he's in love with this money hungry bitch that I can't stand. She's all in his head and his pockets. I might have to fly you up here to piss her off for me."

"Shit, you know I will! I miss that big dick any way, chile!" she said in a whisper.

"Girl, yuck! I don't want to hear about my brother's dick."

"Denie, no bullshit. I know I messed up. Not only is Juan hung like a horse, but he fine as hell, too. I miss him so much."

"Nah, you miss that paper. Money at the Marlins must not be flowing, huh? You shouldn't have broken my brother's heart. He really loved you, Cheri. I think you the main reason why my brother had to get back on top. See Cheri, we came from money. Juan was used to having the finer things in life. When we moved to Florida, Juan was trying to live life right. With you he was trying to be a good boy, until he realized that good boy shit don't keep the chicks. Now he's back, and running shit in D.C."

"Don't put him being back in the streets, and moving up there on me."

"Girl, whatever, I wouldn't expect a white girl to understand. Anyway, you left him for the money ticket, that baseball bread. Trust me, I get it. It's nothing like legit athlete money, so I ain't mad at you. I'm a woman first." I laughed letting her know I was hip to her game.

"So Juan is getting it, huh? I still love him, Denie, but that straight and narrow shit wasn't for me. I needed excitement. All he wanted to do was sit in the house, watch movies, and stare at pictures of his mother."

"He was vulnerable, Cheri. But now he's definitely on top. You fucked up this time, girl. He might have more money than your athlete, chile. Shit, he that nigga. He helped me open my boutique."

"That's a good look. So y'all sell the house down here yet?" Cheri inquired being nosy as usual.

"Girl, yes. That house was sold in less than a month. Now we back at my old house, but I'm ready to move in my own shit. I hate living in my mother's house. It gives me the creeps at times."

"Juan lives there, too?"

"He's back and forth between my house and his condo at the National Harbor. He stays at the condo most of the time, leaving me the opportunity to be with my boo. It's complicated, so I don't want anybody to know about him for now."

"Who is he? I need to know."

"I don't feel like getting into it right now. Us being together gonna make heads spin. Another thing…"

"You just scared to let your guard down. You gonna block your blessings, Denie. You keep on," she warned. "You see how I did with Juan. Now I'm trying to get rid of this damn steroids addicted-ass nigga over here. I ain't being with his ass if he ain't got no bread. Shit, it's bad enough he got a little Vienna sausage penis." She laughed.

She was right. Allen's penis was small as hell, but his head game was sick. That girl would die, if she knew I used to be twirling all over that miniature, little slugger. When I was fucking Allen, I never wanted him. Cheri thought she was that bitch, so I fucked him, just to see if I could.

"Oh my goodness, I miss your crazy ass. You had me wildin out in Florida. Remember our sexcapades in Miami? We fucked that city up girl!" I said, skipping the subject, feeling a little guilty.

"Denie, you know I had to get you on the scene in Miami and get you out of boring ass Sarasota. Oh my gosh, girl guess who I bumped into last week?"

"Who?"

"Lamar. That nigga was ready to pop off on me like I was you. He said he was going to kill you when he caught up with you."

"Why didn't you call me?"

"I tried after I saw him but you didn't pick up. What the hell did you do to that nigga? Shit, he the one that did you wrong, I thought."

I fumed inside. "Fuck Lamar! He thought because he paid for me to go to school I owed him something. You can't cross me and think it's gonna be all good."

"Girl, that's some reality show drama. Lamar tripping, and he doesn't even look the same. He looked stressed out like he lost a lot of weight. I saw him in the mall with that Asian girl strolling their baby in a Louis Vuitton stroller."

"Fuck him and that eggroll bitch," I said jokingly. We both started cracking up.

"Well, girl let me get off this phone because Baby Juan having a fit in the back room. I'll call you later on," I lied, knowing damn well my son, BJ was at home with his nanny, Maria.

"I've heard that before. Give my Baby Juan a kiss for me."

"I will," I said, hanging up the phone. I'd had enough of pretending to be Cheri's best friend. We were cool and all when I needed her but now wasn't the time.

As I stared out of the boutique window and watched the diversity of Georgetown walk down M St., it felt good to be home in my city, Washington D.C. I was happy to hear from my girl Cheri, but I had to face it, life in Sarasota, Florida had been boring as hell. She was a socialite that was plugged in. Miss Cheri was the hottest white chick on the scene and only dated dudes with paper. Just when I began to think about some of the wild things Cheri and I used to do, my phone rang from a blocked number again. I was pissed thinking it was Allen again.

"What Allen?"

"Bitch, I'mma kill you when I catch you! Just cuz you ain't down South don't mean I can't find you!" Lamar yelled in my ear.

"Is this Lamar Bucksley? Star quarterback of the Eagles? Stop calling my damn phone unless you want me to send out a press release of your most recent discovery," I threatened.

"I loved you, bitch. And you gonna do that shit to me! I took care of your bastard son!" he yelled savagely.

"Guess you finally found my letter. Join the club, nigga. You ain't the only dumb athlete I slept with unprotected in Miami. I already killed your ass! Can't trust a big butt and a smile can you? Now stop calling my phone, killing my vibe!" I screamed as I hung up the phone.

Lamar was one of many who got what they deserved for hurting me. I tried protecting him from my demons but he crossed me.

It had been three years since I had been diagnosed HIV positive, and bitterness seemed to be a way of life. My son's father, Javier infected me. He betrayed me, and I didn't trust anyone because of that. Thank God that baby Juan was born HIV negative. Too bad for Lamar. I felt like any man who crossed me, would regret the day they met me. That's just how I used to feel. Now life was different. Florida was my past and I was trying to live life right.

Before we moved back to D.C., I had been dating Lamar. Miami was his hometown and we met during off-season at a club. His swag reminded me so much of my ex-boyfriend, Nelson, which was what attracted me to him. He was sexy as hell; six feet tall, with a baldhead, dark skin, and a muscular body that made me melt. Lamar grew up in the hood and was his family's ticket to a better life.

In the beginning of our relationship, we were really cool and I liked him a lot. From the day we met we were inseparable. He wined and dined me and gave me the world. A black on black Range Rover, bags, shoes, clothes, trips, you name it. He did it. Even paid for me to finish my associate degree in Fashion Design. Lamar had grown quite fond of my son, BJ, and would keep him while I had class. I fell for him hard.

Don't get me wrong, I was hip and knew what came with dating an athlete; the bitches, the drama, but this nigga took the cake, and I still don't get why I did what I did to his stupid ass.

It was off-season. Me and BJ, were staying with Lamar at his condo in Miami. Cheri called, and asked me to ride with her to Orlando for an overnight trip, to see Allen play. Lamar insisted on me going and even offered to keep BJ for me. I knew being around Allen and Cheri together was foul, but I agreed to go anyway. Taking Lamar up on his babysitting offer, Cheri and I headed out. But on our way to the airport, I decided against going. I had never left my son overnight with anyone and felt guilty about it.

Before I knew it, Cheri had dropped me off back at the condo on her way to the airport. As I strutted though the lobby in my six inch Alexander McQueen stilettos, I was ready to make love. Anxious to get to my man, I put the key in the door and was suddenly paralyzed with shock. Lamar's six-foot frame was in front of me, butterball naked, banging some pregnant Asian bitch's brains out. I remember the look on his face like it was yesterday.

"Oh shit! Denie, I thought you were out of town," he had the nerve to say, with a dumbfounded look on his face.

My body remained traumatized as I stared at the man I thought loved me, with his eight inch, bare pole hanging wet from another chick's pussy juice. I was stuck for a minute until I saw that my son was lying on the couch while he fucked this whore. Suddenly, I went into attack mode. I went straight for the butcher block and grabbed a knife. I remembered swinging the knife, wanting her dead, while Lamar had the nerve to stand in front of the bitch trying to protect her.

"Denie, what are you doing!" he asked me.

"Please don't hurt me!" the girl cried, holding her belly that appeared to look like a six-month belly.

"Nigga, I'mma kill your ass. You fucking some bitch while my son laying here. Who the fuck do you think you are?" I said, swinging again.

Luckily, I finally caught his ass, in his right arm. I remembered it so vividly. Lamar yelled, holding his arm as blood poured like a faucet all over his marble floors.

"Look Denie, I don't want any trouble. I just want to leave. I'm pregnant with Lamar's baby and he told me nothing about you. I have been away in Japan caring for my sick father and just got back. Lamar, why did you lie? You told me that was your sister's son."

The woman sobbed uncontrollably holding her stomach.

"Excuse me, little girl, what's your name?" I asked, pointing the knife in her direction.

"Kim. My name is Kim."

"Well, Kim get your shit and get the fuck out of here, right now."

"Naw, fuck that, you leave," Lamar announced boldly. "She's carrying my child. All the shit I do for your ass and you come up in here like this your shit. Get your son, and get the fuck out of my house until I call for you!"

"No, Lamar," Kim interjected. "I'm leaving! I don't ever want to see you again. Some things never change," she said as she gathered her dress and Chanel bag off the floor and left out. Naked and all.

"Mommy!" BJ called out.

Through all the drama, I forgot my son was on the couch in arms reach. The look in his eyes pained me. He looked afraid. Afraid of me. I wondered how long he sat there staring in a state of shock. Immediately, I went to the kitchen to put the knife down to rinse Lamar's blood off of my hands before consoling my son.

"No, Mommy. No! I want Lamar. You hurt Lamar."

I looked up at Lamar and his eyes softened. He knew how I felt about my son. His betrayal damaged the one good thing in my life. I got smart quick. He was gonna pay.

I stayed with Lamar long enough for him to think I had forgiven him. He showered me with gifts. He would have jewelers send me diamonds on the regular; blinged out Rolex watches, dangling diamond encrusted chains and even the $10,000 bracelet that I still wore on my arm 'til this day. Top of the line, was never enough for me. He kept me laced in furs, and Gucci. As long as I was kept, I stayed focused on making him pay.

Of course he continued to lie about the girl, Kim, and how he didn't know if it was really his baby. On our last night together, I devised a hell of a plan. I wanted to send him off right before leaving for training camp. I made him a candle lit dinner, chicken primavera, with my special tomato sauce that contained a good amount of my blood, a Greek salad, and garlic toast. He was gonna pay for what he did.

After making love to him for the first time unprotected, I knew he had crossed over to the other side, right along with me and my other Florida victims. Between the tomato sauce and Lamar dipping and diving in my wet box, I knew he was done. His last words before he left stuck out in my mind…

"You know how long I've been waiting for this day, babe, to feel your love nest? All this time you've been holding back on me, always making me use a condom. I promise that I'm gonna make an honest woman outta you. I'm gonna make you my wife."

That night was different. He made real love to me for the first time ever. Maybe his plans for us were genuine, but it was too late. He had already scarred me. Little did Lamar know, my scheme would change his life forever.

Finally, Lamar was off to training camp and BJ and I were packed up and ready to go back to boring ass Sarasota. Before leaving Lamar's place, I thought I'd leave him a letter to thank him for 'loving me' the way he did.

To My Dearest Lamar,

I just want to thank you for all you have done to help me better my life. You've taught me so much in the past year, and I want to let you know that I truly believe God puts people in our lives for a reason, or a season. You were both.

The season is over. It was great while it lasted. Let me be the reason why you will die of a slow and painful death.

See, someone changed my life years ago and made me look at life in a different scope. I tried to protect you from my demons. You insisted on making love to me, making a baby, one day having me become your wife. Boy please! I don't make love, I fuck! Especially niggas who try to screw me over. You disrespected not only me, but my son as well. The only thing good in my life.

My son is all I have, and you didn't care to love him and respect him the way that I do. By the time you read this letter you would've probably fucked so many bitches up and down the East Coast, and probably fucked your pregnant mistress Kim hundreds of times. I hid this letter in a spot that I knew would take you a minute to find. In your Bible. You must be going through something for you to have finally picked it up. Just when you thought life was hard. It's about to get harder.

Welcome to the world I live in. It's scary living with this big disease with a little name. But you're strong. You'll be alright. And don't worry about you and Kim's baby. Just read a little of this good ole Bible and pray that your child is as lucky as BJ was.

GOOD LUCK WITH YOUR SORRY ASS LIFE!

Peace Out!

Me

Every man that I'd ever come across had been a lying-ass cheater. I vowed to never trust anybody. No matter how my new boo tried to convince me he was the real deal, I kept my side eye open.

It had been three years since my daddy had died, and now I'd turned into a vindictive bitch. No matter what anybody had to say about my father, Rich was real, and he taught me not to trust a soul. Shit, the only person I really trusted on God's green Earth was my son, my pride and joy, BJ. Juan thought he was in my circle of trust, but little did he know, I had it coming for his ass too. In heavy thought, suddenly I was interrupted by one of my employees, Kiara.

"Denie, you have a visitor," she said as she walked hand in hand with one of my clients, Raymond. He was this dude I met a while back from Philly that was paid like shit. He was heavy in the streets. As he planted a kiss on her forehead, she pulled away from his grip and sashayed away all giddy. It was sad. These girls were so thirsty, and pressed to sleep with anybody with money. They made my hustle easy. Ray was fine as hell; he was a Hispanic dude, muscular, cold black waves, and had style. He knew he was hot, and that's exactly why I treated him like the trick that he was.

"Well, hello Raymond. Looks like you had a good night, huh?"

"Lil' mama was cool, but you know I like ass. She ain't give me no head neither."

"That's not my job to make her do shit to you in the bedroom. My job is to get you the girl. Not make her fuck or suck. You're a multi-millionaire. Getting the pussy should be easy for you."

"Why you ain't never fuck with me, with your fine ass," he said leaning in, invading my personal space.

He smelled like Creed, and I was weak for a sensual, clean smelling cologne, but I was a different girl, and trying to do right by my man. "Because I'm taken. Sorry, Raymond, you're a moment too late. Anyway, where's my money?"

"Two stacks, right?"

"Stop playing with me. Kiara was with your ass, all weekend. You know my rates, two stacks a day. So that means your bill is six grand."

"Damn Denie, cut me a break. I had to take the bitch out to eat…"

"You niggas kill me. Always wanting to floss like you make so much paper, but the cheapest, tightest dudes around. You're worth millions, and you can't pay me six g's. Nigga, give me my money."

"Denie, you might be right about a lot of things, but I'm no nigga," he said, handing me a wad of money.

"You're close enough to it," I told him, counting my money to make sure it was all there. I gave him a hug afterward.

"Nice doing business with you Raymond, keep me on speed dial."

"Yo Denie, it's a reason why I hit you up when I'm in town for pussy. You just don't get it."

"Whatever, Ray."

"Man, whatever happened to that bitch Tanya, you used to be with?"

"She bunned up now, with a baby."

"Damn. She was plain, but had the tightest asshole…"

"TMI, Raymond. I don't want to hear about her ass," I said cutting him off."

"Alright man. Just keep me in mind, if she ever wants to let me hit that again. She was my favorite," he said as he left my office, with his fine ass.

Immediately, I thought about Kiara being my next victim. These chicks had no clue they were being pimped out. I put them in a situation to get connected with paid dudes, then they'd have to work their shit to get their coins. I got my bread off the top since I wasn't trying to be up under Juan the rest of my life. Since he'd been taking care of me and my son, he treated me like he owned me, giving me an allowance, while he tricked off bitches on a regular. Little did he know, I didn't fuck with his snitching ass anyway. I had so much shit in motion and Juan had no clue. He was so green, that he didn't realize all the shit that was going on, right under his nose. It didn't matter that he was my brother. He was still that bitch, Lisa's son. I was determined to get my revenge, by any means necessary. His day was coming.

Chapter 4
Juan

"What the fuck? Lil' Man, you shot me. You shot me baby!"

I watched Peaches scream while holdin' her thigh as blood gushed all over her pink sheets. Lil' Man stood in the corner paralyzed with fear as he aimed his gun at me shakin'.

"Look what the fuck you made me do!" he yelled.

"I made you do?" I thought about pistol whippin' the youngster, but I wasn't sure what he was capable of. There was both fear and craziness oozing from his eyes.

Tears poured as he watched blood pour from his mother's thigh like a water faucet.

"Aighhhhhhhh, it burns!" Peaches shouted. "Shit! I need an ambulance. Juan, Lil' Man, call 9-1-1!" Peaches pleaded but her cries fell on deaf ears. Lil' Man was so fixated on me that he couldn't hear his mother's cry for help.

"Put the gun down, lil' soldier. Your mother needs help. You want her to die?"

"No, I want you to die," he spat. "Nigga, I should kill you!"

Lil' Man threatened me like he'd killed before even though he was only thirteen. He aimed his little 25mm straight at me, never takin' his gaze off my naked body. The look in his eyes told me I possibly wouldn't make it out alive. Tears streamed down his ashy, black face and snot dripped onto his lip.

"Lil' Man, put the gun down. Please, son. Put the gun down. I need help. Please, do it for your mama," Peaches pleaded.

"No! You always putting these niggas before me. He just beat your ass and you still giving this nigga a pass," he said, tremblin' in between words.

"Baby, I need help! I'm not thinking about no nigga right now. I just don't want you to get hurt. Your father will take care of Juan."

"You right, Ma. My fatha' a real gangsta. I'mma make sure my fatha' kill yo weak ass. Fuckin' pretty boy ass nigga."

After givin' me a vicious stare down for what felt like hours, reality hit him, and he realized his mother really did need him. Or maybe his punk ass really thought his father stood a chance against me in the streets. Droppin' the gun to the floor, Lil' Man ran to his mother's side and started to cry uncontrollably. The bitch came out of him real quick.

"Ma, I'm sorry. Please don't die, Ma. I'm sorry," he cried as he held her close.

"Get a towel so I can put pressure on it. Juan, call an ambulance!" Peaches yelled.

As soon as I felt safe, I picked the 25mm up off the floor and smacked the shit outta Lil' Man right in his mouth. Not phased at all he tackled me, knocking me to the floor. I wasn't about to fight a fuckin' kid but my gun flew out of my hand and slid by the dresser. We both crawled across the floor and I beat him to it. I went straight into guerilla mode, as I continuously hit him wit' the gun in his nose. Blood gushed everywhere.

"You fuckin' bitch ass lil' nigga, don't you ever shoot a gun at me again. The next time you won't live to see another day," I said, trying to beat all the shit outta his lil' ass.

"Get the fuck off my son!" Peaches shouted.

"Fuck you and your son!" I blasted.

As blood gushed from Lil' Man's mouth, he continued to talk shit.

"My fatha' gone kill your ass, nigga. Watch, he gon' kill you!"

"Fuck you, your hoe ass mother, and your bitch ass Daddy! Peaches lose my number!" I shouted, as I grabbed my shit and ran the fuck out the room.

It was dodge time before the police caught wind of what happened. I damn sure didn't need to get caught up in no shit over a trick. Her son shot her, not me. That bitch wasn't my responsibility. It was time for me to get my ass the hell out of B-more. Luckily, while I was rollin' out of Peaches' house her other kids remained knocked out on the couch.

As I ran to my car, I watched my back to make sure Lil' Man didn't try to sneak up on me. That lil' nigga was provin' to be dangerous. There were a few dudes outside but weren't really payin' me any attention as I slipped into my ride. It had started to snow a little bit and my windshield was covered with ice. I had no time to use an ice scraper, so I put my defroster on blast and jetted off the block. Since it was still dark outside, I was able to dip out unnoticed. The clock in my car read 5:02 a.m. As soon as I got on BW Parkway I threw that little 25mm out the window. There was no way I'd be caught ridin' with it in the DMV.

As I continued down the parkway, I reached in my glove box, and got my throw away phone out. It was my phone for business and the one I'd used earlier to call Julio. I hated havin' to call him again, but thought it would be smart to let him know what was up just in case something went down.

"Yo. My nigga. It's five in the morning," Julio answered with his strong Colombian accent, "what happened now?"

"Man, I can't talk long, but I got caught up at that bitch, Peaches' house."

With concern in his voice, he wanted to know, "Why do you keep getting yourself in these unnecessary situations?"

"Man, I don't need a sermon tonight. I need a friend."

"So, what's up, Juan? Must be urgent since you're waking me from my sleep?"

"Peaches' son bust off at me."

"Hold up. He did what? You killed him, right?" he asked in a matter-of-fact tone.

"Naw, man. I tried to beat the breaks off Peaches, and then the lil' dude came in there bustin' off. He missed me and hit her dumb ass," I said, still speedin', and lookin' in my rearview mirror all at the same time.

I wanted to make sure I wasn't being followed.

"Say what? She dead?"

"Naw, man. She got hit in her leg. I rolled out. I just called you, 'cuz you the only person I can trust. I just wanted to let you know what was up just in case some shit kicked off."

"Juan, what the fuck is wrong with you? You're too respected in these streets to have all this drama around you. We got too much on the line with this new connect. You can't risk us losing this deal. Stop being so sloppy, man. You gonna need to chill my g."

"You right," I said, agreeing with him.

Julio was just keepin' it one hundred. I couldn't risk fuckin' up my money. That's one of the reasons why I fucked with Julio. He was real, extremely business savvy, and intelligent, and always had my back.

"Juan, look…I'm driving down there sometime tomorrow after I run some errands, but for now, you need to make sure Peaches and the kid make it to Hell real soon. You can't ever allow anyone to disrespect you. Ya' feel me?"

"I got you."

"Once one mutherfucker does it, then others will test you. We can't have that. Period."

His tone told me he was serious about me sendin' Peaches and her son to an early grave. But I wasn't about that life. They were harmless.

"I feel you," I lied.

"Bet. Now, I'm going back to bed."

"Bet."

Taking a deep breath, I turned off my throw away phone, and prepared for war with Mecca. As soon as I turned my iPhone on, it started rockin' immediately; 18 text messages, seven voicemail messages, all from Mecca's number. She knew I hated when she stalked me like that. Before I could read one message, my phone started ringin'. When Mecca's picture came across my phone, it was time to put on my armor and get ready for war. It was almost six in the morning, and I knew she was pissed.

"Wassup babes," I said as if I hadn't been out fuckin' all night.

"Juan, it's Shana."

"Shana? Why the fuck you callin' me from Mecca's phone?"

"Juan, Mecca is in the hospital. I've been calling you all night! Where the hell you been?"

"Shana, what you mean she in the hospital? Is my baby okay?"

Silence.

"Shana?"

More Silence.

I panicked. Something wasn't right. "Answer me. Is my baby okay?"

"No, Juan. Mecca started spotting, then bleeding, and more blood. It kept coming and coming, until it got worse. We've both been calling you all night. After she couldn't get you, I went to the condo and took her to the hospital. Shana, to the rescue as usual. When you're not available, out on your missions fucking around, or doing whatever you drug dealers do, I'm there. I'm tired of you putting her…"

"Where the fuck is Mecca? What's wrong with my baby?" I yelled, interruptin' her meddlin' ass. A sense of hopelessness came over me. I felt like the world came crashing down on me.

"The baby is gone, Juan! She's gone! It's all your fault! If she would've made it to the hospital in time they would've been able to save my goddaughter."

"My baby is not gone! What hospital she at?"

"Holy Cross. You..."

Before that home-wreckin', miserable trick could say another word, I hung up and pushed the pedal to the metal as tears escaped my eyes. Mecca's best friend, Shana, hated me and the feelings were mutual. We both knew why she hated me so much, but Mecca remained clueless. Truth was...Shana wasn't shit. Tryin' to drive as fast as I could without killing myself on the icy roads, my mind couldn't focus. Shana's irritating voice didn't make it any easier. The thought of my baby being gone worked on my brain heavily.

Mecca and I had plans. I promised to marry her when the baby came. And now things had gotten crazy just because I chose to be up in a stripper trick. Damn, Mecca, was six months along. Why couldn't my baby girl hold on just a little while longer? I couldn't take losin' another person. My mom, my father, and now my daughter. Something had to give.

Pullin' into the parkin' lot in a panic, I made my way to the ER where Mecca's entire family sat alongside Shana, lookin' like the slut she was, with her bob wig, and dressed in a black tube dress as if she had just come from the club. When I strutted in, I could see tears in everyone's eyes. Their piercing stares made me feel uneasy. There was so much tension in the room, I felt like an outsider.

"Where is she? Where's Mecca?"

"None of your business, son. Stay out of my daughter's life, you hear me?" Mecca's father, Mr. Ross said sternly lookin' up from his Bible out of his black-rimmed reader glasses.

"Mr. Ross, with all due respect, I need to see my girl, that's my baby."

"She doesn't want to see you," Shana instigated, popping her bright red lips.

Ignorin' her, I turned to Mecca's heavy-framed mother.

"Where is she, Mrs. Ross?"

"Didn't my father tell you to leave, punk?" Mecca's brother approached me like he was gonna do something.

"Y'all betta get this lil' nigga before he get himself caught up in some shit he ain't ready for. I ain't got time for this dumb shit. Where my girl at, man?"

"Jr. he ain't worth it. He's a low life," Shana said, pushin' his frail ass back.

"Shana, you would know all about it. Now stay out my business, bitch."

"Have some respect son," Mrs. Ross said, lookin' at me appalled.

"I apologize, Mrs. Ross. I just need to know Mecca is okay. Where is she? Please tell me."

"She's in room nine, Juan. She's in room nine," Mrs. Ross said reluctantly. She breathed heavily as she put her head down and finished reading her Bible.

Not knowin' which way to go, I stumbled over my own feet, almost bustin' my ass. Finally, I made my way to the nurses' station. I stepped up my pace with my shoulders movin', and strutted with that Sanchez swag. Somebody would have to give me answers.

"Which way to room nine?"

An oversized woman pointed, showing me the way. After walkin' the long hall, I finally I made it to Mecca. Her long, black hair was stuck to her pale face as she slept. She wasn't the average girl I would normally mess with. But she had an innocence to her that I loved. Denie called her Miss Plain Mary Jane, but I loved her that way. The puffiness of her chinky eyes was evidence that she had been crying. Shana was right, it was all my fault. As the I.V. beeped, I glimpsed at Mecca's stomach for a strand of hope. Her stomach was still big. Maybe everything was okay. As I approached the bed carefully, I kissed Mecca's forehead not expecting her eyes to open.

"Juan. Juan. She's gone, Juan. Our baby is gone," she whispered in a painful, low tone.

My heart felt like it stopped. There was nothing I could do to heal her pain. There was no fancy car, or bag I could buy to take the pain away. I had no clue how to even take my own grief away. I was heartbroken.

"It's gonna be ok, babe."

"Juan, where were you?" Her voice elevated into a higher pitch than normal. "Why didn't you help me? You said you loved me."

"Baby, just rest. I'm here now," I said, grabbin' her hand and squeezin' it tightly.

"No! Where were you? Shana is always there for me when you're not. It wasn't her responsibility to help me when I was lying there on your hardwood floors bleeding! That was your job! You should've been there, Juan."

"I'm sorry, Mecca. Please stop yellin'."

"Stop yelling? My baby is gone, and it's all your fault!"

"Calm down, Mecca. Just calm down."

"We've got to take her home."

"What? What are you talking about?"

Mecca became hysterical. It was heart breakin' for me to see. The meds had her trippin'. She kept cryin' and sayin' things that made me think she might have to get mental help. Against hospital policy, I got on the bed with Mecca and promised her everything would be okay. After listenin' to her talk her way back into a slumber, I fell asleep right beside her, holding her, never wanting to let her go. I refused to mimic my father's ways when it came to my woman. My baby was gone and it was my fault. I owed Mecca and vowed to dismiss all the other women in my life. I figured for some that would come with complications. But I had to change.

Chapter 5
Juan

Even though my migraines were killin' me, and the last few days had been rough, the meetin' that I'd scheduled would make it all better. A successful outcome would set me apart from everyone else in the city. I compared it to my favorite movie, Scarface, and the scene when Tony Montana met Alejandro Sosa, preparin' him to take over the drug trade. There was nothin' that could stop me from running up to New York for a couple of hours. Atlantic Records was givin' Trey Songz a birthday party, and ironically my new connect wanted to meet me there. I brought Julio in on it, not just cuz he's my partner, but after all I'd been through the last two days, I didn't know who to trust. There was still somebody out there lurkin' and my head wasn't at a hundred percent.

I told Mecca I was goin' to get some fresh clothes and run a few errands. She reminded me not to fuck anybody along the way. She admitted that she no longer trusted me at all, and wasn't sure she wanted to be with me anymore. I'd invested too much time into her and genuinely loved her. Besides she knew too much about me for me to allow her to call it quits. I hated lyin' to her about the trip, but this deal would change our lives.

I sped into the cul-de-sac of my condo at the National Harbor and parked directly behind Julio's yellow Lamborghini. I whipped my condo keys out of my glove box and hopped out. After seeing me walk up to the car, Julio rolled the window down, hidin' behind his black and gold Louis Vuitton Evidence sunglasses. He hit me with one of those gestures that I hated tellin' me to be quiet.

"Va a pasar, ten paciencia," he said, thinking I didn't understand.

Who was he telling to be patient? And what was going to happen? I thought to myself. I kept it cool when he got off the phone, but wanted to ask badly. After he hung up the phone, Julio stepped out of the car in all black, allowing me to notice the Louis Vuitton sweater and black Louis Vuitton sneakers. The nigga was just as serious as I was about staying fresh in the latest gear. He was fly, and the bitches loved him, but this was my show. So, it was a must that I went upstairs, and showed out.

"Man, Juan, wassup," he said, givin' me a brotherly hug.

"Julio, so much shit. I've lost a child, been shot at, robbed, and killed a nigga, all in the last 48 hours. I need us to get up to New York, rub elbows wit' these Columbian dudes, and shoot right back."

"Hold up. You killed the dude? Damn, and your girl lost the baby?"

"Yeah man, I killed that punk ass nigga, Grady. I gotta go clean that shit up, too."

"You left the body there? Dumb, nigga."

"Nigga, I told you shit been happenin' left and right."

"No excuse," he told me disapprovingly and then he added salt to my wound, "You messy."

I wanted Julio to know he wasn't the boss of me, so I kept talkin'. "And then after all that, I thought I was gonna get some pussy real quick before I went home. The entire time, my girl was losin' my baby. Man, I feel fucked up."

As we walked from outside up to my condo, I filled Julio in on all the shit that had happened. He just kept shakin' his head. Once we got in the condo, I was instantly reminded of my loss as soon as the door to the living room opened. There was blood everywhere; all over my twenty-five thousand dollar livin' room set. I had to get Maria over here as soon as possible to clean up, but for now I had to get dressed and handle my shit.

I showered then threw on my all black leather, and snakeskin custom Exclusive Game sweater, and my black jeans. My Buscemi shoes made my entire outfit. I was ready for business. Once I put on my gold diamond bezel watch, and my 24KT diamond encrusted chain, it was on. I looked like I was worth millions. A fuckin' Sanchez. After calling to check in with Mecca, I walked out to my livin' room where Julio stood, lookin' at the pictures of me and Denie on the mantel. I put my fur bomber coat on and was ready to go.

"So, this is your sister, Denie?"

"That's her," I told him hesitantly. "Why?"

"No wonder you don't want me to meet her," he added with a smirk. "She's gorgeous. My kinda girl."

I dismissed the comment and told him the good news."Yo, my dude Shaka, who plays for the Nets, just texted me back. He lettin' us use his private plane, so we can shoot right up and back. You ready," I said as I zipped up my coat.

"Damn straight. Let's make this shit happen," he said as we headed out of the door.

It took less than forty minutes to make it to the port where the private plane was kept. I beamed inside at the luxury and the benefit of flyin' private. It was a must that I bought a plane. The experience was the best. My man really hooked us up. The trip up to New York was seamless. We arrived in less than an hour. Once we landed, a driver in a black Escalade took us straight to Trey Songz's birthday party. During the entire fifteen minute car ride, Julio spoke on the phone in Spanish, about some other shit, I had no clue about. I checked in with Mecca again telling her some outrageous lie about how I had to take Carmen somewhere. Before I could get Mecca off the phone, we finally arrived at the spot, so I just hung up, knowing I'd beg for forgiveness later.

The party was star studded, red carpet and all at the 40/40 Club. Julio chose not to walk the carpet, but I felt it was important to show my popularity. I had to say what's up to all my industry peeps. I mingled a little and hollered at a few rappers I knew. We took a couple of Instagram flicks and then I walked inside. Julio wasn't around so I got a table real quick and had a dozen bottles of Ace of Spade, five bottles of Ciroc, and three bottles of Moet sent over. Of course the bitches followed. I let three beauties inside the ropes of our section, makin' my promise to Mecca extremely difficult. After a couple of minutes, things got out of hand. Trey Songz began performing, and the smallest chick of the bunch started massagin' my shit in front of everybody.

Julio walked over, saving the bitch from getting' fucked in the club. The problem was, he'd already started talkin' to my connect Tony, without me. Tony stood no taller than 5'10" allowing us to stand eye to eye. Walking up on them with confidence, I wanted Tony to know who was runnin' the show between Julio and I. He was my man and all, but I ain't have time for snakes tryna cut side deals.

"Hey, Tony. I see you met my partner, Julio," I said swattin' the chicks out of my section. "Are you ready to meet?" I asked, wonderin', what the hell they were talkin' about, before I walked up. They looked way too chummy.

"This is who we came up here to meet, Juan?" Julio asked laughing.

He finally took off his shades, exposin' his glossy light brown eyes.

"Yep, why. Y'all know each other?"

"Juan, Tony's my cousin," he said lettin' out another laugh, "I already fuck with him."

The music level rose as Trey sang his finale song. But I kept talking loud enough for them both to hear. "Tony, I didn't know you were Colombian."

"Half Colombian," he said dryly.

"Oh well, then that should make things go by smoother," I said thinkin' I would automatically get a pass.

"Not necessarily. It's not that easy. I have a private room set up for our meetin'', follow me."

My blood instantly boiled. Who the fuck was he dismissin'?, I thought to myself? Did he know who the hell I was? I'm far from somebody's peon. I was a boss. It killed me to keep my mouth shut but I had to, to close this deal. If all went well, this connection would send me straight to the top. What baffled my mind was, if Julio and Tony were already connected, then how were we partners? Was Julio really bigger than I knew? What type of shit did he have going on that I didn't know about? My mind raced with questions. Julio was supposed to be my homie. What side shit did he have going on?

As we walked through the party, I made sure to keep my confident swag. Anger filled me, but I didn't show it. By the time we made it upstairs to the private room, two security guards had been placed at the entrance. There was a lot of tension, and I felt a bit nervous as we walked into a room where two Mafia dudes dressed in all black suits stood smokin' cigars, gamblin' at a craps table. Once we were in the room we were told to come over to a long, oak table, surrounded by oversized, black leather chairs. The two older gentleman and Big Tony took a seat, while Julio and I stood. It was understood that you don't sit, unless offered a seat. It was just a silent code I learned from my crazy Uncle Renzo.

"So, these are your guys, Tony?"

"Yea, Dad. Julio is actually a good friend, but Juan is a Sanchez. He's heavy in the game, and..."

"Tony. Enough. Juan, you are Rich's boy?"

I kept staring at Big Tony's three hundred pound frame, and hairy face. He looked as if he hadn't shaved on purpose. "Yes, you know my dad?" I asked, prayin' to God that my father had no type of beef. It was obvious that Tony wasn't the man, his father was. And more importantly, Julio and Tony really weren't cousins. Why did they lie? I had to get to the bottom of that shit later.

"Don't worry about who I know. Take your clothes off," he said as guns were drawn and pointed at me, from the two overweight guys that were once guarding the door.

"Excuse me, what's your name?" I asked the extra thick, bald older Italian man.

"You don't ask the questions around here, son. I do. Now, do what I say, or I'm gonna send your head home in a bag with Julio," he said calmly as he leaned back in a big black leather chair, puffin' on a cigar.

Looking over at Julio, he shrugged his shoulders and nodded, as if I should comply.

Doin' as I was told, I removed my clothing, and was left in my black Hugo Boss boxer briefs and black wife beater.

"Everything needs to come off," he sounded with his raspy voice.

Flashin' back to my experience with Uncle Renzo, when I was raped by Pablo, I started to sweat heavily.

"I don't do gay shit, so y'all gonna have to kill me," I said, lettin' everyone know I would stand my ground. My last couple of days had been so fucked up that I wasn't havin' it. There was complete silence and then suddenly there was a huge roar of laughter.

"Son, I just wanted to make sure you weren't wearing a wire. Put your shit on and let's get to business."

He laughed, as if he was watchin' a Kevin Hart movie. I felt so humiliated as I got dressed. Everyone continued to laugh, as if I were the joke of the meetin'. Why were they fuckin' with me, and not Julio? After an hour long meetin', Big Tony pretty much let me know he'd get back with me. He also let me know that he moved three hundred thousand worth of drugs through the streets daily. He said he only rubbed shoulders with the best, the smartest, and trustworthy people. He wanted to do further checkin' up on me, in the streets. I just prayed no one knew about me tryna take down my father a couple of years back.

As we left the room and navigated towards the door to leave the party, Julio gave me a stiff pat on the back. "You handled yo'self well in there, bro."

I simply whisked his hand off my back. I needed to get back to Mecca. "Let's go," I told him firmly.

"Oh, you out?"

"Um, yeah. I thought you were leavin', too," I asked with my face twisted into a ball of confusion. He knew the plan I had to get back to the hospital.

"Naw, I'mma fall back and catch up wit' Tony. I'll fly back commercial or catch a ride somehow. Hit me up later, though."

"Um, okay. Cool."

"A'ight, lil' homie," he said, as I stood by the door both dumbfounded and pissed off.

Did that nigga call me lil' homie? Who the fuck did he think he was? I thought to myself as I watched them get lost in the crowd.

Chapter 6
Juan

Back on DMV soil, I used the morning to make a little money. I got fresh again. This time I was rockin' sweats and the newest custom Jordan sneaks that hadn't even hit the stores yet. I'd hit up a few of my trusted soldiers and collected roughly fifty grand.

With very little time to work with, I stashed it at the condo and hit the mall to take Mecca an 'I'm sorry for fuckin' up' gift. Before long, I'd hit up Hermes and copped a crocodile Birkin, some Hermes bracelets; then snatched up a few Louis Vuitton bags, two pairs of red bottoms, and a slew of shit from Cusp. An old fling who worked in the store picked out everything for Mecca. As soon as I rushed out of the mall, my phone rang from a blocked number. It could've been Big Tony so I answered.

"Hello?"

"Just in case you wanted to know, I'm alive, bitch!" Peaches yelled sarcastically through the phone.

"Ain't that a shame?"

"Oh, best believe, I'm coming fo' yo' ass, nigga."

"Bet. Until then, stop callin' my phone," I said before hangin' up on her slutty ass.

My migraines were takin' over and picking Mecca up without problems was my only concern. I'd even gotten the red Maserati washed and cleaned up for her since she loved when we rode in it. After two long days of observations, she was finally being discharged. I was determined to make things right. It took damn near two hours to get the final okay after I arrived. After signin' the last bit of paperwork, I wheeled Mecca down to the front door and let her know I was goin' to get the car. After quickly gettin' the car, I got back to the front doors of the main hospital only to find Mecca gone. In a panic, I ran in the lobby to the front desk.

"Excuse me, Miss? Have you seen a girl with a velour sweat suit with long black hair, light skinned, hazel eyes?"

"Sir, she walked down the hall…"

Before she could finish, I heard screams coming from the direction where she pointed. It was Mecca. It was loud, piercing, and had the bystanders talkin' and pointin'.

"Juan, I can't leave her here. She has to go home with us," she cried, barely able to walk. People stared at us with sorrow in their eyes. I wouldn't allow myself to tear up but felt it in my heart.

"It's okay, sweetheart. She's in a better place. We have to go home." I continued to console her before pickin' her up and carryin' her to the car. Tears streamed down my face as I watched my innocent girlfriend scream and holler through the lobby of the hospital. It all had me bummed out and sent me into a funk.

Finally making it to the car, I put Mecca in the passenger seat of the Maserati. Some thick chick stared me down as I reached over to buckle Mecca's seat belt. The bitch blew me a few kisses, but I refused to look her way. It was the car she wanted, not me. I didn't have time for no bullshit.

As I pulled off, things hit me hard. To leave the hospital without a car seat in the back pained me. The car ride home from the hospital was quiet. Mecca was an emotional wreck. She stared out of the window as if my voice was fallin' on deaf ears. I tried talkin' to Mecca again.

"Babe, don't cry. We can make another baby," I said, tryin' to console her.

"I don't want another baby, Juan! I want my baby! It's that easy for you? Just make another one. Do you know how it feels to leave the hospital empty handed while watching happy mothers carry their babies to the car?"

Finally, she turned around and looked at me.

"Where the fuck were you, Juan as I bled on the floor of our condo? Who is she? Was it worth it?"

"No. I mean, I wasn't with anyone, Mecca. I had to handle some business."

"How convenient? You're always handling business. You're lying! Take me to my mother's house."

"For what, Mecca?"

"I don't ever want to step foot in that condo again."

"We can just go to the house."

"Hell no! I hate your sister and I'm not in the mood for her shit."

"That's how you feel. You hate my sister now? What the fuck is wrong with you? My sister is all I have! Don't you ever talk shit about my sister."

"She's all you have? What about me? My baby was all I had. If your ass would've come home that night my baby would be alive."

Her words hit me hard. The hurt in Mecca's eyes made it clear that it would take us a while to get through this one. I'd hurt her many times before, but this was foul. I had to wiggle my way out of it a little bit.

"You're not gonna blame me! That wasn't just your baby. I'm in pain too, shit!"

"Juan, you don't care about nothing but your money, Denie and her baby. That's it. If I didn't know any better I would've thought Baby Juan was yours. That's how far up your sister's ass you are."

"Mecca, now you being real disrespectful. I love you, damn, but you can't compete with my sister. I love her just like I love you. She's family, though. We've been through a lot and she needs me."

"Juan, I need you, too. Can't you see that? She got dudes that can help her. I bet she don't put you in front of them."

As Mecca cried and screamed, I felt helpless. I loved my sister, and no matter what she said, no one could change that. Mecca was right about one thing, she needed me right now way more than Denie. I wanted her to know that I would be there for her and would be the man she deserved.

Mecca finally dozed off. I drove in silence for the next thirty minutes and then she woke up.

"Juan, didn't I tell you to take me to my mother's house?" Mecca yelled as we pulled into the circular driveway of the home Denie and I shared.

"Sweetheart, you need to rest. I will have Maria look after you here. You won't have to lift a finger."

"My mother can take care of me."

"That's my job! Let me help you, dammit!" I said, rushin' to the passenger side to help Mecca out of the car. The wind blew like crazy and the November chill hit me in the face forcefully. After arguin' with Mecca a little, I finally convinced her to come inside. Just as the knob turned, a familiar blast from the past welcomed us at the door. I knew those curly, blonde locks from anywhere. Trouble had arrived.

"Hey babe, I missed you!" My ex-girl jumped in my arms wrappin' her tiny legs around my waist, damn near knocking me down.

"Cheri, what are you doing here? Get off me," I said in shock, but failin' to push her away.

"Juan, who the hell is this white bitch?"

Cheri simply folded her arms across her chest and gave me a seductive look while dressed in boy shorts and a skimpy tank top that allowed her huge breast to spill out.

Mecca continued, "That's what the hell you were doing the other night? I hate you, Juan!"

As Mecca turned to leave, I grabbed her arm. "Baby, wait."

"Juan, baby, I've been in your room waiting for you all night. Didn't you get my text messages? As soon as I heard you pull up, I was so happy. I missed you so much."

Cheri went on as if Mecca wasn't standin' there with us. As we stood in the foyer, I looked up at the top of the circular stairs and saw Denie watchin', as if she'd tuned into her favorite reality show. The smirk on her face told me she was behind it all.

"Take me to my mother's house now, Juan!" Mecca screamed damn near breakin' all the glass in the house.

"No. You're stayin' here," I said, ignorin' Mecca's demands.

"Juan, take that gold digging bitch wherever she needs to go. Get her ass up out my house," Denie yelled down the stairs.

"Come on, babe. This is a mansion, not a house. It is big enough for you to get the rest you need, without them being..."

"You see what the fuck I'm talking about, Juan? You just let your sister say whatever to me, and you don't check her. I'm done with you, Juan. If you're not taking me, I will walk to the main road and catch a cab!"

"Mecca, get out. My girl Cheri will take care of Juan," Denie shouted. "Yeah, Charlie told me your pussy ain't shit. Huh, that baby probably ain't my brother's baby anyway," Denie instigated.

"That's what all this is about? Charlie's broke ass? That's why you're single now. Don't nobody want you, Denie," Mecca said, as if Denie had come across a huge discovery.

"Mecca, for the record, I'm far from single. And about Charlie, I never cared about him. That was your boo! I just fucked him. You loved him."

"I never loved him," Mecca defended, while I wondered what the hell was goin' on.

"Who the fuck is Charlie?" I asked.

"Mecca's baby father. That's not your baby, Juan," Denie instigated.

"Denie, stop it! Both of you stop! She lost our baby. We're just gettin' back from the hospital and walkin' into this bullshit. Mecca needs to rest. Now leave her the fuck alone!" I yelled.

There was complete silence. I guess I'd caught Denie off guard. No matter how much she hated Mecca, her facial expression proved that she now felt bad for her. Of course her pride wouldn't allow her to apologize, so instead she called Cheri upstairs.

Finally, Mecca and me went off to my wing of the house, free of all the drama. I had a lot of makin' up to do, and I knew it wasn't gonna be easy, but I loved her, and I was determined to make things right.

After I got Mecca settled, and gave her all the gifts I'd gotten from the mall, we chilled on the bed. I laid back in bed in heavy thought, thinkin' about Julio and Tony, Cheri being in my damn house, and of course Mecca losing our child. Then there was the big question. Who was Charlie? All I could do was pray that Mecca didn't fuck nobody behind my sister. That shit had me shook. I asked Mecca but she said Denie was just trying to break us up.

At least my nerves calmed a bit. But just when I was finally fallin' asleep, Mecca's cell phone rang.

"Hello," she answered as she tried to turn down the volume on the phone.

With her layin' beside me, I'd already heard a dude's voice.

"Sounds good. I'll call you tomorrow," she said, hangin' up the phone as she turned over with her back to me.

"Who was that, Mecca?"

"My mom."

I couldn't believe she'd lied. What the fuck was she hidin'?

I had no problem whipping her ass if I found out she was fuckin' around on me.

Chapter 7
Denie

Running late as usual, I parked and ran up the stairs of the daycare to pick up my pride and joy. I'd had a long day at my boutique and just wanted to get home to a hot bath. As I got to the front door, the director Mrs. Hailey seemed to be leaving. She was usually the last one there.

"Hi Mrs. Hailey, why are you locking up? BJ isn't in there by himself, is he?" I asked with confusion spread across my face.

"Ms. Sanchez, you called earlier to say it was okay for his uncle to pick him up."

"No, I didn't! I just left my brother. He's at home."

"It wasn't your brother that came, I know him. It was his father's brother, T-Roc."

"T-Roc! No. He's dead! He couldn't have taken my son! Who did you let take my son, Mrs. Hailey?" I yelled in a panic.

"Oh my goodness. Ms. Sanchez come inside. Let's review the camera and call the police."

As we rushed inside I was hysterical. My heart rate had obviously escalated way too high. I felt light-headed and couldn't stop the tears from falling long enough to see my way in Mrs. Hailey's office. My son was gone and I needed to know what the hell was going on. There was no way T-Roc could have my son. As we waited for the police, I paced the floor agitated and frantic. I was in complete disbelief. After waiting for the system to reboot which felt like forever, finally, Mrs. Hailey pulled up the video. There he was, T-Roc holding my son with a huge smile on his face as if he knew he was being filmed. How was he alive? All I could do was scream to the top of my lungs.

"My baby! My baby!" I screamed.

"Denie! Denie! Wake up girl!" Cheri yelled, shaking me from side to side.

"Oh my goodness, where is BJ?" I asked jumping up from my pillow, confused.

"Girl, you trippin'. Baby Juan's in the playroom with Maria."

Cheri laughed, looking at me like I was crazy.

"Give me some of that shit you been smoking."

"Can you go get him for me please?" I asked her in the sweetest voice possible.

"Umm, ok."

Leaning back on my pillow, I realized I had another nightmare. I hadn't had one in months. Maybe it was the loss of Mecca's baby that started playing tricks on my brain. I kind of felt sorry for Mecca but there was no way I was apologizing. I wouldn't wish losing a baby on nobody, not even Juan and Mecca.

It's just that BJ was my world and I loved him more than anything. I couldn't imagine life without him. That's why it always saddened me even more that Marisol just left me on a porch. A fucking wooden porch! Her creeping with my father behind his brother's back got her knocked up with me. I guess my Uncle Los was more important than her raising an unwanted baby. All of the fake shit about how much she loved me and wished she could've raised me herself, yeah right. That self-righteous whore was full of it. Both Marisol and Lisa could rot in hell for all I cared. I was determined to protect my son at all cost.

When Cheri came back in my room without Baby Juan, I jumped out the bed immediately. "Where is he, Cheri?" I rose up on my toes frantically and headed for the bedroom door.

"Denie, chill. Maria is having him clean up his crayons and stuff, then she said she would bring him in here."

"I want him in here, now! Maria! Maria!" I yelled letting everyone in the house know I wasn't fucking around. Just when I heard the patter of feet coming towards my room, I felt a little relief, until I saw it was Carmen. Those damn slanted eyes, made me think of Marisol. It was like I was staring at my biggest enemy.

"What's wrong, Denie? Why are you yelling? Are you okay," she asked worriedly.

"Little girl, stop acting like we like each other. And get out my room, before I cut your dumb ass ponytails off."

"You are so evil. Go to hell," she taunted, rolling her eyes with her hands on her hips. She looked exactly like her whore ass mother, Marisol.

"Carmen, get the fuck out or I'mma..." before I could complete my threat, she ran out of my room calling for Maria like she was gonna do something.

"Girl, you trippin'. Stop treating your little sister like that. You know she your twin," Cheri laughed.

"That little girl looks nothing like me."

"Okay, I'm not gonna do this with you today, so let me change the subject. I need to go to the mall. Let me use one of your rides so I can get me an outfit for tonight. We gonna turn up, girl!"

"Maria!" I screamed again, ignoring everything Cheri said.

I was focused on my son. Plus, I had a secret meeting to get to.

"Look chick, I'm gonna go get in the shower, because clearly something is going on with you."

"Good. Maria!" I continued to yell.

"Yes, Miss Denie." Maria rushed in with Baby Juan in tow.

"When I say I need my son, you fucking bring him to me, comprende?"

"I'm sorry, Senorita. I was bringing your mail also."

Maria apologized at least five times as she placed my mail on the foot of my bed and backed out of the room. Maria couldn't stand me and never had since the days of me living here with Marisol. Her loyalty was to Marisol and that was it. The only reason why she stayed around was to care for Carmen. The feelings were mutual because God knows I had my own son to worry about.

"Mommy, what's wrong? Maria is nice. Why are you mad at her?"

My son held a piece of paper in his hand while he waited for my answer.

"Nothing baby. Mommy missed you, that's all. And BJ, I'm not mad at Maria. Is that clear?" I asked him, kissing his forehead.

"Okay. It's clear," he told me in his sweet little voice that melted my heart. "Can we go to the zoo today for your birthday to see the monkeys?"

"Not today, baby. Maybe later this week, alright."

"Are we gonna have a birthday cake for you Mommy?" he asked, overly excited, jumping up and down.

"No, baby. Mommy doesn't celebrate her birthday. Only yours."

"Why Mommy? You're special and I love you. Look what I made you."

He held up his picture that was extremely difficult to make out. In my eyes, it was the best picture any three year old could illustrate. My son was perfect in my eyes.

"Papi, what's this?" I asked, trying to make out the beautiful stick figures.

"This is you Mommy," he said pointing to what looked like a stick figure with coils of curly hair.

"Oh my goodness! Papi, is this Uncle Juan?" I asked, realizing he'd drawn a big necklace around Juan's neck, and a sports car with crazy looking wheels.

"Yes, and this is all his money right there," he pointed.

I couldn't help but laugh. I was ashamed that my three year old, knew of his Uncle's obsession with money.

"This is the birthday cake, and then this is Lamar. Mommy, I miss him."

"That's so pretty. I love you, Papi! Thanks so much, it's beautiful," I said, trying not to show my irritation at the fact that he still remembered Lamar's ass.

That little guy made my heart melt. He was my reason for living. All those years I resented Lisa for showing favoritism to Juan, and making it all about her precious son. Now I get it; that mother and son bond was deep, there was nothing like it. As he climbed in bed with me, I held him close. BJ made me feel secure. As I ran my fingers through his long, black curly locks, I kissed the crown of his head. He was my blessing.

As I glanced over at my mail, I noticed a pink, Hallmark card. No return address. Uh oh, here we go. Another threat, I assumed. Grabbing the envelope, I peeled it open anxiously. Or maybe it was from my boo this time.

To A Special Daughter, on Her 21st Birthday…After reading through all of the mushy stuff there was a handwritten note on the side. I sat up straight in my bed. Somebody was really fucking with me.

My Precious Daughter,

I miss you so much and wish I could be there by your side to celebrate your 21st birthday with you. No matter how hard it is to celebrate your birthday, know that you are still special. You are officially legal. A woman. Turn up, like you youngins say. Enjoy for me. If I could be there I would. Know that I am watching over you. I am protecting you. Always keep me close to your heart. Kiss my grandson for me.

Love,

Me

Paralyzed with mixed emotions, I called Juan's cell phone but he wouldn't pick up. He probably thought I was calling to mess with him about Mecca, but I needed him. Somebody was really fucking with me and I was nervous. I thought it was probably smart to have Maria get Juan for me. I knew Juan was somewhere in the house.

"Maria! Maria!" I yelled.

"Yes Senorita." She rushed in.

"Can you lay BJ in his room and tell my brother to come here? It's an emergency," I said as calmly as I could.

"Is everything okay?"

"No, I need my brother."

"I think he was getting in the pool, after he worked out. I will get him fast."

"Thanks."

What felt like hours, whizzed by. And twenty minutes later Juan showed up at my door. "Damn, thanks for coming so soon," I said with major attitude.

"What is it, Denie?"

He walked so casually as if I was bluffing. I was pissed at him, dressed in workout gear, all sweaty. He had no sense of urgency, as if a workout was more important.

"If I said it was an emergency, what took you so got damn long?"

"Because I knew it wasn't an emergency, and me and Mecca was in the middle of something. What's up?"

"This is what's up," I said, throwing the card straight in his face.

Juan picked the card up and started reading. His facial expression showed he was puzzled. I gawked at him suspiciously as he read quickly, trying to understand why I was so upset.

"You did this shit, Juan. How could you?" I spat before he could even finish reading.

"Are you insane? Why would I send this to you?" he asked raising his voice.

"Maybe to force me to celebrate my birthday."

I hadn't celebrated my birthday since I was sixteen. That was the day our lives got turned upside down. It was the day Lisa was kidnapped. Ever since, it was just another day.

"No. Denie, I would never hurt you like this. Somebody is screwing with us big time."

I tried to fight back my tears but our history was too crazy. It would all obviously haunt me forever.

"Denie, we both have a lot to deal with. Man, I knew we shouldn't have moved back into this house."

"It was your idea," I roared back, reminding him I had no intentions on living off Marisol's corpse.

"This was just the easiest fix until we got settled and I got on my feet. Something just makes me feel uneasy about this whole thing. Sometimes this house feels weird."

"Like haunted," I agreed.

"Yeah, lately it's been feeling like shit just ain't right. I just can't put my finger on it. I don't know, maybe I'm trippin' but I think we need to come up with some type of plan. We can go on and on about all the bullshit, but the bottom line is we have to be there for each other. The last couple of days have been rough. Man, I've been shot at, lost a child..."

"Shot at? What the fuck happened?"

"A bitch. That's what happened."

"You out here beefing over a chick? Mecca..."

"It wasn't about Mecca. It's the stripper chick, I was hittin'. Her son bust at me."

I just shook my head. "Like father, like son."

Before I could bash Juan a little more, Cheri walked in dressed and ready to go to the mall. Juan had planned a supposedly low-key night out for me, and of course she wanted to look her best to get him back.

"Hey, Juan. Denie, you coming with me?" Cheri burst in the room with her oversized breasts spilling from her Juicy one-piece track suit. She had the gold zipper down just enough to tease Juan.

"That's my cue. I gotta go. But I'm on that. I'll get to the bottom of that card," he said, brushing past Cheri.

"Don't act like you don't miss this wetness, Juan. Stop faking. You not happy with that mixed breed looking chick. She got you stuck on stupid."

"Cheri, I'm not fuckin' you just because that dude ain't hittin' it right."

"Wow, I wonder which head is bigger. Juan, you a trip. Now you think you got some paper you can treat me like this? You all iced out with your diamond, big face Rolex, all your properties and exotic cars. You're Mister Big Time, huh?"

"Denie, you need to school your girl. She got me fucked up," Juan uttered with a slight laugh.

"Juan, I bet my life on it. You'll be swimming in this pond before I go back to Florida. When it does go down, it's gonna be better than you remember. Trust," she ended with confidence.

"Cool, I'mma wait on it. In the meantime my girl needs me. See ya," he said, leaving out of my room, before smacking Cheri on her fake ass.

"Ouch boy! Keep playin', Denie gonna get a show. You know that little girl you got over there can't rock your world like me."

"You know you like it," she teased.

"Like what?" Mecca interrupted.

We all were shocked to see that she had walked up, and had the nerve to be walking around my damn house with a black velour robe on like she lived here.

"None of your business little girl," Cheri instigated walking up to Mecca as if she was gonna do something. Before Juan could get between them, Mecca smacked the hell out of Cheri.

When did this bitch get heart? "Cheri, you better beat her ass," I said in shock as Cheri stood frozen, holding her face.

"Man, come on Mecca," Juan said, trying to control her as she yelled like a lunatic.

"Bitch, you keep coming at my man, and that's what you gonna get every time," Mecca continued.

"And every time I see Juan, I'm gonna make it my business to try to wrap my lips around his nine inches. Trust me. He won't be able to resist me. This is all woman," Cheri said, as she started to strip right in front of everyone.

Juan couldn't resist looking. Me either.

"You fucking cracker whore!" Mecca yelled.

"Yup. I'll take that. I'll even let you slide with smacking me. You best believe, no matter what Juan tells you, you could never break our bond. I carried his first child. You couldn't even get that right. Your failing womb can't even carry a baby, trick."

"Cheri, what the hell is wrong with you? Denie, she gotta get the fuck out!" Juan fired.

It was obvious that Cheri struck a nerve, because Mecca fell to the floor, as if someone had hit her with a ton of bricks. I was in shock. I never knew Cheri was ever pregnant by Juan.

"Juan, with all we've been through, you want me to leave?" Cheri asked while putting her clothes back on.

Trying not to look, Juan ran over to Mecca, who was rocking back and forth on the floor in a fetal position with tears streaming down her face.

"Juan, you told me this was your first baby. You said no one ever had been pregnant by you."

"I've never had any other kids, Mecca. Believe me." He looked over at Cheri and asked the question even I wanted to know. "When did you get an abortion, Cheri? When were you ever pregnant by me? Tell Mecca you're lying."

"Juan, I never got an abortion. My daughter, Ariel, isn't Allen's child. She's yours. Just waiting for us to be a family."

Chapter 8

Denie

After all the drama with Cheri and Juan, I left the house to make some runs, and pick up the rest of my money Raymond owed from the last few days. Raymond, and a couple of dudes he ran with, owed me about ten grand, so I thought it was best I stopped by his hotel room first. He always stayed in the penthouse at the National Harbor. I hoped like crazy Juan didn't catch me over this way. I would have some explaining to do. Pulling up to the valet, I paused to make that important call.

Hello, you've reached Grady, leave a message…Beep.

"Grady, you need to get in touch with me as soon as possible. After looking out for you, you gonna do me like this. I need my money, nigga."

I hadn't heard from Grady in almost two weeks, and I needed my fucking money. Since he wanted to duck my calls, I wasn't dealing with him no more. He could never call me for help again. The next time I saw him, I was gonna spit right in his face.

I hopped out quickly to combat the cold. With only a short, purple velour dress, I'd gotten from Hush Boutique, and a pair of gold sparkle Uggs, I jetted into the building. What the hell possessed me not to wear a coat? After I got on the elevator, I made my way to the penthouse level. Looking at my phone, I read his text, Where you at?

I made it to his door and knocked. He was taking too long so I knocked louder, as if I was the police. Finally, Raymond opened the door, shirtless, with a towel wrapped around his waist.

"Wassup, sexy lady," Raymond said, leaning in, giving me a kiss on the cheek.

"Ewww, put some clothes on. Don't nobody want to see your naked body," I lied, sneaking a peek at his abs.

"I just got out the shower girl, shut up."

"So, you don't have anything to say to me," I said as I sat on one of the stools at the bar that surrounded his kitchen.

"You look like Rudolph, with your red nose," he laughed, as he went in the refrigerator to get a Red Bull.

"Shut up, it's cold outside. Anyway, today's my birthday."

"Aw, happy birthday, how old?"

"I'm finally legal, 21."

"Your bossy ass only 21? I can't believe it. What do you want for your birthday?"

"Something in an orange box would be nice."

"Okay, that's easy," he said, going back into the refrigerator.

"Here, you go. Happy birthday, baby girl," he said handing me a 12 pack of Sunkist.

"Boy, stop playing. I want some Hermes. You got it."

"I only buy Hermes for girls I'm fucking. Since you want to keep being my home-girl, you don't get Hermes."

"Boy, you cheap as shit. You don't even want to give girls you sleeping with a Happy Meal. I might be 21, but I ain't no dummy. Just because you got money, don't..."

Before I could say another word, his tongue was down my throat. For the first few seconds, I allowed him to kiss me, but then an image of my boyfriend came in my head. Trying to push him off me, he wouldn't let up.

"Stop, Raymond. Get off me! Uh, uh, uh, stop..." I said, as I tried fighting back my emotions. Deep down my cat was purring, but I just couldn't let my boo down, by giving in to Raymond.

"You know you want me Denie, stop fighting it," he said, as his towel fell to the floor. We struggled like two wrestlers on the kitchen floor with him landing on top of me.

"Raymond. Please stop. You're hurting me," I said as he held my wrist above my head, and pinned me down.

"Denie, please stop fighting it. Of all the bitches you've given me, they don't compare to you. I want you," he said as he sucked all over my neck. His muscular but slender frame, made it impossible for me to have any wins. His naked body sprawled over me pressing my back into the cold floor. I could feel his manhood resting on my thigh, hard as a brick.

"Raymond, get off me, or I will kill you. Do you really want to die?"

"Denie, I will die for you. I love you, girl. Your dude doesn't have to know," he said as he pulled my thong to the side. I flashed back to Javier and what he did to me with T-Roc. I was being violated once again. As tears streamed down my face, I stopped fighting. Yes, I was attracted to Raymond, but I wanted to do right by my man.

"I'm telling you, you're gonna regret this."

"Awww shit, Denie," he moaned as he entered my vagina with vengeance. As he thrust his large pole in, and out of me, I just cried.

"Why are you doing this to me? Raymond, I'm HIV positive."

"Oh yes, it's so wet," he carried on, not even hearing me.

His calloused hands wrapped tightly around my hips as he pounded my insides and made loud, annoying sounds. I continued to whine, asking that he stop, but he kept going. Finally, he was about to cum, and bust all on my stomach. By this time my dress was around my ankles. I was humiliated.

"Happy birthday, Denie. Now you can have all the Hermes you want."

"Raymond, fuck you, and your Hermes!" I shouted while standing to my feet. "Give me my fucking money, so I can get the fuck away from you, you rapist," I said getting a paper towel off the island to wipe myself off. I felt disgusting. As he handed me a kitchen dishcloth, I spit straight in his face.

"What the fuck is wrong with you?" he asked, wiping his face.

"Fuck you."

"Denie, c'mon. Why you mad? Damn girl, I couldn't resist you anymore."

"Give me my fucking money, before I go off in this bitch," I said, pulling my dress back up. He'd crossed me. Now he would die of a very slow death. Just like the rest of them. Raymond had the nerve to try and kiss my cheek, but I slapped his ass with all my might.

Distraught and angry, I rushed out of the building and bumped straight into Sadique, Juan's main soldier in the streets. Just the man I needed to see. We were supposed to be meeting later in the day for a secret meeting, but everything happened for a reason. He saved me a trip.

"Hey, Sadique, what are you doing around here?" I asked, leaning in to give him a hug. He looked, and smelled so damn good. He was a charcoal, suave brother who talked slow like he was making love in between his words.

"I came to see this chick. Why you looking all wild and crazy?" he asked me.

I shrugged my shoulders.

"What did you want to talk to me about, pretty girl?"

"You know what I told you. Stop playing."

"Denie, that's your brother. Why you tryna fuck with that man's bread?"

I blew a heavy breath through my lips and nose. “Look, you either in, or out. It seems like you wanna be Juan’s peon the rest of your life.”

“Naw, Shawty. I got plans.”

“Ummm huh… Let me know what you tryna do, Sadique. You told me you were in. So hit me up tonight and decide what you gonna do. This shit has to happen sooner than later.”

“A’ight, cutie. What are the chances of me and you getting together?”

“Stay in your lane, Sadique. I don’t fuck with the help…only bosses, nigga. Only bosses,” I said, as I hopped in my Range.

I was sick of men tryna fuck everything in sight. And I was sick of niggas dragging their feet. Juan needed to be dealt with. After running a few more errands, it was time for me to go home and get ready for my birthday celebration. Cheri had been calling me all day. Time was money and that was my focus. If I had to wear something out of my closet, that’s what had to happen. Anyway, I needed to wash Raymond off my body.

As I stepped in the gray marble, multi-jet shower, I turned the water on, and scrubbed my body so hard, I was certain a layer of skin had come off. As hard as I tried, being strong was my only option. Tears streamed down my face, as I recalled being violated once again. Sometimes I felt as though, my family was cursed. Why did so many bad things happen to us?

Once I was out of the shower, I draped myself in my terrycloth Victoria Secret robe and spread across my bed. After a quick nap, I was suddenly awakened by Cheri’s big mouth.

“Bitch, you stood me up,” she said, walking in my bedroom with shopping bags from Cusp, BCBG, and a couple of other Georgetown stores.

“I see you made out. I had a lot of errands to run.”

“Did you forget this was your day? What are you wearing?”

“Girl, something out of my closet.” As soon as I made that statement, Maria walked in, with a huge silver box, that was draped with a satin gold ribbon.

“Senorita, this just was delivered for you.”

“Thanks, Maria.”

As soon as Maria left, I started tearing open the package. A part of me was nervous, after receiving that card this morning.

Inside the box, there were multiple boxes. As I sat on my velvet black duvet, I started to rip open the first box. Inside lay a custom-made leather outfit. Next, were the new black Christian Louboutin

Spike Wars booties, I'd been dying over. Then to top it all off, a cobalt blue Birkin bag to set it off.

"Oh my goodness! Cheri, you see this shit!"

"Um, um…it's cool," she said hating.

Envy filled her face.

My boo surprised me often, but this time he'd outdone himself. Finally I pulled out the gold envelope and found a red heart inside that read:

Babe, enjoy your night and represent your man. Since I'm not partying with you, I wanted to make sure that I sent you off right. See you when I get back in town. XOXO Your 6ft Something Boo

It sucked that he had to be out of town for his game, but this made up for it. My smile appeared to be painted on. It was a huge, wide grin that couldn't be shielded.

"When he gets back in town, I'mma fuck the shit out of him!" I screamed. All my tears immediately disappeared. My day was getting better.

"Girl, you crazy! Who is this boo, Denie?" Cheri pried.

"Someone that I've known for a couple of years, and I finally gave the time of day. I'm so damn happy I did."

"What's the big secret, Denie?"

"Cheri, I'd just rather keep some things private. I told you, it's complicated."

"Is he married or something?"

Now she was getting under my skin. The bitch needed to be slapped, or maybe even pistol-whipped. Why couldn't she just stop prying? "Hell no. Just famous and I'm not ready to be in the limelight just yet."

Reaching into my Chanel Chain Around bag I got my iPhone out, went to my favorites and got my boo on the phone.

"What up, beautiful," he answered after only two rings.

"Hey babe! I love you so much! Thanks for my gifts."

"You're welcome, sweetheart. You deserve it. I'm on my way to my game. Call me when you get in later to let me know you made it home."

"Ok babe. Love you."

"Love you, too."

"I love you. Are you kidding?" Cheri commented. " I have never heard you tell a dude you loved them. Who is this new guy? Girl, you was a man-eater in Florida."

"Well, some things have changed. Maybe I'm maturing. You should try it sometime." I laughed as Cheri purposely ignored my last jab. She was so unhappy in her relationship it didn't make any sense. But I wasn't about to let her rain on my sunshine.

"So, you got a mystery man, huh?" Cheri continued to pry.

"Girl, does it matter?" I said with a smile. That shit was eating her up and I enjoyed every bit of it. Snapping a couple of photos of my birthday gifts for Instagram, I was overjoyed.

My medicine sometimes made me feel a little nauseous, so after taking my medicine, I wanted to have some time to chill. With the weather changing, I felt like I was coming down with something. After lying down for a little while, I gave BJ a bath and read him a story, then it was time to get ready.

Jermaine ended up doing my hair in my beauty suite as soon as my make-up artist, my girl Kym Lee, left the house. My beauty suite was one of my favorite rooms in the house. It was where Jermaine and I acted a fool while he whipped my hair fabulously. Juan had the room remodeled for me last year. It was gorgeous, pink and silver with framed fashion icon photos. There were crystals and sparkles everywhere. It was fun, yet classy and made me feel girly.

I loved the messy, high bun Jermaine gave me. After he put the finishing touches on, he spun me around and gave me a kiss on the cheek.

"Sista, you look gorgeous," Jermaine commented with tears in his eyes. " Girl, do you know how many people I know in your situation who look terrible? But, you're not letting that monster take you down and I love it. You still be looking fabulous, boo-lite! You been taking your meds, right?" he asked in a caring tone.

"Yeah, but sometimes I get real nauseous which is frustrating. The good thing is that I don't look sick. I don't want anybody to find out about my secret. I want to tell my boo on my own time." I paused to smile, thinking about his sexy ass. He's such a good dude, even wanting to adopt my son."

"Shut the front door! Does he have any kids?"

"No, and I don't want to deprive him. It's hard, but I think he's the one. I'm going to marry that man."

"Well, are y'all using condoms, chile?"

"Yes, and he always tries to take them off."

"Oh shit. Chile, I don't know what to tell you on that one. But for now you look great and we gonna have a ball tonight, so let's get outta here."

We all looked good as we left my house and headed to Stadium, a club in Northeast, D.C. It felt weird celebrating my birthday but it also felt good. Juan decided not to come with us because he didn't want to leave Mecca. I wasn't sure how I felt about that kinda betrayal. Fuck that nigga anyway.

The club was packed and we had such a great time. We brought my birthday in right. At the end of the night, I was drunk as hell. Cheri and I actually got along and had a blast. As we came out of the club, I could barely walk but made it to valet. Searching through my Alexander McQueen skull clutch, I finally found my ticket and handed it to the valet guy.

"Umm, ma'am, this car has already been picked up," he said, handing my ticket back to me.

"What the hell you mean? Where the fuck is my truck? It's a black Range Rover Sport, with…"

Just when I was about to go ham on the valet guy, l was interrupted as soon as I looked up. My six-foot something lover, stood there leaning on what looked like a luxurious silver bullet. I wondered how long he stood there watching me act a fool.

"What the…no you didn't! The new drop top Bentley continental!" I said with my mouth wide open. I wasn't sure if I was drunk, or just emotional because it was my birthday, but tears streamed down my face.

"You don't need that old shit no more. I can't have my girl riding around in a whip another dude bought anyway." My babe surprised me. He really outdid himself this time.

"That's your boo?" Cheri questioned. Her expression said it all. "No wonder you kept him a secret. Cornell, Lisa's old boo? This shit is war."

Chapter 9
Juan

For the past couple of days I hadn't been able to sleep. I had those feelings I used to have as a child on Christmas mornin'. Today was the first day I'd be able to prove myself, makin' a major move with Big Tony. Dressed in a black custom Tom Ford suit, and my Chrome Heart black shades, I looked like money. We were meetin' in Phoenix, Arizona for my first test run with product. This deal was huge. Coke on the West Coast was way more reasonable than on the East Coast. That was why it was important for me to make this new connect work. I was gettin' the shit for $20,000 a kilo, and sellin' it on the East Coast for $35,000 a kilo. Big Tony had decided to start me off with 50 kilos to see how fast I moved the shit. In two weeks or less, I could make a quick $750,000. With me having the main distribution on the East on lock, it wasn't gonna be hard to make him a believer.

That was the main reason why I decided to go solo on this move. It was important that I gained Big Tony's trust on my own, without Julio. Especially since I hadn't figured out the relationship between Julio and Tony. I wanted to make it clear, that I was runnin' the show. Julio was my partner, but I was his connection, even if he already knew Tony Jr. somehow. I was pullin' the strings with Big Tony, the one who called the shots.

As I boarded the private plane for a 7:00 a.m. departure at Dulles International Airport, all of sudden I got nervous. Butterflies fluttered in my stomach as I said a quick prayer before take-off. My man Shaka let me borrow his private plane once again. Of course he didn't know the circumstances. If he knew what I was up to, or if I got caught, it would ruin him. But I had to take this chance. Whenever I flew private, TSA never fucked wit' me, so I felt that was the best way to go. When I landed on the tarmac and we exchanged for the goods, I wanted to look like money. It had to be clear to Big Tony, that I was a boss, too.

After over four hours on the plane, I finally arrived to my destination. It was time for me to make shit happen.

"Alright, Mr. Washington, thanks for a safe flight. I will be back in less than two hours," I said to the pilot as I deplaned.

"No problem, Juan. See you in a bit," the pilot responded as he waved goodbye. It was a half past 9:00 a.m., and I had to be at the hotel to meet Big Tony at ten oclock. Luckily, the hotel was at the airport.

As the Suburban Mecca reserved for me, pulled up, I smiled. Mecca was finally coming around, handlin' wifey duties like she was supposed to. I pulled up right on time to the Marriott with my suitcase in hand. Half a mill, just like I promised. It was half down on the cost of the cocaine. The rest I'd pay off after it was sold. Nervously, I made my way through the bright foyer and had a seat in one of the oversized orange chairs. Suddenly my phone rang from a private number just as we'd discussed.

"Hello."

"Juan, I see you've arrived," the unfamiliar voice responded. "The blonde woman that just came into the lobby with the white dress on will show you to the business suite."

I never had time to respond to the Hispanic sounding voice. Just like that, he hung up. As I looked around the lobby, I wondered who was watchin' me. I was supposed to get a call with instructions, but they knew I'd arrived before I called.

"Juan?"

"Yes."

"Come with me," a blonde, Hispanic woman instructed.

As I followed her to the elevator I couldn't help but look at her hour glass shape. She was bad as shit, but the thought of banging her out didn't ease my anxiety. My stomach was in knots. I couldn't believe the moment I had been waitin' for was here. I was moments away from makin' some real bread.

Once we got off the elevator, I felt like I was in desperate need of a ginger ale. I was nauseous as hell. As we approached the door, I could hear Big Tony speakin'. A gentleman opened the door and me and the blonde woman walked in. There were a couple of women half dressed on the red couch snortin' coke, and watchin' television as if they had been up all night. Right behind the couch stood Big

Tony and his protruding gut, while two other guys sat at the long wood table.

"Come have a seat," Big Tony demanded as he took a seat beside me. "So Juan, how was your flight? Everything good?"

I felt like I'd taken a seat next to a hairy lion. "I'm good. It was an early, but smooth flight."

"I see you fly private. You have your own plane?" he asked as I looked around the room in disbelief. How the hell did he know I flew private?

"Um, yes, I mean no. Kinda sorta. How did you know that?"

"Juan, I have eyes everywhere," he said sternly. He just stared at me for the next thirty seconds.

I felt uneasy, until he finally spoke. "Listen, I want to make sure we're clear on a few things. This way, you're responsible for your own death if you fuck up. There are three things I don't play with: my money, my family, and my money, in that order. You can make a lot of money if you fuck with me. But you can also die a painful death if you fuck over me."

"Big Tony, with all due respect, I'm tryin' to eat. At the end of the day, we both want the same things. I'm hungry and I'm ready. That's all I want to do is make this money."

"Sounds good. You really are a Sanchez."

I wasn't sure how to feel about his last comment. It was partially a look of admiration but also a look of pity.

"Now, I have a present for you," he said, motioning his hand for the blonde young lady to come over. She handed me a box that was on the table behind us, where the phone sat. The box was wrapped in silver paper, and had a huge silver bow. As I began openin' the box, I was a little excited. It looked like it could've been a watch inside the box. I had always been a sucker for expensive watches. As I tore through the paper, I got to a nice shiny wooden box. I smiled, just before openin' the box. Instead of a twenty thousand dollar gift, I got the shock of my life.

"Holy shit! What the fuck is this?" I said droppin' the box on the table as two bloody eyeballs fell out. I felt like I was about to have a heart attack.

"Juan, there's no need to be afraid. Just be aware. If you fuck with my money, I will carve not only your eyes out of the socket, but your sister, Denie will be eyeless as well. Capice?"

"Yeah. Capice," I said, watching the eyeballs on the table stare back at me. How in the hell did he know Denie? I was so ready to get the fuck outta there.

"Well, here's the money. You can count it. It's all here. Fair exchange, no robbery," I said, standin' up and handin' Big Tony the suitcase.

After a quick exchange for a half a mill, and 50 kilos of coke, I was ready to be on my way.

"I'll be in touch in the next couple of weeks," I told him. By then I should have the other half a mill."

"For sure. I'm startin' you off small. Show me what you can do, and then the sky is the limit. No more upfront money needed."

"Yes, sir," I said, picking up my fully loaded suitcase, that once was filled with money. It was now filled with the best blow in the country.

As I made my way to the door, Big Tony stopped me."

"Hey Juan, you're forgetting something, here you go. Take this with you as a reminder of what will happen to you if you fuck me over. See, your friend, Star, didn't have such luck, so take a little piece of him with you," he said as he picked up one of the eyeballs that fell out on the table, and put it back in the box.

I couldn't believe it. Big Tony was responsible for killin' my connect; the same dude who introduced me to Julio. Shit, Star was my connect to Big Tony. There was no way I was fuckin' this man over.

I made it back on the plane safely and was soon on my way back to the DMV. As bad as I wanted to take a nap on the plane, the excitement I felt wouldn't allow me to. As soon as we landed, I became edgy after seeing a couple of police in front of the doors of the lobby area.

"Okay Juan, we made it back safely. I'll see you next time," the pilot told me exiting the plane.

"Cool, thanks for a safe flight."

Nervous as hell, takin' my time, I finally got off the plane. As I walked up to the lobby area, I nodded to the police, and kept it movin'. My stomach turned as I prayed to God there were no K-9's in sight. Makin' it thru the lobby and out to the parkin' lot I was safe and sound. Wit' 50 kilos of coke in my suitcase, it was easy to be noid.

Finally, I was at my car and ready to drop my shit off at the condo. It would be safe there for now. It was a little after eight o'clock and the night was still young. There was money to be made, and I was ready to get it. I was supposed to meet Julio at midnight and was already runnin' behind. I dropped the kilos at my spot then jetted to my house to see Mecca.

As I pulled up in my cul-da-sac, I was excited about what the night would bring. Maybe my girl would give me some, I thought to myself as I turned the key and went in the house. Tryin' to surprise my girl, I quietly entered the room.

"Would you stop questioning me? Look, I don't have time for this shit. You should've said something a long time ago," Mecca said into the phone. "Well, so what? Look, I have to go," she shouted.

"Babe, who are you yellin' at?" I asked Mecca, walkin' into the room.

She jumped, damn near dropping her phone.

"Um, my sister," she said, as her fingers scrambled to end the call.

"What's goin' on?" I asked, as I started to take off my suit. Down to my t-shirt, I hoped she would be turned on. My workout game lately had been on point and my six-pack was definitely back. Tryna shoot my shot, I took off the rest of my clothes in front of Mecca, hopin' she'd finally give me some head. She claimed the doctor said, no sex yet. But hell, she had other tools.

"So, what were y'all talkin' about?"

"Who I was talking to, or about, isn't important, Juan. But what is important is you finally telling the truth about who scratched your face up? The scar by your eye still hasn't cleared up yet."

"It's not important," I fired back, to shut her up. I knew damn well she wasn't talking to her sister. I just wasn't in the mood to play private eye. Even though, she probably still wanted an explanation, she wasn't gettin' one. From the blood on my boots to my busted up hand, she knew it was a messed up reason why I wasn't there for her when she lost the baby. She didn't need to know why, and I still wasn't telling her. It would blow over eventually, just like everything else did.

"Babe, I'd rather not discuss things about my business with you. You know this about me. Now, can I get some head before I get changed?

"I'm not in the mood," she spat.

I would have to get a side-chick soon. I damn sho wasn't gonna have blue balls waitin' on Mecca's pussy to get hot.

I showered, changed, and told her I had to go. "Somebody flew in from out of town to meet with me. I'll be back in a couple of hours."

"Juan, do you have to leave?" Mecca whined. "It's eleven o'clock at night."

I had been in the house with her too many days. I'd held off on a lot of my business and hadn't been available to everybody. Unless it involved collecting my cash, it got pushed back. I still hadn't been back over to dispose of Grady's body, and had even missed Denie's birthday celebration.

"Mecca, I got some major meetings happenin' tonight. I'm sorry, babe." I leaned in, kissed her on the cheek then asked the question, "A movie date, dinner, and shoppin' spree, don't give me a pass to go out and handle my business? Somebody gotta pay for it all," I joked.

In my heart, I meant that shit. Time was money.

"I need you, Juan. I feel alone," Mecca stated, starin' at me with tears in her eyes.

Ever since she'd lost the baby she had been puttin' the guilt shit on me heavily. So of course, I fed into her bullshit.

"Sweetheart, I'm here for you."

"So, everything you said to me a few days ago was bullshit. You said you were going to make a better effort in being here for me, emotionally, and physically during this time. Seems like it's the same shit, different day. As soon as somebody calls you about some money, your antenna raises up like a robot."

"In order for you to live the way you do, this is what it takes. It's levels to this shit, and I'm not tryin' to fall. I need you to be strong for me, too. It takes a certain kind of woman to deal with me," I said as I started to put on my fresh, new Tims.

"So what are you saying, Juan?"

"Baby, all I'm sayin' is that I love you, and I want you to be patient with me. I don't plan on livin' this lifestyle much longer, but it's some major shit about to go down, that will set us up for a lifetime. I want more. I don't just want to be a millionaire, I want multi-millions. I'm tryna sit back, and chill in the next year. I'm almost there. It would be nice to have the woman I love, by my side, chillin' right along with me."

I leaned in to kiss her dead on the lips, but she pulled away.

"Juan, I'm not with you for your money. I love you!" With pain in her voice she continued, "With or without the monetary things." She rolled her eyes, and folded her arms. Mecca had become overly spoiled, and I was to blame.

"But the money is a plus, ain't it? Who wants a broke,dude?" I asked, irritated that this talk was lasting longer than needed. I had a meeting that was happenin' in Baltimore in less than 45 minutes. If I had to listen to her complain much longer, I would be late.

"Juan, just stay, please," Mecca whined, followed by the puppy dog eyes.

I stood firm and gave her a kiss on her forehead; that kiss that guys give their girls, when they're headed out to do dirt.

Rushin' up the stairs to get to the main part of the house, I bumped into Cheri's phat ass in the foyer, while tryin' to get out the door. Her ass had gotten bigger over the last few years. Kim Kardashian had nothin' on her. Meanwhile, she was temptin' the hell out of me. Why she was still at my house, I had no idea, especially since Denie hadn't been home. She was walkin' around the house, half dressed, of course. Her white T-shirt, had Pink written across the front, and fell off her shoulder bearing JS, the tattoo of my initials she got, when we lived in Florida. As she turned the corner, once she got to the bottom of the steps, I noticed the tee was barely covering her ass.

"Where you on your way to in a hurry?" she asked, starin' at me with an extra arch in her back. Her nipples were hard, and that instantly had my pole at attention.

"Time is money, young lady," I said, approachin' the door tryin' to ignore her, but she made it hard.

"Juan, why won't you touch me? Did I hurt you that bad?" she asked, with sincerity.

"Naw Shorty. We cool. I'm numb. Can't no chick hurt me. The only women I feel for are Denie, and my mother. Denie my road dog, and my mother's not here no more, so that means, I'm good."

"Burrr, so cold. Well, I miss us. You don't think of me sometimes?" Cheri asked, rubbin' herself between her legs. She knew how to break me. The closer she got to me, the harder I got. I could smell her Tom Ford Black Orchid fragrance that made me weak.

"Is your daughter, Ariel, really mine?" I asked, tryin' not to give in, as my dick got harder and harder.

"Stop trying to skip the subject. Don't worry about Ariel for now. She's well taken care of. Worry about taking care of that big bulge in your pants," she said, grabbin' my manhood through my jeans.

"Whoaaaaa. What are you doing?" I asked, tryna back up. I ended up landin' right against the wall.

"Trying to make you want me. Just like old times."

"Cheri, we can't do this."

"Why not?" she spat.

Before I could answer, she'd already started to unbuckle my Louis Vuitton belt. She was on her knees, with my man in her mouth within seconds. As she sucked, and slurped, I watched her gyrate her phat ass up, and down. I couldn't resist her. The shit felt so good, as she tightened her lips around my piece, and went into overdrive. It felt as if, she had no reflex in her mouth. There was no way I could stop her. I had to have her right there.

"Get up. Get up," I said stoppin' her, as I pulled her up to her feet. Waistin' no time, she started passionately kissin' me all over my neck, and in my mouth.

"Juan, come upstairs."

I followed behind her like a lost puppy with my premium denim, wrapped around my ankles. We didn't even make it to the guest room before we were back at it right in the hallway. I stumbled over my pants, as we fondled each other, and found ourselves on the floor, kissing again. Finally, makin' it to the room Cheri was stayin' in, it was on and poppin'.

"Juan, put that big dick inside of me right now," Cheri begged.

Pulling her thong to the side, I did just that.

"Do you miss this? You miss me, Juan?"

"Hell yeah. You feel so damn good and wet."

"Juan, you're hurting me, but it feels so damn good. I love this big dick. Boy, please don't stay away from me anymore. Tell me, Juan. Tell me I can have you when I need you," she moaned.

"You can have it when you want," I lied.

My thrust got deeper and harder making my eyes roll to the back of my head. Her shit was so tight. It felt like she'd been savin' herself, just for me. Strokin' in and out of her wet box, felt like heaven. I missed Cheri more than I wanted to admit, but I kept my distance. The truth was, she did hurt me.

I was so caught up in her good pussy, everything I had to do went out the window. Cheri straddled my lap, and started ridin' me from the back. As I watched her ass bounce on my stomach, moanin' and shoutin' like she was having convulsions, I was ready to bust.

"Cheri, get up, I'm about to cum…oh shit," I whispered out of breath as I ejaculated all in her.

"Juan, I love you," Cheri whispered in my ear, as she leaned back on my chest.

"Girl, you don't love me. Stop playin'," I said, as I avoided sayin' it back.

"No, I really do," she said sincerely.

There wasn't any time to get caught up in no love triangle shit. I did still have feelings for Cheri, but I promised Mecca I would do right for a change, so I had to put my feelings for Cheri aside.

"Hello, is anybody up here?" a voice sounded, takin' me from my thoughts.

That voice was way too familiar. Shit, it was Mecca.

"Who's there?" Cheri called out.

I gave her the look of death, but then she calmed me down assurin' me, it was all good.

"Oh, never mind. I was looking for Maria," Mecca answered through the door. Her tone warned me that she was already irritated.

Cheri jumped out of bed freshly fucked, with her blonde curly long hair all over the place, and opened the door. My heart sunk to my knees.

"You good, Miss Lady," Cheri instigated, with that 'I just got fucked', and 'I want you to know it' pose.

"There's nothing your hoe ass could do for me," Mecca fired back.

"You sure about that?" Cheri questioned, before slammin' the door in Mecca's face.

"What the fuck are you doin'?" I whispered nervously.

"What are you all nervous for? She's gone," she said, trying to rub on me, as if she wanted to go for round two.

"Alright man, I gotta bounce." I pulled my pants up as fast as I could and rushed into the bathroom to clean myself up. Within the next ten minutes, I found myself sneakin' out of the bedroom, to the foyer, and out to my car. Damn, that shit was worse than ducking the Feds.

Chapter 10
Juan

Finally, I made it safely to my car and onto the main road. It was already after midnight. Cheri's shit was good, but wasn't worth me missin' out on my money. Just when I picked up my phone to call Julio, it rang. He was callin' me. Julio was serious about his business, so I knew what to expect. He had driven down from Philly, so he could catch his flight in the mornin' to L.A. from BWI. I told him we could meet at this new spot in Baltimore that was popping. His cousin was in town also, so I had to hurry up. Julio said his cousin was about to make some major shit happen on the west coast. I wasn't tryna mess that up. The way I'd been lining all my business deals up had been working in my favor so far. This shit was bigger than Los and Rich. It was huge, and I was ready.

"Man, where you at?" Julio belted through the phone.

"Something came up, but I'm getting on 95 now. I should be there in like twenty minutes."

"What kind of place you got me at? This place seems hot?" Julio shot, tryin' to hide his strong Colombian accent.

"You at The Honey Comb Hideout, right?"

"Yeah, man. But this spot looks hot. All types of ratchet dudes and chicks out here."

"Did your cousin make it in yet?" I asked

"Yeah, Blow is here with me. We go back to L.A. in the morning, so we need to get this meeting going sooner than later. You know I like things to go as planned."

"Bet… See you in a minute."

Pushing the pedal to the metal in my Maserati, I hit 120 mph up 95N towards Baltimore. Damn, my gas was past "E" but there was no time to stop for gas. My reserve tank was gonna have to get me there. Turnin' up my Raheem DeVaughn CD, I let my mind get on chill mode, before I got to my business meeting. The song, Wrong Forever came on, and made me think about how I just screwed up again. Mecca was so vulnerable right now. It was scary how she reminded me so much of my mother. Was that why I was so drawn to Mecca? Why would I fuck Cheri right under her nose? Man, I really fucked up. The more I tried not to be like my father with his cheatin' ways, I continued to spiral down his path. Feelin' guilty, I decided to call Mecca to make sure Cheri's hot ass, didn't dry snitch on me.

After callin' Mecca's phone a couple of times there was no answer. I hoped her and Cheri hadn't gotten into it, so I decided to call Cheri's phone.

"Hey Cheri. Wassup?"

"Miss me already?"

Her words made me smile, but I wasn't about to let her know that. "You ain't snitch on me, did you?" I asked, avoidin' her question.

"What I look like? I don't owe Mecca nothing. I'm just down for you, Juan." I loved the sound of those words. "So, we spending Thanksgiving together? 'Cause if we not, I'm leaving for a couple weeks."

"C'mon Cheri. You know I can't spend the holiday with a side chick."

Silence filled the air while I waited on her next comment. When she didn't say anything, I asked, "Do me a favor?"

"What?"

"Check and see if my Porsche out front."

"If you looking for your bitch, she left out right after you."

"A'ight, bet."

"Nigga, bye," she blasted.

What the fuck was Mecca up to? She rarely left the house, and going out close to midnight was definitely out of character. Was she cheating? I thought back to the guy she and Denie were arguing about. Was there really a Charlie, my mind wondered?

Mecca was so insecure, and sometimes came across weak, but there was still a strange mystery to her. The kind of mystery I didn't like. She had become a little too sneaky lately. It was probably my fault, but I promised her I would do better.

Me fucking Cheri was a mistake. And I couldn't let it happen again. I hated that my father did the same type of shit to my mother, and here I am, lettin' history repeat itself. My mother wouldn't be proud of the man I had become, but she would be proud of the man I was gonna be.

Rubbin' my tattoo on my rib, with the shrine I dedicated to my mother I whispered soflty, I love you. Give me a year. It was gonna be a new day. Going legit was the goal and I knew my new situation with Big Tony would put me in position. Before it was all over, I would be an honest man. Gettin' off the exit to the club, I made a right on Pratt Street.

What the hell was going on here? I thought to myself as I pulled up to the valet, at The Honey Comb Hideout. I see why Julio was paranoid. It was crazy outside. It felt like everybody and their mothers were in the parkin' lot. After givin' the valet guy a Ben Franklin and instructin' him to keep my car up front, I texted Julio, to let him know I was walkin' in. He texted me back tellin' me where they were.

As I made my way through the crowd, I saw Julio and his cousin in the VIP area, towards the back. They stood out like sore thumbs; two Colombian men with Black swag. Julio, with his flashiness, all iced up in all black, with shades. He kind of reminded me of Danny Garcia, the boxer, while his cousin looked like an oversized bodyguard. He was huge. In an all black establishment, they definitely couldn't go unnoticed.

"What's up, my man?"

I gave Julio some dap and a manly hug.

"Juan, this is my cousin, Blow," he announced, with a quick introduction.

"What up, Blow. So you guys enjoying the scenery?" I asked, as I looked at all the naked girls around the club.

"A little too many people in here," he told me dryly.

"You come here often?" Julio asked.

"It's actually my first time in here. People been talking 'bout the spot all week."

I looked around admiring my surroundings, right before some strippers walked up to our table askin' if we wanted lap dances. They were all over Julio, but he turned them down. He was focused. That was something I needed to be more of. If they weren't here, I would've been tipping heavy, slidin' hundreds in the cracks of asses, while gettin' my freak on.

"Man, how you pass up that big ole ass?" I asked, jokingly tryin' to break the ice.

"Pussy can't pay my bills," he said sternly. "Now, let's get down to business. We're not trying to be here long."

"This good news won't take long," I shot back proudly. I couldn't wait to shit on the nigga Julio. He thought he was so much better than me. "Big Tony started me with fifty big ones. I gave him half a mill for us. That's why I told you to bring your two hundred fifty. You got it, right?"

"You know it. It's in the stash spot in my ride. We cool."

"Good, so I got 25 bricks in the car for you. We got like two weeks to make this shit happen, so we can re-up and get that real paper."

"That's a bet," Julio said as Blow co-signed with a nod.

"Cool. We gotta divide and conquer, like we been doin'. I'll continue to take care of B-more, D.C., VA and all the DMV, and you got Delaware to New York."

"Bet," he told me, listening intently to my every word.

I'd started to feel like a boss...like Julio finally understood that I was the go-to-guy. His cousin Blow didn't say much. He simply kept his ear to the sound of my voice. After discussin' more possibilities for expansion and ways to move our shit faster, we were interrupted by a loud crash behind us. The next loud crash just missed my head by inches. Someone was hurlin' Moet bottles in our direction.

"Yo, bitch. What's good?" a baritone voice sounded.

We were approached by a very dark skinned, short guy, with a missing eye. The shit was too gruesome to look at. It looked as though someone shot him in his face or something. At first, I thought he'd made a mistake because I had never seen dude a day in my life. But as he got closer, I realized I was his mark.

"Who you talking to partner?" I asked. I had my chest stuck out, face twisted, and my fist bawled up, banging each fist into the other hand.

"Yo bitch ass!" the ugly dude yelled, standing over me.

"Slim, we handlin' some grown man shit over here..." I barked before bein' interrupted by a big hand straight to my face. I jumped up off the break, and rushed the nigga. We tussled a bit, with me able to throw just two punches before we were both grabbed by security. Before they could break us up, we were surrounded by what felt like the entire population of B-more. At first I felt like I was by myself, wonderin' if Julio and his cousin were gonna have my back, until he gave me his infamous nod. Like, I got this.

"Only bitch ass niggas put they hands on other niggas' kids," dude shouted out. "You fuckin' put yo hands on my nephew, Lil' Man. Now, we gon' put our hands on you, punk."

"Your punk ass nephew bussed off at me. You lucky I ain't kill that lil' nigga, and his funky, freak ass mother."

I prepared myself when I saw Peaches' baby father walk in my direction. I wasn't packin' because my hammer was in the car, which was the dumbest mistake I could've made. Glancin' at the poster to my right on the column, I realized that it was his album release party. That's why it was so crazy in the club.

As soon as he walked up to me, I crept away from security and open hand smacked the shit out of him. I had to. They wasn't gonna make me look like a punk in front of my partner. They had to know that I wasn't soft. I needed to make a name for myself. This was the perfect time to do it. Slice fell straight to the ground and before anyone else could jump on me; Julio and Blow flashed their guns.

"Now y'all gonna back the fuck up or we spraying this motherfucker down," Julio said, as he stood over all those short bastards.

"Juan, you gone die, nigga! You gone die," Slice yelled as the bouncers carried him and his entourage out.

I figured we were getting put out next until an unsuspecting figure appeared.

"You guys need to come this way," a sexy, caramel colored woman told us.

I looked her up and down wonderin' where she'd come from. Her body was amazing. It seemed too good to be true, though. What were the chances of a voluptuous woman, comin' to help us get out of there, just like that?

"Sweetheart, we're going out the way we came in. You probably with them niggas," I blurted in a stern tone.

"I'm the owner, Juan. My name is Honey. This is my spot and I'm not trying to get closed down my first week. I got bills."

"How do you know my name?" My face twisted along with the sides of my mouth.

"Who doesn't? I was also a good friend of your father, Rich. He's helped me out a lot and now I've gotta help you. Now, come on before somebody snitches. You're packing, right?"

I searched Julio's eyes to see what he thought. I could tell Blow was all for it. When they both nodded in agreement, we all followed Honey to the back of club, and to an exit door leadin' to an alley where she had valet pull our cars up.

"Thanks, beautiful. Your man must be lucky, cuz you fine as hell," I said flirtin' with the owner. I kept licking my lips, on some LL, or Nelly type shit.

"Thanks for the compliment."

"And again, sorry for the inconvenience tonight," I added as I jumped in my ride.

"Juan, just get out of here. I would hate for something to happen to you," she said, as if she really cared.

Julio told me to follow him up the street a bit to a secluded area. I watched Honey walk back into the club and followed his lead where we exchanged his money for twenty-five bricks. Just like that we were done and on our way to making major paper. It was the start to somethin' big.

"Juan, we out," Julio yelled from the passenger window of the black Escalade.

"Man, thanks for having my back in there. You didn't have to do that."

"Yes, I did. You'll probably have my back one day, too. But one thing homes, you gotta stop fuckin' with this hot, flashy type shit. It brings heat. Hit me up tomorrow," Julio said before Blow sped off quickly, burning rubber.

I was a little embarrassed that I'd put him and Blow in such a compromisin' position, that could've cost them their lives, or freedom. Surprisingly, they were very understanding. My thoughts reverted back to Honey. How did she know my father, I wondered? She seemed too familiar with me, and it had me concerned.

Pullin' off and makin' my way onto the main road, I was instantly irritated. My fuckin' car was damn near on empty. I didn't feel like stoppin' for gas in B-more. Reaching in my custom stash spot, behind the radio, I grabbed my .45 and placed it on my lap, while I hauled ass down the street. As soon as I pulled into the gas station, my car cut off right before I got to the pump. Puttin' my gun in my waistband, I approached the attendant behind the window, then pulled out a wad that made the attendants' eyes dance.

"My man. Put $80.00 on that pump right there," I said, pointin' to the pump closest to my car. "Also, I kind of need your help. My car just cut off. Can you help me push it closer to the pump?"

"Sorry, not safe. Sorry," he repeated in a heavy, Indian accent, not givin' me any eye contact through the bulletproof glass.

"Man, here's $200 just for you. Just need you to help me real quick."

His neck jerked back as he tried to process what I'd just said. His mind changed rather quickly.

"No problem," he uttered, then snatched the two hundred dollar bills up.

Before I knew it, he'd grabbed his old, run down coat and was out of the booth. He kept watchin' me as he slid his cap over his head. It had gotten unusually cold for this time of year so we were both in a hurry.

"Thanks man, I appreciate it."

"You seem like a nice man, but I don't know who to trust out here," he told me while tryin' to lighten the mood. "They try and rob me three times out here. I'm saving up now to get cameras put up. I just got the bullet proof glass installed and that's helped a lot."

He stopped talkin', after realizin' the car was too heavy for only the two of us to push, without exertin' ourselves. All talking shut down until we had the car close enough to the pump.

"Damn, I'm sorry to hear that. All of us Blacks aren't bad people tho. Here's an extra $200.00 for your troubles. I'm Juan, what's your name?" I asked him, as I started pumping the gas tryin' to put him at ease.

His eyes lit up.

"I'm Dezi. I'm sorry, but Baltimore isn't safe anymore. Me and my wife moved to the United States ten years ago for a better life. You people just don't know how blessed you are in America. We try to teach our kids the way we learned life. You have kids? You seem like a good man, Juan."

"Umm…"

Before I could answer, a tinted SUV busted a U-turn and screeched into the gas station at top speed. As the window rolled down, I knew what time it was. Suddenly, somebody started lettin' off rounds. Before I could grab my gun from my waist, Dezi was shot to the ground then riddled with bullets. Blood oozed from his head, and I instantly got a flashback of Grady. I wasn't tryna die.

"Oh shit," I said, runnin' for cover behind the dumpster as I fired back. I could see there were two people in the truck, but couldn't make out their faces from afar. Hidin' behind the dumpster, I said a quick prayer, as I heard footsteps getting closer to me. Now they were on foot, I knew it was either gonna be them, or me.

"Yo, I think he went behind the dumpster. I'mma go that way. You check over there," I heard a raspy voice call out.

All I could think about was my girl askin' me to stay home. Watchin' my life flash before my eyes, I heard the footsteps get closer. I wondered about the likelihood of me survivin' two against one. As soon as the face peered around the trashcan, I bust straight at him shootin' the stranger right in the chest.

"Aighhh…" he said, fallin' to the ground.

Breathin' heavily, I knew what had to be done. Gettin' straight over top of him, I shot him again, straight in the head. Next thing I knew, bullets started flyin'. Tryin' to make it to my car, I felt a bullet fly straight past my ear. My adrenaline pumped while I ran like crazy, dodgin' each and every shot. Still, the next one hit me in my side. I could feel the burning sensation run through my body. It felt like balls of fire ignited my insides. Fallin' to the ground, I knew I was gone. There was nothin' I could do. Just as I looked up and saw Slice's brother standin' over me with a gun aimed straight at my face, I knew I was dead. As I closed my eyes to face my demise, I heard the gun go off and felt a large weight hit my chest.

Chapter 11
Rich

"No, it can't be. What the fuck? Am I dead?" Juan wailed in a panic.

Confused, he tried to make out my face as I pulled the dead body off of his chest. Juan would've been six feet deep, if I hadn't gotten that phone call from Honey. These B-more niggas, must've thought it was sweet. If it was up to me, Juan wasn't goin' out like that. That's why I killed that punk. Two shots to the back of his head, I fried his ass. The bastard never saw it comin'. Little did Juan know, eighty-five percent of the time I watched over him in the wind. He was being protected, and didn't even know it.

My adrenaline was turnt up. Out of nowhere, my usually weak body gained some strength. After strugglin' to get my son off the icy concrete, and puttin' him in the passenger seat of his Maserati, I said a quick prayer. It was important to get us both away from those dead bodies, before the police arrived. I jumped in the driver's side of his car and sped off. Honey followed close behind in her Beamer.

"Awww shit. It's hurting so bad. Fuck," he screamed, as he held his side. Blood was everywhere, and Juan was in a lot of pain.

"You're gonna be alright, son. You're gonna be just fine. Just hold on. I didn't fight for my life to lose you. You're a Sanchez," I preached. "Man, we got nine lives." I drove wildly, and kept makin' him understand everything would be okay. The goal was to keep his mind off the pain.

"Rich, Dad, is it really you? Am I hallucinating?" he questioned.

He became disoriented as his eyes rolled to the back of his head a couple of times, scaring the shit out of me. I definitely looked a lot different from the last time I saw my son. I'd gained at least thirty pounds and had facial hair with a little salt and pepper added in the mix. Although the scars weren't evident in my scalp, they were clearly seen all over my face. I was still sexy as shit though. I'd just aged a lil' bit, with all I had been through over the past three years.

"Rich, is that you?" he asked again.

"Yeah son, it's me. I'm alive. I'll tell you all about it. For now we have to get you to Honey's house. My in-house nurse, Nicole, is there. She'll get you straight."

Reachin' in the pocket of my Helley Hansen coat, I found my Samsung Galaxy phone, and called Nicole. I wanted to get her hip to what was going on.

"Rich, you okay?" she asked, answerin' on the first ring.

"It's my son. He's been shot. Meet me in the parking lot in two minutes."

"Oh goodness! Where? How many times?"

"I think just once. It looks like just in his left side."

"Okay! Make sure he's applying pressure to the wound."

"A'ight. Hurry up!" I said in a panic, hanging up the phone.

Dippin' through downtown B-more, we finally made it to Honey's penthouse. It was in the upscale part of Baltimore, but very low-key. Pullin' into the underground parking lot, we zipped into our reserved parking space. Nicole and Honey rushed over to the car to help with Juan. I still wasn't 100% and suffered major nerve damage, so their help was definitely needed. Nicole was on point with the wheelchair. I had Honey clean up the blood that dripped on the floor leading to her penthouse. I didn't need any of those nosy ass neighbors callin' the police on some concerned type shit.

"Nicole, he's losin' a lot of blood. And he's gettin' weaker," I said in a panic. I was never one to lose control, but this was my son, my everything.

"Oh my God, Rich, he needs to go to the hospital," Honey chimed in before getting to her assigned duty.

"Honey, shut the fuck up! Nicole will take care of him. I can't afford for him to go to the hospital. That's giving the cops ammo to ask too many fuckin' questions. You got this right, Nicole?" I asked, rushin' behind her as Juan's skin grew paler by the second.

"Rich, I'll do my best," Nicole panted. "I really won't know until we get upstairs."

Rushin' onto the elevator we were able to get inside the penthouse unnoticed. Juan was losin' consciousness. As strong as I was trying to be, I was afraid of losin' my son. As soon as we entered the penthouse, I tore off my coat, remainin' by my son's side.

After we got him from the wheelchair, to the bed, Nicole went to work, tearing off Juan's clothes.

"Juan, you good man," I told him, as we made our way to the nurse's suite that I recovered in for months, after Marisol failed at killin' me. When I was released from the hospital, there were still a lot of health issues that I needed extra care for. It was a good thing we kept the suite after my recovery.

"Call my girl. Call Mecca," Juan mumbled.

"Juan. Nobody can know about me. Not yet. Let's focus on keepin' you alive for now," I told him. I held his hand while Nicole suited up ready for work.

After over an hour of hard work, Nicole came through and saved my son. I would be forever grateful to her. As she added the final touches, stitchin' him up, I knew he was gonna be ok. Especially when she gave me the sky free nod. He just needed a lot of rest and pain medication for a day or so. I owed both her and Honey big time. I stared at Juan in disbelief. The thought of being able to touch my son again was a dream come true. Once Nicole switched Juan's IV, I felt some relief. My nerves were all fucked up. I needed Honey to make me feel better.

"Honey! Honey!" I yelled from my son's bedside.

"Yes," she said runnin' in.

"Suck my dick. My nerves are fucked up."

"Rich, right here?" she asked, looking over at Nicole and then Juan.

"Don't question me. Not now. Not ever." I gave her that face that said 'don't fuck with me'. "And why you looking over at Nicole like it's her turn. She just saved Juan. She's busy. Now come on and suck me off now," I demanded.

Just like a good girl she got on her knees and pulled my manhood out of my pants. She jerked it a few times before dripping spit on the tip, then she started going to work. Up and down on my shaft, she sucked me off like a chocolate Popsicle. "Got damn, girl," I complimented while lifting my ass as much as I could. I wanted her to get it all. "Ooooohhhhh, shit!" I shouted, not giving a fuck that Nicole watched closely. "Your skills, baby! Your skills." Closing my eyes, I could feel the nut at the tip of my dick, as I blasted off right in her mouth. As usual, she sucked and swallowed everything my dick offered. Once I opened my eyes, I looked over to see Juan awake and in disbelief. He just stared at me as if the muscles in his mouth wouldn't allow him to talk. I zipped my pants back up as Nicole took over.

"Now, Juan, you're gonna have to take it easy for a while. I got the job done, but I don't want you to have a set back," Nicole uttered, taking his attention off of me.

She gave him specific instructions to ensure he had a healthy recovery. It was clear Juan couldn't believe that Nicole was unbothered by what had taken place between Honey and me. I laughed inside. He had no idea. Nicole was used to it, and many times took part.

"Son, you scared the shit outta me," I interjected. I shook my head from side to side. It was somethin' I couldn't control due to being shot. My nerve condition took control over my body quite often.

"Dad, you're alive. I still can't believe it."

"No doubt. It's me. I'm here, baby," I said, staring at my son.

Juan kept glarin' at me through his glossy, confused eyes. It touched my heart that he called me Dad. I hadn't heard him say those words since he was around fourteen years old. He had really grown into a man; a handsome one at that. Instead of curls, or those braids I always hated, he now had wavy hair. His light mustache showed maturity. He looked just like me in my younger days, and definitely upgraded his diamond earring game. His diamond was easily over four carats. He looked like a Sanchez. My boy. I stared at him proudly.

"Man, you know I ain't goin' nowhere. I've been watchin' you, Juan. I'm proud of the man you've become."

"Man…I missed you Dad. I missed you so much. Mannnn, I still can't believe you saved me from them niggas. You popped Slice's brother for me. He woulda killed me if it hadn't been for you…and I love you for that."

"I love you too, son," I said, as I limped over to him and held him the best way I could, without hurtin' his wound that Nicole had stitched up.

"Dad, this the second time you saved my life. You might not have been there when I wanted you to, but you damn sure on time when I need you. Denie is gonna be so…"

"Juan, she can't know I'm alive," I interrupted.

"What's the big secret? Why did you stay away from us so long? Marisol said she killed you. She said she killed you and Trixie."

Juan asked me so many questions, that he'd begun to jumble his words.

"Ain't that a bitch, both of my kids' mothers set me up. They were workin' together. Trixie lured me to Atlantic City not knowing Marisol was gonna try and kill me. She ended up poppin' Trixie. Them foul bitches both dead. Hahaha, look who's still breathin'."

"Whatever happened to your daughter, Juanita?"

"She around. I make sure I send checks to the bitch, Toya, Trixie's daughter. She probably thinks it's some type of Social Security. She don't know no better. Sometimes, I ride by her school and see her from a far. She looks just like us. She's a pretty little girl."

"How old is she?"

"She just turned seven, October 26th."

"Damn, that's fucked up. I got a lil' sister that don't even know me."

"She can't miss what she don't know she have." I laughed. But the way Juan's face twisted, I knew he had more questions. He didn't find my joke too funny.

"So gettin' back to Marisol, she found out about Los?" he questioned.

"Naw, but I told her ass when she had that gun cocked at me. She tried to kill me because I robbed her ass."

"Are you serious?" Juan asked, becomin' more alert as he listened so intently.

I stared straight ahead for moments until Juan interrupted me.

"What happened, Dad? C'mon, tell me."

"When she was ready to off me, she got all emotional crying and shit, asking, how could I kill Los? She said he loved me. First, she popped me in my shoulder. She was so fucking emotional talkin' 'bout how it was my fault that Denie was sick, and blah, blah, blah. She was cryin' and shit, then shot me two more times. One bullet grazed my head and the other hit me in the jaw. See look," I said, showin' him the inside of my mouth.

I paused to show Juan the rest of my wounds.

"What the fuck? I guess it ain't meant for us to die," Juan chimed in.

"All I could think about was getting back to Denie, to get her away from that bitch Marisol, as I laid on the beach. I was determined to live, and come back for my daughter. Some white couple found me on the beach not long after Marisol shot me. I recovered for months in New Jersey. Honey was the only one I could trust, so I called her. She's been by my side ever since."

"Don't forget about me," Nicole chimed in.

“Nicole, too,” I said with a smile.

“So how long you been in B-more? How are you here, and I never once seen you?”

“Juan, I stay out the way. Once I got back from Jersey, I planned on killin’ Marisol. The entire time in the hospital, I devised different plans on how she was gonna die. When Honey brought me back here, I went past her house and saw it was vacant. I had Honey call Maria, and she said Marisol died. I figured somebody in Renzo’s camp got to her so…”

“I did it,” Juan interrupted.

“What?”

“I blasted that whore. I killed her for what she did to you, and what she did to me.”

Juan started to get a little excited. The mention of Marisol’s name hit a nerve. I hadn’t realized he hated her so much.

“Son. You more like me than you think. I didn’t realize you hated Marisol so much.”

“Fuck that bitch. I thought she killed you,” he said, rollin’ his eyes back. I wished I could take away his pain, physically and mentally as he let out a quiet moan. “Nicole, I need some morphine, or somethin’. This shit hurt.”

“Juan, I thought you were dead. I can’t…”

Juan kept watchin’ me, waitin’ for me to finish. But for some reason my thoughts were hard to verbalize at times.

“It’s ok.” Juan nodded. He understood.

“So, how’s my baby girl and my grandson doin’?” I asked, tryin’ to keep him from gettin’ even more upset.

“She’s Denie. She hates my girlfriend of course, but she’s a good sister, and an even better mother.”

“I can’t believe she’s a mother.”

I allowed a small amount of water to well up in my eyes. That faggy, cryin’ shit wasn’t in my character, but I missed my daughter.

“So, it was you?” Juan asked, as if he had discovered somethin’ big.

“What?”

“If you ain’t want her to know you were alive, why did you send her that birthday card?”

“Naw, I never sent her a card. Shit, I don’t want her to know I’m alive.”

“Who the…Man, somebody fuckin’ with us,” Juan said lookin’ puzzled.

"I've been keepin' tabs on y'all since you been back in D.C., but I ain't send no card. Anyway, why y'all leave Florida?"

"That daughter of yours was off the chain in Florida. She got me caught up in a beef down there with some dude she infected."

"Man, what the fuck?"

"She was wild'n out in Florida. Denie was fuckin' with some Dominican dude named Marcus that was paid out the ass. He was spendin' on Denie, and they were cool. I think he had a wife, and Denie found out, or some shit like that. The wife somehow found out where we lived, and popped off at our house on Denie one day. I had to man handle the bitch a little bit, and get her outta there. Denie fucked with him a little bit longer, and next thing I knew she had moved to Miami, with the football dude named Lamar."

"Dude that played for the Eagles?"

I nodded. "That lasted a little over a year then she was back in Sarasota. After she was back not even two weeks, I came home, and walked in on Marcus beating her, and me and him got into it. He told me Denie had given him HIV, and he was gonna kill her and Baby Juan. That nigga was so irate and out of control. I popped his ass right there on the spot. We had to move because that nigga was way too connected down there. He was a Blood, and his boys would've killed us all."

"You did right. Man, what the fuck is wrong with Denie?" I asked with so much hurt in my heart. She needed me, and I had to figure out a way to make my way back in her life.

"Javier fucked her up. She's calmed down a lot, but she had been hell to deal with."

Juan kept shakin' his head, making me feel like there was so much more I didn't know. But the mentionin' of Javier's name sent chills up my spine, and caused me to have a little panic attack. As my limbs started to wave out of my control, Nicole was right by my side with my medication.

"Rich, calm down. Take this," she instructed, handin' me a glass of water and my pills. As my hand shook, I got the glass to my mouth.

"I don't need help, Nicole. I got it," I said, movin' her hand off the cup as she tried to help guide it to my mouth.

My son started to tear up a little, as he stared at me with pain in his eyes. He knew I was fucked up. Hell, I knew I was fucked up, but it was nothin' that some physical therapy couldn't heal. As I motioned to Juan to finish what he was tellin' me, he carried on. But reluctantly, he kept watchin' me to see if I was okay. Juan caught me up on a lot of shit I had no clue about. From Denie's shenanigans, to how he came up on Marisol's fortune. I wondered how he was able to be gettin' the bread he was gettin', but I would've never guessed Marisol's Clinton, Maryland stash spot was how.

"Dad, I did somethin', and I don't know how you gonna take it."

"What son?"

"I killed Grady. I had to."

"What? Juan, why?"

"I looked out for him and he tried to rob me. And," Juan said with extra emphasis, "there was some chick pullin' out of the driveway when I pulled up. I think she was with Grady."

"A chick, huh? You get a good look at her?"

"Naw."

I just shook my head and listened to all the stupid mistakes he'd made. After fillin' me in on every detail I reached over and rubbed the top of his head. "I'm glad you popped Grady, son. That nigga needed to go."

"Good, 'cause I need your help."

"Anything, what?"

"I need you to help me get rid of his body."

"What the hell, Juan? Where'd you leave him?"

"He's still in the Clinton house. I had gone through so much in the past week, I hadn't made it back to take care of him."

My son still had a lot to learn. Who the fuck would leave a dead body in a house, and forget about it? Shit, I couldn't believe it. My son killed Grady. I ain't fuckin' with the nigga like that no way. Grady being dead was best for so many reasons.

All that talk about the Clinton house made me remember about a fortune that was right up under Juan's nose. I knew I had to get my hands on it. My son was back in my life now and he needed me. We needed each other. Little did Juan know, I had my eyes on the prize. He owed me anyway.

Chapter 12

Denie

Seeing those words written across my iPhone had me boiling inside. I breathed heavily while trying to read the entire story.

"Would you stay off the internet, babe?" Cornell asked me with agitation in his voice. "We had a great dinner. Please, don't let those gossip sites ruin our evening. I have more in store for my baby's 21st birthday."

Cornell knew I would be going the fuck off shortly about the new headlines on the Necole Bitchie website. It read, 'Cornell Willis Dates His Dead Ex-girlfriend's Daughter.'

"If they're gonna say shit about me, first get their facts straight. That bitch ain't my mother!" I said pissed off. He tried to touch me, but I moved away.

"Denie, do I look like I care about what the media says? If I did care, you would be a secret."

"I was a secret until the other night," I said pouting, looking over at my fine ass six-foot-something, caramel boo thang. "It's been over a year that we've been seeing each other," I added.

"You were never a secret. I just don't believe in letting others in on my personal life. Surprising you at the club with your whip was for you. To show you I love you."

"Well, I love you more," I said, staring out of the window of his Lamborghini.

He was right. After all this time it was meant for us to be together. The night I stood Cornell up and went out with Javier instead replays in my mind often. Trying to spite Marisol when he came to the house that night smacked me right back in the face. If I hadn't been chasing a fast car and a handsome face, I wouldn't be staring a death sentence in the eye. Even though I pursued Cornell in the past to get back at Lisa, I'm glad we made our way back to each other. I bumped into him at the Porsche dealership one day and it's been good ever since.

Besides my son, Cornell had been the best thing that had happened to me. He gave me hope. If only there was a cure for HIV, we could live happily ever after. For now, I had to find a way to keep him safe. I didn't know how long it was gonna be before he wanted to stop using condoms, but I loved him too much to hurt him like I hurt the others.

"Babe. What's on your mind?" Cornell asked, as he reached over and held my hand, getting onto I-495.

"Nothing."

"Something's bothering you. Are you still upset that Juan hasn't called you?"

"No, it's all good." I lied. There was no way I would let Juan get away with not calling me or getting me a birthday gift but that wasn't what I was thinking about. My mind had drifted off, thinking about what chick I would hook up one of my new clients with. Spending time with Cornell kept me from staying on top of my game. Plus, I wondered if Sadique was going to call me about our deal. My thoughts bounced all around while I stared glossy eyed out of the window. I decided to text Sadique.

Nigga, what's up? Are we doing this or what?

Surprisingly, he texted right back.

Denie, I ain't fuckin' around. I'm fallin' back wit' that shit. You know the sayin'- Never bite the hand that feeds you. He a good nigga to us both. Don't cross him.

Angry, I threw my iPhone into my Celine bag and sighed heavily. So not only was Grady not fucking with me, but now Sadique was out, too.

Fuck you- I texted back quickly damn near breaking the phone. After finally looking up, I realized Cornell was taking the exit to my house.

"Why you taking me home?" I asked, sounding a little irritated. He knew I wanted to spend the night with him. I knew the Wizards weren't playing and he had a couple of days off, so I wondered why he didn't want to spend the evening with me.

"Because you need to go home. Trust me, it's what's best."

"For what? It's still my birthday," I said, trying to milk that thing as long as I could. My birthday had passed almost three days ago, but we had been celebrating the entire time. He wanted me to feel special and was doing a great job at it.

"Here, put this on. Time for another surprise," he said as he threw me a blindfold.

As we rode in silence for what felt like eternity with my eyes covered, the car finally came to a stop.

"Take the blindfold off."

As I uncovered my eyes, I was paralyzed with disbelief. We were in front of an estate with a green and white 'sold' sign in the front yard. As the black iron gates opened there were red rose petals that filled the entire circular driveway. As Cornell pulled up to the front door, I sat in my passenger seat in disbelief at what was in front of me. There was a big gold ribbon on the front door of the gorgeous cobblestone mini-mansion.

I put my mink coat on quickly before he made it to my side of the door. I stepped out of the car in awe.

"Cornell, is this for me?"

I hoped he would say yes. Not answering my question, Cornell led me into the home where yellow rose petals filled the foyer. The mansion was breathtaking. It was like one of the homes I had seen in the Billionaire Magazine. It was just like the house on my vision board.

"Cornell, talk to me. Is this for me?" I asked again.

"The red roses that filled the driveway represents all my love. The yellow roses in this foyer, represents the joy you have brought into my life, and our friendship that will last forever."

As I stood in the foyer under his trance, he closed the door, and dropped to one knee. Grabbing my hand, he finally started to speak again.

"Denie, I've never met anyone who's made me feel the way that you do. You are my soul mate, my best friend, and all I need in a woman. I love both you and BJ, and I want you guys in my life forever. Denie, would you give me the honor of making you my…"

"Yes, Cornell! Yes!" I answered before he could say another word.

Just when I thought things couldn't get any better he pulled out a flawless canary yellow, 10-carat diamond ring. It paid to have a dude with an eighty million dollar NBA contract. I'd hit the jackpot. No longer did I need Juan. Fuck that bastard. It was BJ, Cornell, and I against the world. So many things ran through my head, as I took it all in.

"You don't need anything. Come upstairs and let me show you what I've been up to for the past couple of weeks," Cornell said, leading me up the dual staircase. I kicked my Gucci heels off so fast, and followed behind my king.

The bedroom was completely furnished. There were gold linens and a California King bed with more rose petals. An unspeakable joy filled my insides once I made it to my closet.

"It's 1500 square feet of any designer you can think of," he said, assuring me that my life was going to be nothing but sweet.

After giving me a partial tour and me seeing all he had done for BJ and I, we made our way back to the bedroom where a bottle of Ace of Spades sat on ice. Cornell and I made it back to our new bedroom. He started kissing me up and down my neck, instantly causing my temperature to rise. My body felt as if it were literally melting.

"Cornell, what are you doing to me?" I managed to ask between the tears. I placed my arms around his neck, "I don't deserve you, babe. I've been such a terrible person."

Deep down inside my guilt started to take over me, and I didn't know why God had blessed me with such a good man.

"Babe, everyone grows and learns from their mistakes. You make everything in my life better, and I want you around forever. I need you to know that I accept you wholeheartedly, flaws and all."

"You promise? No matter what? For good or for bad?"

"I promise baby," he said, kissing me on my forehead.

I loved when he did that.

"Please don't ever leave me, Cornell."

"I won't. I love you."

He looked straight into my eyes. I knew he meant every word, and I loved him even more for his honesty. As he removed my black velour dress, he stood over me and stared, as if he had discovered a piece of fine art.

"You're flawless, Denie. And you're so beautiful. Can I make love to my wife to be?"

"Yes. Let's christen this spot, baby."

Removing my panties, he spread my legs open, and started to flicker his tongue across my clit, which sent me crawling up the golden satin sheets. Pulling me back down to him, and pinning down my legs so I couldn't escape, he devoured his tongue into my love box. Sucking me like I was his last meal, I found myself cooing like a baby.

"Cornell, oh my goodness. Ahhhh, it feels so good." I moaned as he held me and continued to suck my loving. "Babe, I'm about to cum. I love you so much," I said as I released. Just as I came, he stopped as my body quivered for more.

"Cornell, why did you stop? I was cumming."

"I don't want you to cum like that. I want you to cum like this," he said, taking his pants off exposing his ten inches.

"You have a condom?" I asked, as my wet box jerked, wanting him inside my wetness.

"Babe. You're about to be my wife. I would marry you tonight if I could. I want to finally feel you. Let me make love to you…raw, Denie. It's you and me against the world, right?"

I should've been mature enough to reject his request. But I was too selfish. Hot, horny, and in love with Cornell, I said nothing as he pushed his thick, love inside of me. I couldn't stop him, or maybe I didn't want to. He plowed through my wetness like a power drill, as my walls held on to him for dear life. He stroked me long, and hard for what felt like forever. I could no longer hold back anymore. What kept playing in my head was him saying, I will love all of you forever, flaws and all.

Maybe he will.

Maybe I should've told him why I wanted to use a condom.

Maybe I should've made him stop.

But I couldn't. I loved him, and as bad as I wanted to protect him from my demons, life with Cornell meant he accepted all of me like he promised. After fighting with my conscience, I allowed my fiancé to make love to me until we came together. I wrapped my legs around Cornell and let his love pour inside of me. He filled me with his loving and I loved every inch of it.

While we both laid in each other arms, I took in everything around me. This was all I ever wanted. Just to be loved back, the way I deserved, with no ulterior motives. Caught in a trance, I thought about my new life and felt blessed. I was finally happy.

From afar, I could hear the constant ringing of my cell phone in my handbag. Quickly, I jumped up just in case it was Maria calling about BJ. As I scurried through my clutch, I found my phone.

"Hello," I answered out of breath.

"Denie, it's Mecca. Have you heard from Juan?"

"No. And, why are you calling my phone? He's probably up in something," I fired.

"That's a given," she blasted nastily. "He did some foul shit that he thinks I know nothing about and now he hasn't been home in days. He didn't even call yesterday. It was fuckin' Thanksgiving! I'm just worried about him," she ended in defeat.

Mecca was right. Juan loved her and would never go even a day without calling her. Since he missed my birthday to stay with Mecca, I really hadn't been speaking to him. For the past couple of days I'd been with Cornell. I hadn't even seen my son. Juan not calling her for days wasn't normal. Something just wasn't right.

"Oh my God! Denie!" Mecca yelled.

"What?"

"Turn on the news! Turn to channel 8."

"Cornell, turn on the TV. Turn to channel 8." I motioned to him quickly.

Three unidentified men, were found shot to death, two nights ago at the Dezal gas station here in downtown Baltimore. We reported earlier that it appears to have been an attempted robbery. There was one gun found on the scene…"

"Denie, Juan was in Baltimore. Suppose that was him?" Mecca started screaming.

"Calm down! I'm gonna call him now. I'll call you back as soon as I know something."

After hanging up on Mecca, I called Juan's cell phone. The phone rang and then went straight to voicemail. I called back twice, still getting no answer. Eventually, I threw the phone across the bed and ran my fingers down Cornell's back. His body was beautifully sculpted as if it was too good to be true.

"Babe, you not worried about Juan?"

"Yeah. But that nigga is grown."

Cornell stood up and walked toward the bathroom, unfortunately for me, knocking my clutch to the ground. Instantly, my heart felt like it had stopped. No life. No pulse. Nothing. I just froze while he picked each item up from the floor. Seeing the bottle of medication on the floor had me stumped as Cornell continued to talk.

"Grown? Shit, I'm grown, but you wouldn't be worried if you hadn't talked to me in three days?"

"That's different. He's probably with some girl," I said, swiftly making my way over to Cornell. But it was too late to grab the medicine.

"Babe, what's Reyataz? You not tryna take no birth control behind my back, are you?" He laughed.

The sad thing was there was nothing funny. All the hiding, ducking, and dodging I did to keep my HIV status a secret, I would've never thought he would find my medication this way. I was good at landing on my feet though. Rich taught me that.

"No, Cornell. That's Cheri's. She left it in my bag the other night."

"Oh. Well get up and let's make some phone calls t[illegible] check on Juan."

I dodged a bullet for now. Hopefully, he wouldn' [illegible] on the Internet researching. That was a close call. Now it wa[illegible] [illegible]ne for me to act like I gave a fuck about where Juan was, or if he [illegible]s alive. Maybe that would get Cornell's mind off what he found in my purse.

Chapter 13
Juan

Who would've ever thought spending time with my dad would be so emotional? It felt so weird that he was still alive, but it made me happy that he was ready to get back in the business. The family business. We'd talked non-stop since I'd gotten shot. Except for the time span where Nicole would have me doped up on pain medication that made my eyes roll to the back of my head. A few times it had me thinkin' somebody was sucking my dick.

Life with him seemed crazier than before. Yet, I really didn't want to leave his side. I'd missed four days of servin' my people, tryin' to get rid of my new product. But spendin' those days with my father, while I recovered was priceless. I got him caught up on my dealings with Julio, and my new connect, Big Tony. He asked a lot of questions and analyzed everything. My father suggested that I not tell anyone about being shot, not even Julio. I didn't really agree with it, but knew he had my back. Things always worked out better when I listened to him. Besides, everything happened for a reason.

I got to know more about Rich than I knew my whole life in that short time span. Some things still never changed. He still was up to his old shit with the chicks though. He had no love for women, and even made Honey suck me off. He was off the chain, which was where we were different. I loved Mecca and would never treat her like Rich treated Honey, or my mother. Strangely, I allowed him to convince me not to charge up my phones, knowin' Mecca had probably been callin' like crazy.

Rich stayed full of surprises though. After catchin' him up on how much money I was makin', he hit me with words that would change my life forever.

"Son, it's time for us to make this shit happen, together."

"Together?" I questioned.

"Yep. Just you and me son. True Sanchez soldiers."

Damn. I lit up like a fuckin' bulb on a Christmas tree. It felt so good to know he needed me. "Alright man, well I got some good news that might get us closer to our goals."

"Wassup?"

"Man, I just closed probably the biggest deal, this area would ever see. That's why I gotta get out of here and get back on these streets."

"With who?"

"The dude Big Tony I was tellin' you about. He hit me off. But I need to get empty quick and re-up. I gotta show that man that I'm ready and capable of some serious quantity."

I could tell by the look on Rich's face that he was proud of me. That shit felt good down on the inside.

"Son, that's a good look. You feel like he good peeps?" he asked leanin' in close to my face. "And, can you trust him?"

I got excited. "Man, he's a hustler's dream connect. He is who everybody in this game tryna fuck wit'."

Rich started drilling me. "How much bread we talkin'?"

"Well for now, he started me off on some short shit, until he can feel like he can trust me. But, eventually, a cool five mill, a bi-weekly thing. That's 10 mill a month."

"Oh yeah, son. I want in. I got $250K right here at the house."

His offer wasn't really a request. It was more of a demand.

"Dad, I got you for sure. Once I come back, on the next move we good."

"Who goin' with you?" he asked, lookin' skeptical as hell.

"My man Julio. He's who I been fuckin' with. We went half."

Disappointment showed all over Rich's face. "How much you know about these dudes?"

"Enough to know we about to eat," I said, dismissin' him slightly.

"Well son, this is what I'mma do," he responded standin' and leavin' the room for about two minutes. He showed back up in the livin' room with a gray, Puma duffle bag. "I'm your new, silent partner. You got that?"

I nodded. Not sure how to handle things.

That's $250K. Now, let's get back our Sanchez reputation, and make this shit happen," he said pattin' me on the back.

"Bet. Let's do this."

He was actually helpin' me and didn't know it. I had missed a week of business and time was money. I needed to pay Big Tony soon whether my shit was sold or not.

"Dad, I love you and thanks for savin' my life. Once again," I said, givin' him a big hug knowin' I needed to leave. I held him so tightly. I didn't even want to let go, feeling all mushy inside once again. I needed him now more than ever. For so long, I'd felt like I was in the world alone. Now, I had my dad back. Even though he had the same ruthless attitude, and had lost a little swag, he was still Rich. His nerve condition put a couple of years on him, but in his mind, he was still that nigga. And that's all that mattered.

"Son, I love you. Take care of your sister, and remember, don't let her know I'm alive just yet. She can't know. Not yet, Juan. I can trust you, I know. You've proven that."

I nodded, then opened the door to leave.

"I promise you, I'm gonna be a better father to y'all. Just give me time. I promise you that," he ended as his head started jerkin' side to side.

Whenever he got excited that happened. It made me sad that my father was really fucked up. I'm sure that his brain injury had been frustratin' for him. He wasn't the same Rich physically, but mentally he was still rugged, and still my dad, ruthless and ready for war. The only real soldier I knew.

As I slowly climbed into my Maserati, still in a lot of pain, I moved carefully. My father was alive… That was all I could think about and so badly, I wanted to tell the world. Startin' with Denie, but I couldn't. That was all I ever wanted was to make things right with him. What's crazy was that's all he ever wanted, too. Thinkin' back, I thought about how proud he looked when I told him I was the one that killed Marisol. I did it for him, and that was enough to let him know he could trust me. I wasn't a snitch anymore.

Takin' my time drivin' home, I thought it was best I just waited to face Mecca and Denie. I didn't know what type of excuse I could give for not only being gone for almost a week, but missin' Thanksgiving. That was gonna be an even bigger problem. Calling them would've meant too many questions over the phone. How was I gonna explain being shot? Fuckin' with a bitch always got niggas caught up. It seemed like Rich and I were the walkin' billboards. My phone rang again. This time from a number I didn't recognize. Maybe it was Rich, I thought, as I answered it on my Bluetooth in my car.

"Yo." I answered a little incognito.

"Motherfucker, you gone die! You killed my cousin and my brovah!" a raspy voice yelled through my speaker.

"Who the fuck is this?" I said, trying to make out the voice.

"Nigga, you know who it is. It's Slice. Don't get this rap shit twisted, I'mma gangsta and I'mma make a zample out ya ass!"

"Come get me, you short, faggot, bitch," I yelled back, feelin' like I had just popped a stitch in my side.

"First, you disrespect my son, you got my bitch shot, and now my brother and cousin dead. Nigga, they my blood!" he yelled.

"Man, I don't know what you talkin' bout. Get off my horn with that hot shit. And you call yourself a gangster rapper. Haha!" I instigated, addin' salt to his wound.

"You a dead man walkin', Juan. You and dem Spanish niggas gon get it!" he yelled, just before I hung up on his ass.

Now, all over some pussy, I had to watch my back. Not only did I have to worry about the Feds, I had to worry about this troll tryna get back at me. I knew what I had to do. Dude had to go. One day soon it was goin' to be a sad day in the rap game because he was gonna die. My phone rang again, and I was ready to go in on that bitch ass nigga, Slice.

"Nigga, stop callin' my motherfuckin' phone…"

"Damn my nigga, it's like that?"

"Awe shit, my bad my nigga. I thought you were somebody else," I said apologizin' to my main dude down Newport News, Virginia who I supplied on a regular.

"Man, I been tryin' to hit you up all week, but yo' man Julio came thru. Man, I need to re-up already."

"What you mean, my man Julio came thru?"

"Oh, I thought it was cool. Whenever I can't get you, he always looks out."

My antennas were up. "Naw, it ain't cool. That nigga foul as shit," I shot. He knew I was pissed off. I had to make moves fast and he was fuckin' with my territory, and hadn't said nothing. I had a week to move shit to get my paper. Bein' out of commission for a week fucked me up.

"Man, I ain't tryin' to get caught in the middle of nothin'," my boy commented reluctantly.

"Naw, my nigga it's all good. Just hit me only, from now on. I got some more shit too, so let me know when you ridin' back up."

"Bet. Just gimme a day or so."

Laying back in my ride, I was instantly pissed off. That nigga Julio was cuttin' deals behind my back. All I could think about was who else he'd served without me knowing. I couldn't contain myself any longer, so I decided to call Julio.

"Juannnnnnn. What's up, baby boy?" Julio said answerin' the phone with some loud ass Reggaeton music in the background.

"I had a little emergency, but I'm good. I need to holler at you about somethin' in person," I belted dryly.

"Cool. I'll call you tomorrow and let you know when I can get down there from Philly."

"Bet."

"I'll hit you later. I'm taking my little Philly hoe to the movies."

"Yeah, whatever, nigga," I sounded and hung up. That lying motherfucka must've forgotten he told me he don't go to movies...too dark and too easy for niggas to run up on him.

Chapter 14
Juan

Russ Parr's voice snagged me out of the daze I'd been in. I liked to listen to The Russ Parr Morning Show from time to time if I roamed the streets during the early morning hours. Flipping back between 93.9 and listening to Huggy Lowdown, they all helped to get my mind off things. The new Drake song rocked through my speakers, Just Hold on We're Going Home… That song was so appropriate because I couldn't wait to get to my damn house. After leaving Rich's place and dropping his money off at my condo, I was winded. The bullet wound had done more to me than I anticipated. It had been a long week and I still needed more rest. Flipping through the radio stations again, trying to dodge commercials, I landed on 92.3 Baltimore radio, and was stopped in my tracks by Rickey Smiley's news.

Police have a person of interest that they would like to question in the triple homicide that went down last week at Dezel Gas Station. Hell, I thought they all just shot themselves but it seems as though Slice, the Rapper has given police a name that they haven't revealed yet. Umm, when did gangster rappers start snitching? They laughed and joked about the comment before going onto other news.

Fuck, I said to myself as I turned onto my street. Did he have somebody on the phone, I wondered? When I pulled up to my gate neither Denie nor my Porsche were in sight. I figured Cheri had left to be with her daughter for Thanksgiving, so I knew she wasn't inside. The question was, where the hell was Denie, and Mecca? Did they even care I had been gone a week. I wondered where they could've been. As I got closer, I noticed two unmarked cars in the driveway. A part of me wanted to pull off, but I didn't know who was watchin'. My heart felt like it had dropped to the pit of my stomach. Still, I boldly hopped out of my car and approached the front door. Before I could put my key in the door, Maria opened it as if she was expectin' me.

"Senor. Someone is here. They want to talk to you. Let me take your coat."

"Who? Why the fuck you let them in?" I whispered harshly. "Get the fuck off me," I told her, refusing to give up my coat. I didn't want any signs of me being shot to show. My coat was the perfect camouflage for my unwanted guests.

"Everyone has been worried. I thought they knew where you were," Maria whispered back.

Not trying to look hot, I slowly made my way to the family room where they were sitting. As I walked in, two men stood up, one white, one Hispanic, dressed in suits, looking like JC Penny's models. They looked as if they weren't a day over twenty-five. Extending my hand, I addressed the white guy first.

"Juan," I said nodding.

I shook his hand and then the Hispanic man's hand. It hurt me to even raise my arm slightly, but there was no way I'd let the pain show on my face.

"Hi Juan. I'm Detective Wallerby and this is Detective Santiago," the white detective said as he took his seat.

"Hi Juan," Detective Santiago chimed in as he sipped his coffee in one of Maria's favorite mugs. They had a little spread going on the oversized coffee table filled with donuts, croissants, and jelly-filled pastries. Now, I was even more concerned on how long they'd been in my damn house.

"What can I do for you gentleman?" I asked, trying to remain calm.

Slowly, I sat down, making sure I didn't show any expressions from the pain. I didn't know what I was more nervous about, them finding out I was recovering from gun shot wounds, or the gun tucked between my waist.

"You okay?" Santiago asked, looking as if his antennas just popped up.

"Yeah, I'm good. What's up?" I looked that fuckin' narc straight in the eye. I thought about how Rich would handle the moment. So I sat up straight and gave the most confident look I could give.

"Have you heard about the triple homicide that took place in Baltimore on Tuesday?" Wallerby asked, switching from talking proper to his ghetto voice. He really was trying too hard.

Now I was irritated.

"No, I'm sorry Sir. I haven't been in town. Now, what does this incident have to do with me?" I asked, trying to speak as proper as possible to make him feel like the jackass that he was.

"Well, at first we thought that it was an attempted robbery until one of the victims family members assured us that you had something to do with the murder. Do you have someone who can vouch for your whereabouts on the night of November 27th?" Wallerby continued as Santiago watched me intently, waiting for me to flinch.

"Sure, I was out of town with my girl…" Before I could continue Mecca rushed in the front door in a panic, stopping to mean-mug me. I reached out to hug her, with Mecca taking longer than expected. It felt as though I could hear every stitch in my side pop as we embraced.

"Juan, where have you been? When I pulled up and saw those sedans, I thought they were here to say you were dead. When I saw the news…" Cutting Mecca off before she could incriminate me, I just kissed her.

"Babe. I told you I was going out of town. These gentleman are here questioning me about a murder in Baltimore," I said, squeezing her arm as I hugged her tighter.

"What's going on here?" Mecca asked, directing her attention to Santiago.

"Handling business. Seems like your boyfriend had been doing the same, since it's clear he wasn't out of town with you," Santiago responded in a matter of fact tone then continued to go in even more. "You're his woman right?" he instigated.

"Last time I checked," Mecca said, rollin' her eyes at me. She then shot me a look that let me know she was ready to blow her top.

"Look detectives, do I need a lawyer? Unless I'm being charged, I have nothing further to say."

"You might. For now, just know we'll be in touch," Wallerby assured me, looking over his black-rimmed glasses.

"Can I get you more Colombian coffee, sir?" Maria asked as if she wanted them to stay a while. Even with me cutting my eyes at her, she stood anxiously waiting for their response to more coffee.

"No thanks Maria, but you have been a doll. I would love to have one of you at my house. Wish I could afford a Spanish maid," Wallerby shot in a racist demeanor.

"She's Hispanic. Spanish people are from Spain. You do know that, right?" I wanted him to know I was educating him. Then I looked toward Santiago to let him know he was a sell-out for allowing his partner to speak to Maria that way.

"Gracias por su colaboracion. Sorry for your loss. It's good that you care for what's her name?" He snapped his fingers a few times before continuing, "Carmen. Yeah, taking care of Carmen the way you do."

Santiago shook Maria's hand trying to appear sincere.

"Cooperation? What loss?" I asked with a puzzled expression. My words also let Santiago know I understood Spanish with no problem. Growing up half Colombian, I didn't have a choice with my grandparents speakin' Spanish fluently on a regular.

"Oh Senor. I told them about Senora Marisol. I really miss her," Maria said looking down.

That bitch, Maria was really trying to win her Academy Award. She didn't like Denie or me but needed her fucking job. And if she cared about her life, I hoped she would stop the bullshit. I knew she was being spiteful. It was written all over her face.

"Alright, gentleman, show's over. It was great talking to you both," I said as I ushered them to the foyer. I'd had enough. But before leaving, they both handed all of us business cards.

Looking Mecca straight in the face, Santiago flirted. I didn't like what I saw going on between them.

"Next time your boyfriend here goes on a business trip without you, I'm just a phone call away."

"Get the fuck out my house!" I yelled, pushing them toward the door, and slamming the door behind them.

Next thing I knew the slap came. It landed across my face with a strong sting.

"Motherfucker, where were you and who the fuck were you with? I've been in this fucking house pacing the floor back and forth, worried sick about you! I've lost five pounds thinking someone had killed you!"

I knew I'd have to deal with Mecca's bullshit, but she wasn't my main concern at the moment. Ignoring her, I directed my attention to Maria.

"What the fuck did you tell them?" I asked, looking at her right in the eyes.

"Senor Juan, I didn't tell them anything. I just miss Senora, that's all," she said shaking, as if she was about to have a seizure.

"Leave her alone, Juan," Mecca interrupted.

Continuing to ignore her, I got so close to Maria that she could feel my breath on her lip. "I'm going to ask you one more fuckin' time, what did you tell them bastards?"

"They ask me questions, I don't know. I scare. You scare me, Juan," Maria said, shaking her head.

I back-handed her so hard she fell to the floor.

"Noooooooo," she wailed, while holding her face. "Please, nooooo, Juan. Pleaseeeee don't," she begged while on her knees.

Smack! Smack! I continued to beat her slender frame with my fist while she screamed almost as defenseless as a young child. Her body lay flat to the floor as I straddled her, putting a terrible whipping on that ass. She needed to be taught a lesson.

"You don't fuckin' talk to the fuckin' police or let nobody in here without my permission. Do I make myself clear?" I yelled, smackin' the shit out of Maria one last time right before her nose bled.

"Juan, what the hell are you doing? Stop it! Stop Juan," Mecca yelled, trying to stop me from whoopin' Maria's ass.

Ignoring her, I grabbed my gun from my waist, and put it straight to Maria's head. I had been waiting for this day. If it wasn't for Carmen, Marisol's daughter, she would've been dead. Me, nor Denie wanted to take care of her, but she shared Marisol's estate with Denie. We were stuck with Maria, especially since she loved Carmen so much.

"No, Senor. Please, no kill me. Please no," she cried.

"Don't make me kill you, Maria. You almost sent me straight to fucking jail letting those bastards in here," I told her before looking up and seeing Carmen and BJ staring at me in fear. Quickly, I placed my gun back at my waist. I let Maria up.

"I hate you, Juan! You killed Marisol! I know you did!" Maria shouted, getting up from the floor, then usherin' the kids out of the foyer.

"Come here, BJ." I charged, pullin' him from her grasp.

She continued with Carmen out of the room. I could hear Carmen ask, "Are you okay?"

I focused my attention on BJ. He was my heart. "Your Uncle was a little upset, and I am sorry you had to see that. You know I love you, right?"

"Yes," he answered, looking at the floor.

"Look at me Lil' Juan. You know I love you like you my own son. I will always protect you and will never hurt you. You know that, right?"

"Yes. I love you, too," he said huggin' me.

I loved that lil' dude.

"Now go tell Maria to give you a Popsicle," I said, brushing my hand across his curly bush.

"Alright."

He ran off as if nothing had happened. My nephew was a soldier. A true Sanchez. Nothing like his faggot ass father, Javier.

"What the fuck is wrong with you, Juan? I can't be with someone like you. You just beat a woman who's old enough to be your mother," Mecca said, looking at me as if I were nasty as scum.

"Mecca, fuck you! Maybe you don't need to be with somebody like me. I'm from the streets. I mean damn, we all make mistakes, I get that. But that bitch almost sent me straight to jail. It's more to the story… you wouldn't understand," I said, walking towards my room. She followed behind me, talking shit.

"And guess what? I don't want to understand. I'm done with you! You've been out fucking a bitch all week. And you think I don't know? You think I'm stupid?"

She paused in the foyer that linked my wing to the rest of the house. Standing with her weight on one foot, she crossed her arms, waiting for my response.

"I know everything. Let's stop bullshitting. I even know about you and Cheri."

My face became flushed and I knew not to say another word. I pled the fifth. I wasn't sure what she really knew, but the way she rested her hands on her hips with confidence told me I needed to get my lies straight.

"Maria told me she saw you and Cheri go into the bedroom upstairs. She's even got you on video downstairs, before you went up to fuck her. And don't lie, Juan. I'll go get her phone now and show you. For once, stop lying to me."

"That bitch, Maria," was all I could say before Mecca got close up in my face.

"I even knocked on the door when it was all happening. You didn't even have the decency to stop at that point," she spat. "I remember the look Cheri had when she came to the door. Do you know how embarrassing that is?"

"Mecca, I didn't…"

"Hold up. What the fuck? Juan, you're bleeding," Mecca hollered with concern.

I had to play my get out of jail free card while her eyes zoomed in on my side and the blood that trickled to the floor. "I wasn't with a bitch, Mecca. Somebody tried to kill me the same night I left here going to a meeting. I almost fuckin' died."

"Why didn't you go to the hospital?"

"I did. But guess what? You were hardly even here when I called for you. I needed you."

Damn, that shit sounded good.

"Did you fuck Cheri, Juan?" she asked so matter-of-factly. She wasn't letting up.

"What do you think?" Damn, I didn't know how to play things. I asked myself, what would Rich do? Then I sprung into action.

"I'mma give it to you straight, Mecca. I did feel her up but I didn't fuck her…."

Before I could say another word, Mecca smacked me with an open hand and ran toward the front door. Her tears had turned into loud outburst full of wailing and despair.

"You're a liar! Maria saw you, it's on video, and Cheri told Maria everything! All of the details! I heard every last word! You're a liar, a cheater, and I don't want to have anything else to do with you!"

Her tears flowed heavily. It was clear my bullshittin' ass ways were breaking her down. Damn! I had some makin' up to do. I knew Mecca was hurt, but just like I'd been up to no good, Mecca was up to something, too. And I was determined to get to the bottom of it. She'd take me back eventually though.

Chapter 15
Rich

The damn phone had been ringin' over and over again, interruptin' me from the marvelous head I was receivin'.

"Hello. What the fuck is it?" I asked while the phone fumbled between my fingers.

"Dad. We need to talk. Them people came to my house. I'm outside your joint," Juan said in a panic.

"A'ight, I'll have Nicole come down and get you from the lobby. You by yourself, right?"

"No, I got my girl with me."

"What the fuck you mean?" I yelled. "I don't know that bitch."

"Dad, she's not a bitch. Besides, I had to tell her. She ain't gonna tell nobody. Man, she was ready to leave me so I had to go find her. I had to prove to her I wasn't lying about a few things."

Hanging up on his dumb ass, I got up and slipped my sweatpants on. I freshened up while Nicole headed down to get Juan from the lobby. I was mad as shit. I ain't know the bitch, and didn't have time for no chick hottin' up my spot. In less than five minutes they were at the door. When they came in, I noticed the chick had on a blindfold.

"Fuck is this about?" I asked, greetin' my son with a pound.

"I knew you was gonna be pissed off, so I blindfolded her so she wouldn't know where you lived. Mecca, go 'head and take it off," Juan instructed, guidin' his girlfriend through the foyer and into the sunken living room.

"What the fuck? This bitch look just like your mother." I looked at Juan shockingly.

"Dad, don't call her a bitch. This is my lady. Mecca, please excuse my father. He's suffered from a lot of trauma and has outbursts from time to time that are a little wild. Mecca, this is Rich. Dad this my girl, Mecca."

"How are you, Sir?" she said reaching out for a handshake.

Grabbin' her hand, I pulled her close, damn near yankin' her arm off. I had to see if she felt like Lisa, too. Holdin' her close it felt like Lisa all over again… before Lisa was ruined by all the bad things that destroyed our relationship. Juan's girlfriend, looked so innocent and pure. She was very pretty, light- skinned, long hair, dimples, freckles, light eyes and all.

"You feel like Lisa. You even smell like her."

"Dad, what the fuck is wrong with you? Let her go," Juan said, pullin' my hands off of Mecca.

"My bad. I'm sorry, Mecca. Did I make you uncomfortable?"

"Sort of," she said in a soft-spoken voice.

"Well, Miss Innocent. Juan gave you the details, right? You don't know I'm alive, right."

"I know nothing," she said as she sat on my oversized black leather couch.

"Where did Nicole go? I need her to look at my stitches. I popped somethin'," Juan said as he took off his coat anxiously. The nigga was filled with anxiety.

"Where Honey at?" Juan asked.

"She went to fill my prescription. She should be back in a little while. Calm down, son. Just sit for a few seconds."

"Naw man, I need to ask her if she's seen that clown, Slice. That nigga called my phone talking reckless; sending fucking death threats. He needs to go."

Juan was clearly upset. I knew it by the way he clasped his hands together repeatedly. That's somethin' he always did when stress had him by the balls.

"Look son. We gotta be smart about how we handle this shit.

"There's no way to handle it, other than killin' him."

"See it's that irrational, young, immature way of thinkin' that got you into this in the first place." It was time to set Juan straight. He could sense the disappointment in my voice and face. "See, when you fuck a nigga's bitch, then beat on her and her son, these are the consequences."

Mecca's eyes grew to the size of fuckin' golf balls. Maybe Juan hadn't told her, but I didn't give a fuck. Any bitch who signed up to be with a Sanchez needed to roll with the punches. My next sentence was just for Mecca. "I hope Peaches' pussy was worth it. She kept you from bein' with Mecca at the hospital that night, and now her baby father tryna smoke you."

"I'ma handle the nigga," I shouted as Nicole grabbed Juan by the arm and took him with her.

"Well, let's get you cleaned up," Nicole said to Juan.

The soft nigga barely wanted to leave the room. He kept lookin' at his chick with multiple "I'm sorry faces". None of that shit worked. I could tell by Mecca's expression that I'd filled her in on shit she didn't know. And that Juan would've never told her. I left Mecca in the livin' room to sulk and followed Nicole and Juan to the health suite.

"What the fuck would you do that for?" Juan blasted as soon as I walked into the room.

"Because she needed to know. That's why!" My head shook more than usual, but I'd had it with Juan and his kindness to women. "If your chick gon' be with you, she gotta be ride or die. Not ride when shit's lovely. She gotta ride until the breaks fall off. You feel me, lil' nigga?"

"Dad, you supposed to be with me, not against me."

I stopped talking for nearly three minutes. I needed to calm my nerves. I sat watching Juan get fixed up by Nicole, while I sat in the chair breathin' heavily, as if I were havin' an attack. Nicole knew it wasn't my health in jeopardy. I was simply angry at my son. As soon as Nicole said she was done, I sent her to entertain Mecca as Juan and I discussed what needed to go down.

"Now, who the fuck came to the house?" I asked him sternly.

"Some detectives. I think Slice told them I had some type of connection with the murders. Hot ass nigga. I need to leak that the nigga is a snitch to fuck his whole rap career up," Juan said, forgettin' that his ass was a snitch himself not too long ago.

I must've shot him a dirty look because he cleaned that shit up real quick. He didn't really know how to take me since my demeanor had changed for the worse.

"I mean, I know I did some foul shit in the past, but I know betta now."

"I'm glad you've learned, son," I said after listenin' to Juan go on and on about the detectives.

"But this the kicker right here," he continued, "Maria let the motherfuckers in and was talking to them before I got there."

"Man, I never trusted that bitch. You might need to kill her ass. She don't have no loyalty to nobody but Marisol and Carmen."

"You know I fucked her ass up."

"Why the fuck you do that? She live in yo' shit and can send you straight to jail. What were you thinkin', Juan?" I shook my head with pity.

"She told them something about Marisol and I just reacted. I don't know what she said but they thanked her for her cooperation. Then after I whooped her ass she flat out told me I killed Marisol."

"Man, you gotta kill her, Juan. Tonight. Send your girl somewhere and get rid of that bitch." I quickly devised a plan to get that bitch out the way. Juan was on board. Now that was done, I was on to my next convo with Juan. We needed to get focused on getting this money.

"Juan, your girlfriend is ready to go," Nicole peeped in to say. "I tried to tell her it would be just a few minutes longer, but she's really upset."

"Dad, I gotta go." Juan jumped and headed to the door.

"Son, remember these words. You can't be a boss if your bitch is callin' the shots. You feel me? But you go 'head 'cause I need some pussy anyway," I ended, giving Nicole that look she knew so well. "So, I'll holler at you, unless your girl is into girls?"

"Naw, we good. I'll call you once I drop her off."

"Cool. Love you son."

"Love you, too."

As soon as I heard the alarm sound, I knew Juan and his lil stuck-up chick was gone. Now it was time for me to release some tension. Honey still hadn't gotten home yet with my seizure medication, but I needed some pussy.

"Nicole, come up here and fuck me," I yelled from the loft. Havin' two girls had its perks. I could get sex, meals, and anything I wanted anytime I needed it. Like the obedient girl she was, she called for me from the bedroom. When I walked in the room she was already ass naked. My shit got hard immediately. Looking down at my gray sweatpants my man was already at attention.

"You got a banana in your pocket or you just happy to see me?" she joked.

"Man, I wanna get up in this pussy. I love fuckin' you Nicole because your ass and tits are real," I said as I filled her head up.

"Not like Honey's fake shit, huh?" she said, kissin' my neck.

"You ready for me, babe?" I said, ignorin' her comment.

"Lay back, Big Daddy."

She pushed me back onto the bed. Pullin' my sweatpants off she got on top of me and got busy.

"That's right, ride it baby. Ride that thing, Nicole."

"Rich, it's my turn," a voice sounded. It was Honey, startlin' us both, standin' in the doorway with that jealous look I hated so much. Obviously, neither of us heard her come in.

"Hold up, Honey, I'm about to cum," Nicole said as she tightened up around my shaft. Her natural double D's bounced as she rained on top of me. She was so wet and moist and felt so good. Sometimes I wished that it could be just Nicole and me, but I needed Honey to handle business.

"Get up, Nicole," Honey roared. "And I mean, now! What you think, y'all making love? That's my dick," Honey yelled, pushin' Nicole's limp body off me.

I was still rock hard. Honey knew I could go for even more hours, so I didn't know why she was trippin'. She was right, sex with Nicole felt like lovemakin'. Me and Honey fucked.

Takin' her clothes off within seconds, Honey jumped on top of my hard pole and went to work.

"Who's pussy is wetter, Rich?" Honey said, as Nicole watched nearby on the satin sheets beside us as she pleasured herself.

"Man, do what you do, Honey. It ain't no competition. Fuck me man, shit."

"You want me to fuck you. I'm gonna fuck you and I'm gonna fuck you good."

One thing I loved about Honey was that when it came to sex she aimed to please. After ridin' me for a few facing me, she turned around. I knew what time it was. As I continued to lie on my back, she strategically placed two pillows behind me. Like it was nothing she wiggled my big pole until it finally fit in her ass. Up and down she stroked ridin' my dick.

"Honey, this shit feels so tight. Fuck me, bitch. That's right. Fuck me."

"You like it, Rich?" she fired back.

"I- I – I –I love it."

As she continued ridin' me, Nicole started kissin' me all over my neck and on my chest.

"I love you, Rich," Nicole said, starin' me deep in my eyes.

"I love you, too. Oh shit, I'm about to nut, fuck!" I moaned as I felt the head of my dick about to explode.

"Oh shit, Nicole, I'm about to bust." Suddenly, Honey got up and left me for dead.

"What the fuck you doin', man? I told you I was about to nut."

"You told Nicole, not me. You let that bitch make you cum since you love her so much."

"Are you serious? I was just sayin' the shit niggas say when they about to nut."

"Yes, I'm serious. I always knew you had a thing for red bitches but I still brought Nicole around to help your ass. I didn't think lettin' you fuck her that night would bring us here. Now you tellin' my friend that you love her! I'm the one that's been here for you, taking care of you. Not her!"

Nicole ignored Honey, placing my dick in her mouth finishin' what Honey started. This was a regular thing. For the past couple of months, Honey had grown even more jealous of my buddin' relationship with Nicole.

"It was all good at first. Now you wanna enforce rules. You right, you shouldn't have brought her around. She helped me recover. Can't I love both of y'all?" I asked, trying to rectify the situation.

"Bitch, stop sucking his dick! Do you see me talking?" Honey said, pushin' Nicole.

"Honey, stop putting your hands on me," Nicole shouted, getting up like she was ready to square up.

"Nicole, you know I will whoop your ass. I wish you would."

"Rich, it's all good. You don't appreciate me. All I do, but it's cool. I'll find someone that does."

"Where's your loyalty, Honey?" I asked, tryin' to get in her head.

"Loyalty? Are you kidding me? Do you realize that I risked my life for Juan? Just for ushering him out the back door of my club, I'm a target. These niggas have been coming to my club every other night pressing me out about Juan and you sit here like I haven't been loyal. You're a joke," she said, puttin' on some thigh high leather boots and a leather motorcycle jacket.

"Why the fuck haven't you told me those niggas been pressin' you?"

"I did. Your lame ass has been so far up Nicole's ass that you never paid me attention."

"What they say?"

"Does it matter now? They haven't been back." She continued to get herself together.

"Rich, come back to bed." Nicole sat back in bed instigating and watched the show while her hard pinkish nipples sat erect. She looked so damn edible but for now my focus was making things right with Honey. Couldn't fuck up the money. I joined her in the master bathroom.

"Honey, don't be mad at me," I said, movin' her long hair to the side and kissin' the back of her neck. She smelled so damn good. I wanted her again. This time I wanted to taste her. As I tried to pick her up and put her on the sink my leg gave out and we both fell. My head started rockin' side to side again and I felt like I was strugglin' tryin' to breathe.

"Rich. Rich, are you okay? Nicole, get in here, I think he's having another seizure!" Honey yelled.

I couldn't say another word as my tongue felt like it was slippin' to the back of my throat. As my eyes rolled to the back of my head, I passed out.

Chapter 16
Juan

Mecca's whinin' and cryin' hadn't stopped; not even once since we'd left my father's house. We argued for ten minutes straight, only taking a break when I stopped at my storage unit to scoop the $250 grand my father had given me. I needed it to meet up with Julio. It was the first time in hours that I felt a sense of relief. The chaos between Slice's threats, Maria's deceit, and Mecca threatening to leave me had become too much. Besides, I was still in pain.

I hopped back into the Porsche only to have a gun aimed at my head. "Oh, shit," was all I could mumble. My breathin' escalated. I kept trying to think of words to say that would make her put the gun down. Mecca had been so emotional for the last two days I knew she was at her breakin' point.

"Mecca, c'mon babe. Put the gun down. I know you're upset, but I love you, girl. I thought we got all this straight."

"Shut the fuck up!" she shouted with snot drippin' from her nose. "How can we straighten out all those fuckin' lies you've been feeding me?"

Her face had turned an even brighter red since I'd gotten out the car. And her eyes that had once looked at me lovingly, now looked at me with spite.

Hate.

Pure hate.

Who would've ever thought my girl, my woman, my lady, would be holdin' a gun to my temple? I thought about asking for forgiveness, and telling her it would never happen again, but knew it wouldn't do any good. I'd been apologizin' nearly an hour for fuckin' Peaches the night she lost the baby. She felt like if my father hadn't dry snitched, I wouldn't have ever confessed. She was right.

"You son of a bitch! I hate you, Juan! She shouted as the gun shook between the palms of her hands. As the tears flowed she kept tellin' me how much she hated me. "You ruined my life and all I ever did was try to love you! You fucked Peaches', Cheri, and God knows who else....all while I was sufferin' inside. I lost my damn baby, Juan!"

"Nooooo, Mecca, it wasn't like that," I pleaded, with my hands now on the steering wheel. From my peripheral vision, I had a close up on her brittle nails. I kept trying to steal a glimpse of her eyes. I wanted to speak to her through them. I wanted her to know that I really did love her. "Mecca, you know you don't want to kill me, baby. You're not a killer. So just put the gun down."

"You don't know what I'm capable of, Juan. You really don't know!"

She hauled off and spit in my face, dropping the gun simultaneously. I thought about beatin' the shit out of her. But she was balled over in the seat crying, and holdin' her stomach like she was having a nervous breakdown. Sadly, it was one of those moments I remembered about my mother.

My cell phone rang interruptin' everythin'. It was Julio, so I had to answer.

"Yo, what up, bro?"

"Juan, my nigga," he said all too lively. "It's time to re-up. Where we meeting at?"

"You tell me. I just need to get your half, then I'll hit Tony up. He's in town already."

"Yeah, I know. I'm about to meet Tony in a couple hours. We hitting the West Coast tonight to see Big Tony."

"What the fuck do you mean?" I asked irritated.

"They had been tryin' to get at you all week, that's why I had to hit up some of your folks cuz you weren't answerin' the phone. Shit is pumpin'. I just hit up some folks in B-more, now we about to be out."

"What the fuck you mean you hit up some of my folks? Nigga, this is my territory. My shit. That's exactly the shit I needed to holler at you about. Where you at?"

"At Red Maple in Baltimore."

"Stay right there. I'll be up that joint in 25 minutes."

As bad as I didn't want to take Mecca with me to handle business it was important that I got this money to them for Big Tony to redeem myself. There was no way I could lose this connect or let Julio cut me out of the deal. He wasn't takin' over my shit. Thank

God, I wasn't too far from B-more. As we pulled out of the storage place parkin' lot and headed to Red Maple, Mecca shot me a dirty look.

"Where are we going? Take me home!"

"I will, Mecca. I just need to drop this money real quick."

"I don't want to be a part of your drug transactions."

"Look, I gotta make a quick move. I know you're upset, but I gotta do this."

"I'm not going to jail for you Juan, just so we're clear."

"Mecca, chill man, damn."

As I turned up my Kanye, I let the music drown out Mecca's whiny voice. She was mumbling shit under her breath about how she was done with me, forever. I simply drove as fast as I could, so Julio wouldn't roll out. Within thirty minutes, I'd made it to Red Maple. Grabbin' my cell, I hit Julio up.

"Julio, I'm right behind your car," I said as I pulled behind his Lamborghini.

"Bet. I'm comin' out now," he said before he hung up.

"Juan, I'm getting out. I'll just catch a cab," Mecca stated.

She'd stopped cryin', but had a revengeful look in her eyes. "Mecca, we still have some things to resolve. Just hold tight. I'mma drop you off at your mom's joint when we leave. Just give me five minutes." I popped the trunk, and got out the car.

"Wassup my nigga," Julio said, givin' me dap.

"Hey. Look man, I don't feel comfortable with you fuckin' wit' my folks. Goin' forward, you handle your peeps, I handle mine."

"That's cool. I was just tryna help out my nigga. If I eat, you eat. Don't forget we in this together."

"Aight, well my girl trippin' so here is the bread," I said, handin' him the gray Puma duffle bag my father had given me. "Tell Tony, I said what's up."

"Cool. I'll hit you up later."

As I got back in the car, Mecca rolled her eyes like she was twelve years old. I didn't have a clue how to make things right. She made me feel nothing was ever enough. She started askin' questions about my father, about who Julio was, and what did I get from the storage place. She'd never done that before.

"Mecca, look, are we gonna work on our relationship, or what?"

"Hell no. Not until you come clean with me about everything. Our entire relationship is built on lies."

It was time for her to go back to her mother's house, so I could concentrate on my business. Just as I was about to let her know, my phone rang from a private number. I pulled out of the parkin' lot and answered.

"Hello Juan, baby."

"Hello, my beautiful queen," I said as a broad smile fell across my lips.

"Who the hell is that?" Mecca yelled, as I continued to talk on the phone, ignorin' her.

"How you feelin'?" I asked her after hearing her cough multiple times.

"Oh, another bitch, huh!" Mecca blasted.

"I'm not doing good, Juan. I'm in Johns Hopkins, and I need you to come up here."

My smile faded. "Johns Hopkins? You're in Maryland? When did you get back from St. Louis?" I hit my grandmother with question after question. "I thought you were still out there with your sister."

"She bought me back here a month ago. She told me not to call you because you were on her side."

"Whose side, Grandma?"

"That evil monster left me to die all alone. The doctors in Johns Hopkins are better for cancer patients, you know. Guess she don't wanna help me wipe my tail no more, haha. Juan, I don't know how much longer I have. My doctor said a day or two."

"You can't be serious."

"I am baby. There's nothing more they can do. I need to see you. I should've called you weeks ago."

"Grandma, I'm comin' right now. I'm turning my car around right now and coming to see you. Don't you worry."

"Okay, baby please hurry. I don't think I'm gonna make it through the night," my grandmother said in a faint voice, as she coughed even more.

"Don't talk like that, Grandma. I'm turnin' around now. I'll be there shortly," I said trying to keep calm. Hangin' up on my grandmother, I turned my car around pullin' straight through the authorized vehicles only road and made a U-turn.

"Juan, what's wrong?" Mecca asked, as I drove frantically down BW Parkway.

"It's my grandmother! Mecca, she's the closest thing I have to my mother. She's been in town all this time and I didn't know. She's dyin'. I can't lose her."

"Why would God want to take my grandmother away from me?" I asked out loud.

"To make you appreciate the good in your life," Mecca stated, followed by the rollin' of her eyes. Obviously, she attempted to deliver some subliminal bullshit.

I ignored her antics. She'd better be thankful that I didn't beat her ass for pullin' that gun on me. Reality set in. My grandmother was dyin'. After a silent car ride to Johns Hopkins Hospital, my mind raced. Mecca wasn't the down ass chick I thought she was. Maybe I'd hurt her so much she no longer cared. Strangely, I thought about Cheri as I made the left onto Loch Raven Road. I wanted to call her so bad. I knew she'd be supportive. I started to sweat.

"Juan, are you okay," Mecca, finally spoke.

"Yeah, I'm alright," I lied.

"You're sweating really bad," she said, lookin" at me with deep concern.

"Just a lil' nervous. That's all," I replied, pullin" in the garage and parked.

"Everything's going to be okay… Just like you told me about our daughter."

I didn't know how to take that comment so I kept walking. Fast.

"Can I ask you something, Juan?" Mecca questioned in a matter of fact tone.

"Shoot."

"Your grandmother has lived a long life, and here you are upset beyond disbelief. She's still alive."

"I still haven't heard the question, Mecca," I cut her off, annoyed.

"Why is it that you weren't this upset about losing your own child?" she yelled.

"How the fuck are you sittin' here comparin' my grandmother dyin' of cancer to you having a miscarriage?" I shot back.

"Never mind, Juan. You don't get it."

"You right. I don't," I said, gettin' onto the elevator. Her fuckin' tears began again. I was sick of her. Lovin' her had become too difficult. As I got off the elevator, I was so upset, I couldn't think straight. Once I got to the information desk, I got my grandmother's room number, then made my way to the other set of elevators. Once I finally made it to her room, I peeked in and saw her lyin' in her bed, sleepin' peacefully, connected to a breathin' machine. She looked like she weighed less than ninety pounds. She had lost so much weight. My grandmother had always looked so young, but this disease had taken her under. As she slept, the machines were at work, doing their magic. Tears escaped my eyes, as I stood there, and thought about my mother. I never got the chance to tell my mother goodbye. Now the only person that loved my mother the way I did was slippin' away from me.

"Grandma, it's me, Juan," I said, watchin' her open her eyes. I tried to hide my tears, as I quickly wiped them away.

"Juan, is that you," she said through the breathin' mask. As she looked up at me, with her glossy eyes, my heart melted.

"Yes, Grandma, it's me."

"What took you so long? I told you I was about to die."

"You not gonna die, Grandma. Not yet," I said, feeling like so many important pieces to my life were slipping away.

"Where's Lisa? Why didn't she come? She still mad at me?"

"Grandma, my mother isn't here. She's gone," I said, no longer able to hold back my tears.

"Juan, she's mad at me. She's mad. I let Rich talk me in to putting her in that place. She left me in St. Louis. I tried to get her away, Juan. Away from that Rich."

It broke my heart and I knew that my grandmother's mind had gone. It was sad to see her speak about my mother as if she was alive. It saddened me even more that she was hurt thinkin' my mother wasn't visitin' her in the hospital.

"My daughter hates me, baby," she cried.

"Grandma, my mother loved you," I cried.

Takin' off my coat, I decided to get in bed with my grandmother to hold her. She needed me more than ever. Her sister had sent her off to die, and I was all that she had. As I got as comfortable as I could, behind my grandmother, I held her without disturbin' any of the tubes.

"Grandma, you know I love you, right?"

"I love you, too. How is that crazy sister of yours doing, Denie?"

"She's actually doing a lot better. Over the past couple of years, we've gotten closer."

"Juan baby, don't trust her. I know you might've forgiven her for what she did to your mother, but I haven't," my grandmother said in between catching her breath.

"What did she do?"

"She tried to poison her. Sweetheart, she's the reason your mother went crazy. She tried to kill her with poison. She tortured my daughter with letters while she battled losing her mind…" before she could finish her sentence she started to rub on my face. "Juan, I love you so much. You've always been my favorite. When I found out that you were alive, I was so happy. I didn't tell your mother right away. Do you think that's why she's mad at me?" she ranted on again. "She came to see me once."

"Grandma, she didn't come here. She's dead. And she's not mad at you. She loved you. You have to believe that. What else did Denie do?" I asked, realizin' that my grandmother had more info that I needed to know.

"Denie's here, too? No, get her out of here, Juan. She's evil and means us no good."

"She's not here, Grandma. I'm here. Juan's here."

"Warn Lisa. Tell her Denie's here," she wailed. "She's done so much to you already, baby! That bitch is evil!"

Just when I got her to calm down by reminiscin' on a few past memories of her and my grandfather, a gorgeous, very curvy, nurse came in.

"Hello, you must be Juan, I'm Taylor."

She smiled as she reached out to shake my hand. She was very pretty. Her warm cocoa complexion, with very deep dimples, made her smile glow even more. My piece got hard lookin' at her cleavage in her blue uniform. "Yes. How did you know?" I asked as I wiped my eyes and diverted my attention from her breast.

"First Lady always talks about you. Her handsome grandson."

"Oh, so you think I'm handsome, huh?" I flirted.

"You are handsome, b-a-b-y," my grandmother chimed in with broken pronunciation. Her speech had begun to slur and she seemed to be fadin' out.

"First Lady doesn't forget anything," Taylor laughed.

"So, does my grandmother talk about my mom a lot?" I asked.

"All the time."

"What's gonna happen to my grandmother? Is she really as bad as she says?"

"Juan, I told you they said…" She gave a long pause. Before continuing, "I'mma die. Taylor, take care of my baby, Juan," my grandmother struggled to say. Both Taylor and me looked at each other confused.

Then Taylor continued. "Her situation is delicate. She has good days, but they are far in between. Today appears to be a very good day, but in a matter of seconds, things can change. The doctors are not expectin' her to make it much longer. Not only is she suffering from lung cancer, but she's got a long list of other health issues as a result of the chemo and radiation."

"Does that mess with her mind? She keeps speaking about my mother, as if she's alive."

"Well, before the Dementia really got worse, she would speak of her daughter often."

"Oh, Jesus," First Lady moaned. "He answered my prayers. Lisa, is that you? I'm so sorry baby, for everything. Now, do you see, Juan? She didn't want you to know. She's back, Juan. She came back to her…"

As I looked up to the door, I was in shock. It was Mecca. My grandmother started crying uncontrollably. Her body shook, then she began gaspin' for air. All of a sudden her body started shakin', right in my arms. The machines started to beep and I was suddenly instructed to get out of the bed with my grandmother. After minutes of listenin' to the doctor and nurse talk, I heard a long, annoyin' beep. My grandmother had flat lined. She was gone. The only connection to my mother was gone.

"Grandma, noooooooooooooooo! Please don't leave me! You can't leave me!" I screamed.

Her eyes were closed. She was at peace, no longer in pain from the cancer. Another loss under my belt. As I cried and cried, the first person that comforted me came as a bit of a surprise, it was Taylor. She held me as we both cried. After a brief embrace she looked at me and held my chin up as I sat in the chair at my grandmother's bedside.

"Juan, your grandmother was a good woman. I will miss her dearly, but she's no longer in pain. She's in a better place."

"Hi, I'm Mecca, Juan's girlfriend. You are?"

"I'm Taylor. I have cared for First Lady, I mean Juan's grandmother, since she came here over a month ago. I just grew very fond of her. We used to talk a lot. I'll let you all mourn properly."

"Yes, thanks," Mecca said coldly, as she placed her hand on my shoulder.

"I'm sorry if I intruded," Taylor said in a sincere tone.

"No, you didn't. Thanks Taylor. Thanks for being there for my grandmother when no one else was. Thank you."

"I was just doing my job." Taylor said after wiping away her tears.

"You said you were leaving, right?" Mecca interrupted as Taylor exited the room.

"What the fuck is wrong with you?"

"A bitch has her hands wrapped around your neck, consoling you, and you ask me what's wrong with me?" Mecca snapped.

"Mecca, my grandmother is laying here dead, and you want to start an argument? Are you serious? Besides, you said it was over between us, so keep your word. Now get the fuck out. Now!"

As I watched Mecca leave the room, I turned my attention to my grandmother. She looked so angelic. Deep down inside I wanted to believe her. I wanted to believe my mother was alive. A part of me felt anything was possible. My father came back to me. Maybe my mother would, too. For now, Denie had some answerin' to do.

Chapter 17

Denie

"Denie, girl, guess what happened last night?" Chaz, one of my employees, belted as soon he walked in the door of the boutique.

"What drama do you need to fill me in on Chaz?" I said, shaking my head, laughing. He always knew any and everything going on in the city.

"Girl, you know…" as Chaz spoke, his words fell on deaf ears. I was in la-la land trying to process that my life had finally felt right. With all the bad I had done, God still found a way to bless me with my son, and Cornell. It started to feel like I was gonna beat this HIV thing. Deep down inside I felt like Cornell was the one. He deserved to know all my secrets, because for the first time in life, I found true love. It was true. We were meant to be and there was no way I would allow a disease to keep us from being together. Things were going great in my life. Deep down, it just felt too good to be true.

Chaz kept talking as I put the final touches on the windows to prepare for my grand opening next week. I was quite pleased. Kinycole Dé cor had come in andmade magic happen, with all the upholstery, decorations, and accents. My street team had done their part with promotions.

"Denie, did you hear what I said?"

"Huh," I said, embarrassed at the fact that I hadn't been paying him any attention.

"I asked if you were excited about the grand opening?"

"Overly excited! Everything is taken care of. Now all we have to do is sell a lot of shit." We both laughed.

"OMG! Is that a rock on your hand? Okay, Miss Thang, I need details. What the hell is on your hand?"

"I'm engaged," before I could say another word, I got a phone call from a guy I barely knew. He did some quick name dropping and asked if I could get him a chick for the night. He seemed legit, saying he'd gotten my number from a dude I knew well. So, I rattled off the prices. I had the perfect girl in mind but was interrupted by a loud crash of glass that sounded from the front of the store.

"What the hell was that?" I asked, running in my six-inch heels to the front of my boutique.

"Juan? What the fuck is your problem?" I belted as he walked towards me in a deep rage. Before I could say another word, he grabbed me by my neck, and pushed me straight to my office with force.

"What the fuck did you do to my mother?"

"Get your hands off me, Juan!"

"Denie, should I call the cops?" Chaz asked in a panic. He had his hands planted across his mouth while standing at the door of my office.

"No, Chaz. Just leave. I'll call you."

"Are you sure?" he asked through the door.

"Get your faggot ass outta here!" Juan yelled.

"Juan, get your hands from around my fucking neck!" I yelled. I could barely breathe.

"Denie, how could you? Why did you do that shit?"

"Juan, what the hell are you talking about?" I said, trying to figure out what he knew.

"You poisoned my mother and made her go crazy!" he yelled with rage. Finally removing his hand from my neck, he paced the floor back and forth.

"Where did you hear that nonsense, Juan? I didn't do anything to that bitch," I fired back.

"My grandmother died yesterday. She told me everything about your ass. You tortured her, and now you…what the fuck is that on your hand?"

"I'm marrying Cornell. He's going to be my husband. I'm sure your mother is turning over in her grave, but I love him," I said as I scanned my office, to see what I could hit him over the head with.

"You a disrespectful whore. You and Cornell some shit. Wait 'til I see that nigga. I'mma fuck his ass up!"

"Your punk ass ain't gonna do shit. You're not gonna mess up what good I got going on in my life. You need to be worried about your bitch. That's the whore, and that's real talk, you Fed-loving, hot ass nigga!"

"Hot! You called me hot? You want me to throw your past in your face, Miss HIV? You want me to be hot and tell your new boyfriend…"

"Fiancé," I corrected.

"Whatever the fuck you wanna call him. I bet Cornell don't know about yo' shit. I bet Cornell don't know."

"Don't know about what?" Cornell asked. He waltzed in ready to save the day. His tall stature towered over Juan.

"Nigga, you figure it out. You figure out her demons on your own. You think you can fuck my mother, now my sister, and think it's all good?"

"Juan, you've slept with somebody's mother and sister before. You supposed to get a pass? Your mother fucked up and chose drugs over me. Your sister? Shit, we just happened."

"Yeah whatever, y'all just happened. She went after you to get back at my mother!"

"And I'm glad she did, Juan! I love her. She's more of a woman than Lisa ever was…"

Before Cornell could say another word, Juan punched him square in the face. As they threw punches back and forth, I panicked. Trying to break them apart, I fell and hit my head on the edge of my metal desk. Blood poured from my head. Finally, they stopped fighting once they heard me scream.

"Juan, what have you done! Denie, are you okay? Get something for her head, Juan," Cornell ran to my rescue.

"Fuck both of y'all. I ain't helpin' her with shit, and I damn sure ain't fuckin' with her blood."

The room fell silent for a moment while Cornell tried to process what Juan had said.

"Denie, lose my number and let that nigga take care of you from now on. This boutique is the last thing I'm ever doing for you. I'm out."

"Really Juan? Fuck me? Stay the hell away from me. You can have that house. I'm getting my son and getting the fuck out of there today. I don't need your ass," I yelled as he left.

No matter how much I played tough my feelings were hurt. I ain't fuck with the bitch nigga for real, but his words still stung. He was really close to letting Cornell in on my HIV status. He must really be mad at me. I had never seen him like this. Was it because of First Lady dying? He wasn't even that close to her. I didn't get it.

"Babe, come on, get up. I have practice but I can call and tell them I have an emergency if you need to go to the hospital?"

"Cornell, all I want right now is to hug my baby boy. I want to go pick him up and let us all cuddle in our new house together. I just need to get out of here."

After calling the maintenance guy that I hired to board the front door, Cornell and I headed to the house to pick up BJ from Maria. I had been so caught up with my new engagement and the boutique that I hadn't seen my son in a couple of days. My son was my world and I was feeling a bit guilty that I hadn't been to the house to see him. I didn't even see Cheri before she left. My last few days had been dedicated to spending time with Cornell while he had time off.

"How you feeling, babe?" Cornell asked as he reached over to hold my hand. All I could think of was how angry Juan was. If he wanted to blame anyone for Lisa's downfall he needed to blame Lisa. No man out here was gonna have me so gone that I would get caught up in drugs. That's for weak chicks.

"Denie, you good?" he asked again.

"I'm sorry, just got a lot on my mind. I'll be alright."

"Well, let me help you."

"You're helping me in more ways than you know."

"What's the big secret, Denie? What was Juan talking about when he said, he bet I don't know? You need to tell me something?"

"Cornell, Juan doesn't even know what he's talking about. He's still mad at me for all the stuff I did to Lisa. Lisa did some really bad things to me when I was young that I never told you."

"What? What did she do?" he asked afraid of what I might say.

"She held me at gunpoint and tortured me. She even cut my hair off just to get back at my Dad, for cheating on her."

"What type of sick shit is that to do to someone you raised as your child?"

"I was no better, though. Juan's mad because my grand…I mean Lisa's mother, told him that I poisoned Lisa. I planted boric acid in her drawer. She sniffed it thinking it was cocaine. I did other things to her also, that I'd rather not say."

"Denie, what else did you do?" he asked looking at me, like it was now or never.

"When she was in the hospital, I sent her pictures of us, from the night we met in the club. I wanted to make her jealous."

"So, I was a game to you?"

"At first you were. But now, I am glad things happened the way that they did. I love you so much. Besides my son, I can't think of loving anyone more than I love you. Cornell, you are a God send."

"Well, Denie, you do have a colorful past. Are you ready to tell me about BJ's father?" he said as he turned down the street, of the house I once called home. I couldn't wait to get the hell out of there, and start a new life with my man.

"The things that he did to me are too painful to even repeat. If you think what Lisa did to me was sick, brace yourself, you ain't ready."

"I can take it. Tell me."

"The problem is Cornell, I try to bury it so deep, that it's too painful to relive through telling you. Please respect my wishes, babe," I said as we pulled in front of the house.

"Denie, you are about to be my wife. There should be nothing you can't tell me. I vow to love you unconditionally."

"I'm going to hold you to that. Just not today, I want to just see my son right now," I said, before getting out of the car.

Walking to the door, I couldn't wait to see my little man. As soon as I opened the door I called for him.

"BJ, Mommy's home."

"Do you need me to help you carry anything to the car? Any of BJ's favorite toys that I didn't buy for the new house?"

"All this shit can stay here. You've given me all that I need," I said, giving Cornell a kiss before walking into the kitchen. No one was home. Reaching for my phone out of my Chanel bag I called Maria. She didn't answer. After calling her five times still no answer, so I left her a message.

Maria, it's Denie. Call me back ASAP. You know I have a real big problem when you don't answer your phone. I miss BJ. Bring him home as soon as possible. Bye.

As soon as I hung up, Cornell called my name.

"Denie, come here quick!"

"What's up, babe," I said, running to the living room.

"It's a letter, from Maria," he said with a confused look on his face.

As I grabbed the letter from Cornell I read it in disbelief.

Denie,

I am taking Baby Juan and Carmen out of this house. Marisol would never want them to live like this. Juan is a bad person and so are you. You never wanted to be a mother anyway to Javier's son. I will care for them from now on. Do not contact me.

Maria

"Cornell, she took my baby. She took him, Cornell." My body stood paralyzed with mixed emotions.

"We'll find him. I'm calling the police."

"She could be in Colombia by now. Cornell, I can't live without my son," I cried. "Please find him," I wailed, more and more until I fell to the floor.

Chapter 18
Juan

If Denie called my phone one more time, I was gonna choke her ass out. There was nothing she could say that I wanted to hear. Hittin' ignore for the umpteenth time, I slowed down so my father could catch up to me. As he limped to the car, it broke my heart. Through all his loud moans and shakes, I still saw strength. He was the strongest man I knew. That's why I jetted to him for advice on the way shit had been going. I needed to tie up so many loose ends, starting with disposin' of Grady's body. It was long overdue. And nobody else could be trusted.

"Dad, why didn't you call and tell me you had a seizure?" I asked, leavin' his condo in Baltimore. Nicole and Honey had filled me in on his last episode, and warned that he had to take it easy.

"I'm alright, son. This shit happens all the time," he said, shuttin' the passenger side door. "Why you ain't tell me your grandmother died? Hell, I would've paid my respect," he laughed.

"Yeah, right, what's funny?"

"Naw, for real, it ain't funny. I can't believe First Lady died," my father said as we rode to the stash house in Clinton.

"Mannnn, it was weird how she kept speakin', like my mother was still alive."

"Juan, don't get your hopes up, boy. She's dead. I saw her in the coffin. Lisa killed herself, son. She in hell burnin' like a mother…"

"Slow down. That's my mother you talkin' bout." I shot his ass an evil eye.

"You know they say, if you commit suicide, it's a wrap. You going straight to hell," he fired with confidence. "I'm just sayin'. Anyway, why y'all cremate First Lady? She ain't have no money to get buried?"

"Man, you know I woulda paid for her to have a funeral. But her sister said that's what she wanted. I wasn't tryna argue with nobody. I'ma just pay my respect at the memorial."

"Don't be crying and shit. That's for weak niggas," my father laughed. He was still so insensitive. Even after all he had been through. It seemed like he had gotten worse.

"What the fuck you expect? My grandmother died. Have a heart for once."

"Ah, come on, Juan. Y'all wasn't even all that close. That heifer was a rude bitch. She made my life a livin' hell, and I ain't like her."

"She was all I had left of my mother. I guess you don't understand," I said, decidin' to just let it go. Talkin' to him about anything concernin' my mother was worthless.

"I lost my mother, and my wife. I get it. I understand. But what I'm tryin' to say son is, you can't waddle in the shit. You gotta grab life by the horns and ride that shit out. You gotta be a man out here. To your bitch, and your sister..."

"Me and Mecca are done. And fuck Denie!"

"Hold up, son. What do you mean?" He barked like he was ready for war.

"My grandmother told me what Denie did to my mother. She made her go crazy," I told him. He needed to realize his daughter was fucked up.

After tellin' my father what First Lady said about the poisonin', he looked relieved. Like I said something he wasn't expectin'. Which made me question, was there more? Deep down, I knew he always loved Denie more, so I had to accept it. But if there was more, he wasn't the person who'd tell me.

"Lisa made herself go crazy, not Denie. Son, you can't blame Denie because Lisa decided to fuck my brother. Then get caught up on drugs!" he yelled, as if he had pissed himself off talkin' about the situation, all over again.

"Rich, when are you gonna take accountability for what you did to my mother?"

"Oh, I'm Rich to you now. Dad sounded so much better."

"Well, Rich, Dad, whatever way you wanna slice it. Answer the question. When are you gonna say, I fucked up my wife and my kids?"

"That's how you feel? You feel like I fucked everybody up, huh?"

"Look at our lives. My mother is dead. Denie has HIV. I'm in the streets and could get snatched by the FEDs at any moment. How could the Sanchez' be any more fucked up than that?"

"Your mother killed herself! Denie chose to fuck a nigga that I warned her about! And as for you, I always had enough money so that you didn't have to choose the streets. You like wearin' them diamonds and drivin' fast cars and shit, right? You should be thankin' me."

"Did you forget when you got locked up back in the day? I had to take care of the family. That's when Denie spiraled out of control."

"Did I not try to shield you from this life, Juan? Take accountability. You chose this life."

"It was all I knew. It was all I saw," I yelled.

"So, you mean to tell me if I was a trash man, you would've been a trash man, too?" He held onto the smug look on his face.

"Maybe not a trash man, but maybe somethin' just a little better than a trash man, like some type of business man or somethin'," I said imaginin' what life would be like, until my vision was suddenly squashed.

"No, you wouldn't have. You a Sanchez, boy!"

"Well, sometimes I wish I didn't have that name."

"Listen to me, son. Uncle Renzo brought me into this life. He made sure me and Los carried on the Sanchez legacy out here on the East Coast with pride and integrity. My father was a good man. His brother still made a way to turn me into the man I am. The man you are ashamed of, but you've become. No matter how you might resent me deep down inside, you are just like me," he said, lookin' me square in the eye.

Strugglin' not to show any emotion, I listened to my father talk. His words were chillin' and made my soul shiver. He was right. There was no denying it.

I'd mastered this game better than my father or Los. No matter how much I hated my Uncle Renzo, he had paved the way for us, and I fucked it up. With my mother in my ear, I helped take down his organization. Luckily, it's a new generation out here on these streets, and I was able to bounce back without too many people really knowin' my history. In heavy thought as I drove down I-495 approachin' the Branch Avenue exit, I decided this was the right time, to let my father know that I was the ticket to gettin' the Sanchez reputation back where it belonged. Just before we got to the house, my phone rang. It was Julio.

"Hello."

"Nigga, what you trying to do, get me killed or somethin'?"

"What the fuck you talkin' bout?"

"Man, your money wasn't right. That shit was counterfeit. Now, Big Tony wanna get at you."

"Nigga, my money wasn't fake. Fuck you talkin' bout?" Instantly, I put Julio on speakerphone so my father could listen.

"Well, my money was straight. So yours was the counterfeit shit. It was the money in the Puma duffle bag that wasn't right."

"How do I know that?" I fired. "How do I know you ain't settin' me up?"

"Look my nigga, I'll let Big Tony deal with you about that. I just wanted to hip you to what's going on. I felt like I owed you that. Strap up."

"Naw, nigga. You..." I tried to say.

Click.

He hung up the phone so abruptly. I didn't know what to believe. Julio's tone and demeanor was too convincin'. I was beginnin' to believe the money I'd given him really was fake.

"Rich. What the fuck have you done?"

"You believe that nigga? He probably tryin' to set you up. That nigga probably tryin' to take over your shit. He wanna rob you of $250 thousand, but your simple ass giving me the suspicious eye. "

"Man, he said the money that was in the Puma duffle was counterfeit."

"Juan, how easy would it be for him to switch the money out?"

"You really think so?"

"Man, fuck that. The next meetin' you have with these clowns, I'm there. Fuck that, ain't nobody fuckin' over my son. We gotta get the Sanchez name back. We need to let these motherfuckers know the Sanchez's aren't to be fucked with."

My father leaned over to give me a pound. But I refused to lift my hand. My insides were twistin' all around. And hundreds of thoughts bounced around in my head while I drove crazily through the streets. My father began speakin', but I didn't hear one word. I was so unsure about everything as the many emotions rushed through me.

By the time we pulled up to the house in Clinton, I was finally able to answer a few of my father's questions. The entire time he'd been fillin' my head on how we'd get at Big Tony's crew. With reservations about the entire money situation, I had to stay focused.

We had a job to do. No matter how my father might've let me down in the past, he assured me that his money was straight.

"Have I ever let you down?" he asked as we stepped out of the car.

I shook my head. He was right. He'd always been there for me.

"I love you, son. Now, let's take care of this nigga, Grady."

It was cold as shit. For it to be around noon, the sun wasn't doin' the temperature outside any justice. Moving the body during the middle of the day, while most people were at work and school, was my father's idea. We drove my Escalade pick-up, to make it easy to just throw Grady in the back. My father was always prepared. Where he'd gotten a mail cart from was unspeakable. But it was the perfect thing to move Grady's body. We both worried about the smell. Leaving a decayin' body for that long was the dumbest thing I'd done in a while.

"Come on son, let's go in through the back."

I followed my dad's lead. Just as I always imagined, I was now the co-captain, learnin' while my father taught me. Dead motherfuckers wasn't my expertise.

As soon as I unlocked, and opened the door, the funk hit me in the face like a sack of bricks. It smelled worse than a house full of rotten meat, and caused bile to rise up in my gut. Weak and out of my league, my stomach could no longer handle the stench. I started throwin' up everywhere.

"Aww shit, Juan. Man up," my father said, shootin' past me, going straight to the living room.

He paced the floor, searchin' from room to room, while I moved around, lookin' for something to wipe my mouth.

"Where the hell you put the nigga? Shit, I smell his ass, but he ain't in here."

My eyes bulged damn near out of the sockets. What the fuck did he mean? Finally gettin' myself together, I made my way through the kitchen, into the livin' room. Coverin' my nose, I stopped at the spot where I left Grady's body. It was gone.

"What the hell!" I said in disbelief.

"Don't tell me you ain't make sure the nigga was dead, Juan?"

"I did. His brains were on the floor. I shot him in his head," I said, tryin' to convince my father that I knew how to kill a man.

"We've both been shot and survived trauma, son. So, either you didn't get him good enough or that bitch you saw leaving the house came back to help him."

My dad pulled his nine millimeter out and started searchin' the rooms while I allowed my hands to massage the sides of my head. This shit was fucked up. When Rich reappeared he ran down his plan.

"Look, I'm about to get Honey to get a storage place around the corner on Branch Avenue. We can load up the Escalade and move your shit outta here, pronto. You gotta debt this place for good."

"Okay." As he started preachin' about how I ran my business, I jetted down to the basement to gather up all my money and coke. As soon as I got to the wine cellar, I felt like passin'out.

"Dad! Come down here!" I shouted. "My shit is gone."

"What? What the fuck!" he asked, makin' his way into the basement. I could hear him givin' Honey instructions as he hit the bottom step.

"Most of my fuckin' coke is gone. Man, that was over a quarter mill worth of shit," I told him with frustration.

"Are you serious?"

"This is crazy. I hope nobody hit my condo, too." I had about six hundred thousand in my condo, I thought to myself wonderin' why so much bullshit was happenin' to me.

"Listen, we'll check all your other spots later. For now, let's load up what's left."

One thing I could say, my father definitely had a ride or die chick. Honey came through with usin' her name to get a storage unit in less than an hour. She called sayin' everything was straight. She'd even gotten me a lock and a key. Once we got the Escalade completely packed, I realized I had lost over half of million dollars worth of shit with only about eight hundred thousand worth of shit. My mind was still messed up from losin' First Lady and now with the robbery, I was messed up.

Who the fuck could've robbed me? I kept asking myself as we left the house in Clinton. The first person that came to mind was Julio. I thought about it the entire ride over to meet Honey. Rich didn't say much. He just let me sulk. But Honey hugged me saying everything would be okay. She knew my mind was heavy. I kept wondering if the same female I saw leaving the spot the night I blasted Grady had anything to do with this.

After we moved everything to the storage unit we were back in the truck. Makin' my way onto Branch Avenue, I tried calling Julio immediately from my throw away phone, I didn't get an answer. I decided to tell my father what I was thinkin'.

"I think Julio fucked me," I said bluntly.

"Exactly," he responded while starin' out the window.

After bangin' on the steering wheel a couple of times, I tried to find the words to match what I felt. But Rich knew exactly what was needed.

"Kill him," he uttered.

"Just like that."

"Yeah, just like that."

"But I don't know for sure, and…"

"What do you really know about this half-breed?" my father interrupted. "And where'd you meet the nigga?"

"Well, you know the dude Star, from LA that got killed last year?"

"I heard of him. They found his body in Philly, right?"

"Yea. Well after he died, Julio and me decided to fuck with each other. I figured he's Columbian and I'm half Columbian." I paused. "Look, Dad, I don't want to jump to conclusions."

My father was in deep thought before speakin' again. "Do you think I know this nigga?"

"Naw, he like my age. Maybe a year or two older at the most."

"You got a picture of the nigga? What about this Big Tony dude? Are they connected?"

"They know of each other thru Big Tony's son, but not really.

"You got a pic in your phone of the nigga?"

"You know what? I do. We took a picture one night on my phone. Mecca was trippin' thinkin' I was out with a bitch. She made me text a pic to prove we were together. Hand me my iPhone out the glove box."

Once I turned my phone on to show my father the picture, I ignorined the fact that Denie and Cheri had been callin'. I scrolled through my pics, still keepin' my eyes on the road as I made it on to I-495.

"Hold up, go back," my father interrupted as he tried to catch a quick look at a titty pic Mecca sent me.

"Hell no!" I laughed for the first time in hours. Finally getting to the picture of Julio, I showed it to my father. "This him," I said as I diverted my attention back to the road while he analyzed.

"Juan, this dude looks very familiar to me. You say he Colombian?"

"Yep."

"What's his last name? Who's his family?"

"I don't know."

"Why in the hell don't you know? You can't fuck with nobody on these types of levels and know nothin' about them. Set up a meetin' with this nigga. I wanna meet him. Fuck it, I don't care who knows I'm alive now. Ain't nobody fuckin' up my legacy, thinkin' they can fuck with my son."

As he ranted again, my phone started ringin'. It was Denie. When her picture popped up on my phone, my father's eyes instantly watered.

"Start with her. Let her know you're alive. She needs you, because I ain't fuckin' with her."

"Answer it Juan. I just need to hear her voice."

"Fuck no, you answer it."

It was too late. The phone went to voicemail.

"Here, she left a message. You can listen to her voice now all you like since you afraid to let her know you're alive."

As he pressed play her annoyin' voice rang through the Bluetooth in my truck.

"Juan, I'm at the house. I know you mad at me, but I need you," she cried out. "You can't let me go through this alone. I can't live without my son, Juan. I'll kill myself first."

"Without her son. What the fuck is wrong with my grandson? Juan, call her right now, nigga. Call my daughter!"

Denie's voice sounded like she had lost her best friend. I was afraid to know what to expect. If my nephew was dead I couldn't live with that. First a nigga robbed me, now my nephew, if me being in the streets… I just couldn't bear to finish the thought. As I turned the car around and headed to my house, I tapped on Denie's name. The phone only rang once, and she answered.

"Juan, come home! Please come home," she begged in between sobs.

"What's wrong, Denie?"

"I left you a million messages. BJ's gone. He's gone, Juan."

"What the fuck you mean, he's gone?"

"Maria took him. The police issued an Amber alert, but it's been 48 hours."

"I'mma kill that bitch," my father yelled with tears in his eyes.

"Juan, who was that?" Denie asked the question as if she knew, but needed confirmation.

"Denie, it's complicated. But I'm on the way," I told her while lookin' at my father start twitchin' in the passenger seat.

"You just sounded like Daddy," she said, as she started to cry uncontrollably. "Juan, I need my Daddy. My son is gone and I can't deal. Maria could be in Colombia by now. I can't live without my son!"

As I pushed the pedal to the metal, my father lay slouched into the passenger seat, twitchin' out of control. His nerves were runnin' wild as he made noises that he couldn't control.

"Dad, you alright," I asked wonderin' how bad his convulsions would get.

"I'mma kill her, Juan. I'mma kill her."

Chapter 19
Denie

My heart was heavy. There was no way I could handle living without my son. At least Juan had showed up to support me. He'd put our differences aside to help me deal with police and finding BJ. Taking my brother's advice, I decided to take a long, hot bath in my Jacuzzi. As I ran the bath water and turned on the jets, I dropped some Lavender bath salts in the water, to help relax my body. Looking in the gold, foiled-trimmed mirror in my bathroom, I couldn't believe what I saw. In a matter of days, I had lost so much weight. I still had curves, but my eyes looked a little sunken. Letting my hair down from my ponytail holder, I shook my head from side to side, and let my hair fall loose. I finally took off my black velour Juicy romper, that I'd had on for the last three days. I lit all the candles in the bathroom. With every flicker from the torch, I said a prayer for my son.

I heard my phone make a sound letting me know I had a text. Realizing it was from Skeet, a dude who wanted me to supply him with a chick, my lips made a slight frown. I texted back, letting him know things were shut down until further notice. The only thing on my mind was getting my son back. I didn't have time anymore for being the middleman between thirsty men and weak chicks. Besides, with Cornell in my life, I didn't need the extra income anymore.

As soon as I turned off the phone and my skylights, I walked towards the Jacuzzi to get in. But the unexpected touch startled me.

"Damn baby, you scared me," I said as I almost jumped out of my skin.

"Juan let me in."

"How'd that go between the two of you?" I asked Cornell smugly.

"Cool. He just told me where to find you."

"Glad to see he could put his differences aside right now. What are you doing here? I thought you had practice."

"Baby, I couldn't focus at practice. I had to come be with you. The Wizards organization understands what I'm going thru. My coach said they'll use their assets to help find BJ."

"Are you serious? How?" I asked with a glimpse of hope, as I made my way into the water with Cornell's help.

"I'm their franchise player. They're willing to do anything for me. At every game, they plan to bring awareness, by having BJ's picture on the monitor. The good thing is, my fans are concerned. There has been an overwhelming response from the community."

"But babe, suppose she's already out of the country?"

"There has been no sign of her leaving, so think positive," he said as he took my loofa sponge and started to wash my back.

"I love you so much, Cornell. Babe, you're the best thing that ever happened to me. You've changed my life. Just when I thought my life was complete, this happens. The most devastating, and the best things in my life, are all happening to me at once. I just don't get it. I've been horrible, I know, but why would God take my son. He's my life," I started to cry as I laid my head back into the water."

"Denie, what can I do to help you? I just want to take your pain away."

Before I could respond, he kissed me. Maybe that's what I needed because once we started kissing I needed Cornell. I needed him to take all my pain away. The more intense our kissing became the more emotional I got. There was no way I could fight back my tears. As I cried, Cornell kissed me all over my body, as if he knew where it hurt. Water splashed, as I pulled Cornell in with me, clothes on and all. As he kicked off his shoes he never once stopped kissing me. As I pulled his drenched clothes off his body, I cried, and cried.

"Cornell, why me?" I sobbed.

"Baby, let me just take your pain away. Just for an hour. Let me take it all away," he said, as he lifted my body up to the edge of the Jacuzzi. As Cornell devoured his face into my love box, I let out a passionate scream, and moan.

"You like when I suck this pussy?"

"Cornell, I love it," I said, making my way on his pole and went to work. Water splashed everywhere as I rode him like a stallion. Cornell reached his hand down to the drain to let the water out, as I continued to flex every muscle on his pole. I needed to feel him. I needed to feel better. If only for an hour like he said. As the sound of the water draining from the Jacuzzi played, we made our own music, between all the moaning, and I love you's.

"Denie, when I told you I loved you unconditionally. I love you. Flaws and all."

"Cornell, I believe you, I cried," as we both came together.

Cornell held me tight, as we laid together, in the empty Jacuzzi. So many thoughts raced through my head. After taking that short trip to ecstasy with Cornell, I was back to reality, real quick.

"Come on babe, get up. Let me massage your body, and get you dressed."

"Thanks for everything. I just can't believe that Maria would just take my son like this. Why now?"

"Babe, we're gonna get him back. We need to be trying to explore all options. Starting with BJ's father…"

"He's dead, and I hate him."

"Why every time I ask you something about him, you get like this? Don't let anybody have that much power over you."

"He was a faggot, and I hate him. That's all you need to know about him."

Before our disagreement could go any further, Juan was knocking at the door.

"Yea," I yelled, putting on my pink Ugg slippers.

"You decent?" he asked through the door. Peeping his head in I could tell by his face expression he was serious.

"You need to come downstairs, right now."

Cornell and I rushed downstairs, behind Juan. As I got to the family room, I was confused. Some chubby Spanish girl with short curly hair stood there. She looked like she was in her early 20's.

"Who are you?" I asked.

"My name is Guadalupe. I am Maria's daughter."

"Where the hell is your mother? What has she done to my son?"

"Look Denie, my mother didn't like you, I know, but she loved your mother. She would never harm Carmen, or BJ. She loves those kids like they were her own."

"When I get my hands on Maria…"

"Babe, chill. Listen to what she has to say. Maybe it's something that she knows, that could lead us to BJ," Cornell interrupted.

"Yeah Denie. Cool down," Juan agreed.

"The last time I saw my mother, she had a broken nose, compliments of your brother Juan here," she said, looking at Juan with disgust.

"What happened, Juan?" I asked, confused.

"Maria let the police in here and was talkin' to them. She tried to say I killed Marisol. I didn't think she would take the kids behind that shit," Juan defended himself.

"So this is all your fault, Juan? My son could be in Colombia by now, all because of you. That's how you get me back, huh?"

"Denie, I didn't make that bitch do shit."

"Look, my mother would never hurt BJ."

"What makes you so sure? She hates us," I yelled.

"He's family. Javier was my mother's nephew. She would never hurt BJ."

"What?" I asked.

"Look Denie, what Javier did to you was awful. That's why my mother wanted to do anything she could to help you."

"What do you mean? You are related to Javier?" I said again with narrowing eyes. The mention of his name made my blood boil.

"How do you think my mother met Marisol? Jade, Javier's sister was who helped get my mother this job."

After Guadalupe went down memory lane for what felt like forever, I finally snapped.

"Bitch, if you can't tell me where your dumb ass mother took my son, get the fuck out of my house!"

No longer able to hold back my tears, I ran up the stairs and into my bedroom. Letting out a loud scream, I cried and cried. As I laid, sprawled across my bed, I buried my face deep into my satin pillows and let it all out. There was no describing the pain I felt. It was so deep.

On my back, staring at the ceiling, I prayed to God.

God, please help me. I need you now, more than ever. When I asked for you to send my father back to me, I knew that was a far reach. Now, I need you for real, Please bring my son back to me.

"How strong is your faith? I don't think it's such a far reach."

As I wiped my puffy eyes, I wondered if my mind was playing tricks on me. I knew the voice. I just didn't believe it.

"Who are you?" I asked, preparing to let out a scream, as the tall figure got closer.

"It's me, Denie. It's your Daddy."

Chapter 20
Rich

"Daddy, is it really you?"

"Yes, my baby girl. It's really me," I said, reachin' out, grabbing my daughter tightly. This was all I ever wanted…to hold my daughter again.

She touched my face as if she couldn't believe it was really me, I reassured her.

"Denie, it's really me."

"But how, Daddy? How is this possible?"

"I laid there on the beach, and fought for my life, baby. You kept me alive."

"Daddy, it's really you, Daddy," she yelled as she cried like a baby in my arms.

After getting her caught up on all that had gone on in my life, and how I survived, I saw a glow come over her. It was like I gave her hope.

"God answered my prayers. I prayed every night. I've had some dark moments Daddy, and I needed you. I prayed for you. God sent you to me in my darkest moment. I love you soooooo much," Denie said with so much emotion, as I held her, as we laid down together.

"Daddy, why did you stay away so long?"

"To be honest, Denie, I was afraid. I didn't want you guys to reject me. And I didn't want anybody tryin' to kill you or Juan because of me being alive. When Juan found out about me bein' alive I made him promise to not tell you. He was the one that told me you needed me. So, I'm here now. Let's focus on that. We need to focus on getting my grandson home."

"He's so precious, Daddy. He has our dimples." She smiled proudly.

"How are you handlin' your situation? Does your new man know about you bein' HIV positive? You know I don't like his ass."

"Daddy, I love him. He's a good man."

"How do you think he's a good man? He's been with both you and your mother. I'm sorry, I mean Lisa."

"Daddy. He's good to me, and BJ. I can't help who I fell in love with. He's the best thing that has ever happened to me."

"You used to say that about Nelson. Now…Cornell."

"Daddy, he respects me, and that's what matters."

"Well any man that still stays with a girl, knowing she's HIV positive, I gotta respect."

"He doesn't know."

"If he loves you like you say he does, he'll love you, no matter what. You need to tell him. You wearin' condoms, right?"

"No."

"Come on Denie. I'm gonna be honest. If I found out a chick fucked me, knowing she had HIV, I would kill her. The bitch would die of a brutal, ruthless death. With all that Juan has told me about your Florida escapades, you're lucky to be alive. Now you've made it ten times harder to tell him," I said, as I let out a loud squeal. My head started shakin'. It scared the hell out of Denie.

"Daddy, what's wrong with you? Daddy, please. Are you okay?"

"Baby, I'm okay, it's just my nerves from being shot," I laughed, just to assure her, that I was okay.

After givin' her a lecture, I felt I had gotten through to her, but I knew she wasn't gonna tell that boy nothin'. I really didn't give a fuck about him. I just didn't want anybody to hurt my daughter. She filled me in on how she got the dude Lamar. He deserved what he got, after fuckin' over my daughter like that. What was sad was, my daughter had more heart, than my son. She was the female version of me. She was ruthless. After a long heart to heart Denie started to get sleepy.

"Daddy, please stay with me," she mumbled.

"I'll stay until you fall asleep. Then I will be back in the mornin'. I have some shit to take care of."

"Some things never change. Your grandson is missin'. I just got you back, Daddy. You can't leave me."

"Babe, by the time you wake up in the mornin', I'll be here. I promise."

Finally, she was asleep. Quietly, I got up and made my way downstairs. Juan and Cornell were in the family room, watchin' football.

"She's sleepin'. Look, I'm happy to see that you two can be civilized. No bullshit, my daughter needs strength around her right now. Can you two handle that?"

"Rich, I love your daughter. If I knew you were alive, I would've asked you for her hand in marriage, before I proposed," Cornell said, shockin' the hell out of both Juan and me. We had been so caught up in so much, that we had no clue.

"Why didn't she tell me?" I said still in shock.

"With all that's going on, she has been preoccupied."

"Well, my nigga. Get it right this time. Take better care of my sister, than you did my mother."

"Trust me, Denie's good. I bought her a house right down the road. She's gonna be good. We're gonna be alright. For now, my focus is bringing our son home," Cornell said with confidence. He really did love her.

"Juan, I gotta go. Let me hold one of your rides, so I can roll."

"Cool, take the Escalade. Shit, you can have it. The keys are in the top drawer of the wood cabinet, in the foyer."

"Alright, see y'all tomorrow."

"Rich, I know how much you mean to my girl. Thanks for coming through. You are what she needed," Cornell said, as if he held rank with my daughter, more than me. If he was tryna have a pissin' match he was way outta his depth.

"You ain't gotta thank me. That's my daughter. You just better take care of her. Don't hurt my daughter."

"She's good. Trust me," he said, gettin' up to shake my hand. He looked me straight in the eye which I liked.

No matter how much I tried to forget about Marisol it wasn't easy. It felt a bit eerie, bein' in her house, without her there. Don't get me wrong, that bitch deserved to die, but it was no way to deny how I missed both Marisol and Lisa.

Denie was right. Some things never changed. I was still the fucked up nigga I only knew how to be. And I just couldn't help it. Yeah, I gave my son $250K in counterfeit money, but damn I ain't know street niggas pay attention to that shit. We never did. I was tryin' to get rich quick. Shit, who would've thought they would've found out? Anyway, it was important that I protected my son from them niggas, and helped my daughter, too. Juan would still have to give me my $250K back though.

As I got in the truck, I pulled out the gate and called Honey. We had shit to do, and tonight was the night to get it done. Grabbin' my phone, I called Honey.

"Hello."

"Honey. You almost at the storage unit?"

"Of course. You texted me an hour ago. I'm always on point. Pulling up now," she said unhappily.

"A'ight. You got that extra key to get in the unit, right?"

"Yes, Rich," she said dryly.

I didn't have time for that female emotional bullshit. Feelings had to be put aside if we planned on makin' moves. "I should be right behind you," I told her. "Probably be there in a half hour."

"Rich…"

"Yeah?"

"Ummm… never mind," Honey hesitated.

"What is it?" I snapped, irritated by her always wantin' to talk at the most inconvenient times. She drove me crazy when she did that shit.

"Why do you do this? You betray everyone you love. I can't think of one person, you haven't hurt. With all Juan has been through, why are you doing this to him?"

"Honey. He gonna be a'ight. He don't know how to handle this shit. It's too much for him."

"If he knew all you've done to him, it would destroy him."

"Don't worry about my son. He's my seed and he'll be okay."

"Rich, you don't see nothing wrong with robbing your own son? It's fucked up. That boy worships you," Honey yelled.

"Didn't I take care of Grady? That was for Juan. His body will never be found. All because of me! I saved his life. You always talk about the fucked up shit I do. What about the good?"

Little did she know, I was on point. When I didn't hear from Grady after a couple days, I double backed to the spot and found him dead. I had to act surprised when Juan first told me. But that's what hustlers do. We hustle mutherfuckers.

"I see the good, Rich, that's why I love you," Honey continued. "Deep down inside, you're a good man. But I've only seen that man when you were at your lowest point. No matter how much you snapped at me out of frustration, I still knew that you cared. When you were fighting for your life, and when you had to learn how to walk again, I was there."

Blah blah blah, I wanted to say. I wanted her to shut the fuck up.

"You say that I always see the bad in you. Do you ever see the good in me? You always so far up Nicole's ass. While she sits back like a princess. I'm your ride or die, Rich."

"That's what this is all about? Are you jealous?"

"No. I just want you to look at me, the way you look at her. I'm the one who's been there for you," she started to yell again.

"Man, I know you not cryin' and shit. You gotta be strong, Honey. Don't let no nigga, not even me, break you."

"You insensitive bastard. Fuck you. You cursed your daughter, and don't even know it. Your daughter's life is fucked up because of you. Your lack of respect for women is the reason why your daughter got that shit! She will never be happy, all because of you. You fucked her up. I be damned if you gonna fuck me up. After this last drop I do, I'm getting as far away from you as I can. You and Nicole can live happily ever after!"

Just like that, the phone went dead. I didn't bother callin' her back, because I knew as soon as I gave her some of this good dick, she'd be just fine. I knew I was wrong for all that I had done to Juan, but it was for his own good. I ain't want him fuckin' up all the money. I wouldn't say I robbed him. It was more like I moved his shit in another place.

As I took my exit, I thought about everything that Honey said. Was I that fucked up that God would punish my daughter? That was the type of shit both Lisa and Marisol would say.

As I pulled in the parkin' lot, I saw that Honey's car was still there. I had to fix things with her, because there was no way Nicole could do for me the things Honey did. We had chemistry in the bedroom, but she was far from being a ride or die, like Honey. Maybe I just needed to tell her, that I appreciated her. That can't be so hard.

I parked next to Honey and headed down to the unit. It killed me that she was so trustin'. The unit was wide open making us both sittin' targets. As I got closer, I called her name. My dick got hard at the thought of fuckin' her in a room filled with all my guilty pleasures; drugs and money. But first, I would check her for not closing the bay.

"Honey, where you at? I said as I reached the unit. "Honey! What the fuck?"

I ran over to her after seeing her lying on the cement floor, bleeding like a gutted pig. She lay on her side, panting slowly as if it hurt to breathe. Honey had been shot a couple of times in her chest and face. Whoever blasted her knew what they were doin'. "What the fuck happened?" I asked. But inside I wondered who she was workin' with?

Tryin' to calm down I sat on a box. I could feel a panic attack comin'. "Rich…" she attempted to say.

I stared at her with a blank look on my face. Who was tryin' to fuck with me? "Honey, who did this to you?"

It was clear she couldn't answer me.

"H-e-l-p…" she managed to say with her eyes open, beggin' for a chance at life.

I knelt down beside her, knowin' not to touch her. I wasn't about to go down for her murder. "Who did this, Honey?"

Before I could get any information from her, she closed her eyes, and took her last breath. She was gone.

Chapter 21
Juan

As I got in the shower, I was in deep thought, while the hot water massaged my tense muscles. So much had happened to my family all at once. Durin' these difficult times, I needed Mecca by my side. But I guess she meant every word when she said she was done with me. At least Cheri had called a few times, constantly showin' a nigga love. Just wasn't tryna go back down that road again.

After a long hot shower, I prepared for what was goin' to be a big day for me. Out of all the bad shit goin' on in my life, things were about to get better. After talkin' to Big Tony, he was convinced that I hadn't fucked over him. He agreed that somehow someone else had either given me that money, or Julio fucked me over. Still, he wanted his bread. Either way, he was out 250 grand, and wanted me to come up with the money. I had a couple of days to give him his cash; so I would have to take money from the stash we moved to the storage place. I'd have to deal with my Dad later on the money he thought he'd invested. He was gonna have to chuck it up to the game; that money was now a loss.

Julio was meetin' me up the street at the Chick-fil-a, so we could ride to the airport together. Some chick he was fuckin' on the side, was bringin' him to meet me. I felt a little guilty leavin' town at a time like this, but I had to redeem myself with Big Tony. Hopefully Denie would understand. My life depended on it.

It was important that I looked like money. So, after puttin' on my Versace boxer briefs, and tank top, I threw on my Givenchy sweater and my Balmain biker jeans. Looking in my full-length mirror, I was pleased. I definitely looked like money. My jewelry was the added touch; my 24kt gold chain with diamonds was a no brainer. Breakin' me from my daze, my phone rang. It was Cheri.

"Yo, wassup? You still comin' here to be with Denie?"

"Yes, I'm on the plane now. My flight takes off from Florida in less than fifteen minutes. Can you pick me up from the airport? I didn't want to bother Denie or Cornell."

"I'm about to go to L.A. I can have a driver come get you."

"Why are you leaving? Your sister needs you, Juan."

"She has you and Cornell. I'll be back in a couple of days. I gotta get that money, babe."

"For us? You gonna make me move up there for good and take care of you."

"Yeah. You just might have to do that," I said sincerely. "I'll see you when I get back."

Once I got packed, I put my Louis Vuitton duffel bag near the front door, and shot Denie a text message. I didn't want to face her. She was upstairs in BJ's room, where she'd been spendin' most of her time, lookin' at pictures of my nephew. She'd lost so much weight. It pained me to see her like that.

Rushin' out the house, I jumped in my Audi R8 and jetted. As I pulled up to the Chick-fil-a, Julio got out of the white Mercedes truck and walked over to my car.

"Wassup, my nigga, man this young bitch cook me no food and I'm hungry as shit. Let me run in and get me a sandwich real quick, since the drive-thru wrapped around the building."

"Aight. I gotta make a stop before we head to the airport, so be quick," I said, rememberin' that I had to run by my storage unit. As I waited for Julio, I saw Cornell's Bentley pull beside me. Denie was in the passenger seat. Cornell rolled the window down.

"She had to have a chicken biscuit, and insisted she ride with me," he said, shakin' his head, gettin' out of the car, and makin' his way inside.

Guilt consumed me, as soon as I saw Denie. "You a'ight, babe?"

"I'm good. I just needed to get some air," Denie said through the window.

"Look, I didn't wanna tell you, but I gotta go to L.A. for a couple of days. I'll be back by the weekend."

"Do you really have to go?" she asked with hurt, pain and sorrow filled eyes.

"I don't want to. But there's somethin' I must take care of. Cheri's on her way though. You talked to Dad, right?"

"He called a little while ago apologizing for not being here when I woke up. He said he would be over later."

I jumped out the car real quick, and leaned in to give Denie a kiss on the cheek. "Here comes my man, so I'm about to be out. You need me to wait until Cornell comes back out, before I leave?"

"Naw, I'm…what the fuck? Raymond?" Denie's brows twisted into knots. "What are you doing with my brother?"

"Denie, this my man Julio. His name isn't Raymond," I said laughin'.

"That bitch ass nigga's name is Raymond. Tell my brother who you really are, motherfucker!"

"You know my sister, man?"

"Naw, I ain't never seen her a day in my life. Sweetheart, my name is Julio," he stated smoothly.

"Yeah, okay," she said once she saw Cornell comin' back to the car. "You go 'head before I tell the both of them what you did to me."

With little time left, I followed Julio to the car. He seemed more than confidant that Denie had the wrong guy. The entire way to the storage place, I thought back to Denie's facial expression when she spotted Julio. She seemed certain that she knew Julio. I believed her. Julio was up to no good.

Somethin' told me there was more to the story. I just needed to figure out why he lied and what the hell he did to my sister. For now, I had to stay focused on my money. As I pulled into the parkin' lot of the storage facility, I thought it was best that I let Julio stay in the car. Zippin' up my coat I walked around the bend to my unit. Once I opened the door, and before I could get all the way in, I was devastated. It was empty. All my shit was gone. First my stash spot, now my storage unit. Before walkin' any further into the unit, I called my father immediately.

"Hello," he answered half sleep.

"Dad, somebody fuckin' robbed me again."

"What? You shittin' me."

"Man, it's empty in this motherfucka!"

"Man, that's messed up, damn. I mean Juan, no bullshit, I know you been takin' a lot of losses lately, but you gonna have to make a way to still pay me."

"Pay you for what?"

"For the money Big Tony tried to say was counterfeit."

"Nigga, I just got robbed and you talkin' bout your money. Man Fuck!" I yelled, ignorin' my father. I wasn't payin' him shit. Man, right about now, I had bigger issues.

"Calm down, Juan."

"Man, I can't keep calm. Man, just go back to sleep, I'll deal with this shit on my own," I said pissed off.

"Man, I'm good, I ain't hardly sleep. Shit, I've been up worried sick about Honey, all night. She never came home. Now, I'm hopin' those Baltimore dudes you was beefin' with hadn't been followin' her. They've been comin' up to her spot lately, sendin' death threats. Maybe they followed her to the spot."

"Why you just now tellin' me?" I fired loudly, as I turned on the light and walked into the unit hopin'there was somethin' left.

"She ain't want me to say nothin'. I was gonna lay back and pop them ni…"

"Oh my God! Dad, Honey is right here."

"Put her on the phone."

"I can't, she's dead."

"She's what?"

"She's dead."

"What the fuck is your bitch doin' in my damn storage unit?" I demanded and I wanted answers.

"That's what the hell I'd like to know. Shit, was the joint broken into?"

"No, she had to have had a key. The door was locked."

"Man damn, Juan you sure she's dead? Man, she can't be gone."

"Fuck this bitch. You told me she was cool. Your ride or die."

"Yo', Juan for real tho', I don't even want to think like this man," my father said, with pain in his voice.

"What?"

"Maybe Honey was behind this shit. The only thing I could think of is, maybe who ever she was workin' with, killed her. Fuck!"

"Dad, now that I think about it, the night I killed Grady, there was a car that scurried out of the driveway. There was a girl drivin'. You don't think Honey was workin' wit' Grady, do you?"

"Naw, Juan. She ain't know Grady like that. Man, I loved that girl. How could she do this? Son, I gotta go. I gotta… just be safe," he said as if he was about to hang up.

"Hold up, man. I need you to come take care of Honey. I need to shoot out to L.A."

After listenin' to my father black out, I let him know he needed to handle the shit with Honey; her body and everything. After thinkin' hard, my father said he had an idea of who Honey was workin' wit'. He assured me, they'd be dead before I got back from L.A.

It was imperative that I found out who that bitch was workin' wit. I needed to play my father close for now to get to the bottom of this, but losin' almost a million dollars worth of shit, wasn't okay wit' me. Somebody was gonna die.

Closin' the storage unit, I hurried back to my car as if nothin' happened. I couldn't miss my flight. Especially with me losin' over a million dollars worth of shit. It was more important than ever, that I got to L.A. It was hard to not let Julio in on what was goin' on and what I'd just discovered. I decided to keep everything to myself.

After a long flight, I couldn't get much rest, as my brain rattled constantly. Visions of Honey's body kept flashin' through my mind. My head was heavy, and I had a lot of time to think. Another thing that stayed in the forefront of my mind was, Denie's face when she saw Julio. I knew what needed to be done. I'd texted Denie a few times before the flight took off. She assured me she knew Julio, and that there was much more to tell me about him, as soon I got back. I was now lookin' at his ass totally side-eyed. At this point, I didn't know who to trust.

Straight off the flight, our driver met us and took us directly to meet Big Tony. Once we arrived at Maestro's, I felt a pit of fire burnin' in my stomach. Every time I had to meet with Big Tony, for some reason I got nervous energy. That nigga made my stomach bubble, like I had to shit or somthin'.

The hostess showed us to the room where the meetin' was being held. When we walked in, Julio was greeted by Big Tony, and his son, with open arms. Once they got to me, I got a handshake. Instantly, I felt uneasy.

"So, let's cut to the chase. Juan, do you have my money?" Big Tony said before I could even get in my seat good.

"Yes, it's right here," I said, handin' it to one of his peons that ran to my side to fetch it for him.

"You got the money pen, Tony?"

"Yes, father," Tony said, as he started to strike the pen through the money instantly before he could get the bag open good.

"The money is all there and it's good," Tony assured his dad.

"Big Tony, I'm a man about my word. I don't fuck around when it comes to business. I don't know how that fake shit got…"

"Look Juan, no more excuses. No more fuck ups. Plain and simple, you got one more chance, or Denie and Mecca are dead. That simple," Big Tony said with straight face, starin' me straight in the eye. How did he know about Mecca? That motherfuckin' Julio was a snake. He had to have told him all my business. Now it was clear that he couldn't be trusted.

"Well, now, that I've made myself clear. Let's eat," Big Tony said, as everyone laughed and started to mingle.

After discussin' our game plan to get the work from Cali to DC, we were good to go. Julio let Big Tony know he secured a driver, which was the first I heard of that. I knew that him and Big Tony's son was cool and all, but I put him in this arena. I was pissed and just wanted to go back to my hotel and chill. It was getting late. After the meeting was adjourned, we all headed to the lobby. Tony and Julio was talkin' about goin' to some rooftop club in Downtown L.A. I was tired and jet-lagged and really didn't feel up to it.

"Come on man, Juan, don't be a pussy. Let's turn up. You can rest later," Julio belted. He usually was laid back and more reserved, but being around Tony, he was someone else.

"Aight. I'll have one drink. Then I'm goin' to the hotel."

"Bet."

After a short twenty minutes, Tony, Julio, and me arrived to the club. It was just after midnight and the club was turned up already. The white dé cor was sexy and chickswere everywhere. It was a mixed crowd for sure. Wiz, Juicy J and Miley Cyrus' song, J's On My Feet, blasted through the club, as women hung from the ceilin' on some Cirque de Solei shit. We made our way to our private section, on the rooftop, where there were bitches half dressed, fuckin' and suckin' each other. It was one big orgy.

As soon as I sat down, the waitress handed me a glass of champagne. Not really trustin' my surroundings, I put the glass down, and poured me a shot of Ciroc. Wasn't nobody slippin' me shit. I had to pour my own spirits.

"Let's make a toast, before we get up in some pussy fellas. Here's to real niggas and loyalty. Now, let's get this money," Julio yelled boastfully just before his cousin Blow walked in, dressed in all black, lookin' a lil' shabby.

"Wassup Juan," he said, givin' me dap.

"Wassup Blow. I ain't know you was comin' thru."

"Man, once I got the call saying they had the private rooftop reserved, I knew what that meant; bitches and coke. So, I told Julio I was on my way," Blow laughed, before makin' his way over to Julio and Tony. It was like they were havin' their own private meeting.

"Wassup wit' all this one off talkin' shit, my niggas?" I asked Julio and Tony. I couldn't take it any more.

"What you mean?"

"I thought we was all partyin' together. Shit, first y'all say y'all cousins, then y'all grew up togeth…"

"Man Juan, chill. All that shit you sayin' ain't important. We all boss niggas gettin' money and bitches. Tonight that's all that matters. Now let's turn up," Julio said tryin' to get off subject.

Any other time I would be down wit' gettin' some pussy, but I felt uneasy. It felt like deja'vu. Bitches doin' lines, and suckin' each other off, wasn't the combination I was tryna fuck wit. I hated seein' chicks do drugs. It took me to a dark place.

Just when I was gettin' up to get another shot, I spotted a familiar face, and I just couldn't remember where I knew her from. She was over in the corner laid back on the couch, gettin' her pussy sucked. I tried to wreck my brain, until I heard someone call her name, Mandy. That's it. It was her. The bitch that set me up for my Uncle Renzo. A part of me wanted to go over there and strangle her with my bare hands, but I was on Cali turf. I had to be careful.

Pourin' me another shot, I was ready to go. Once I put the bottle back in the bucket of ice, I looked up and Big Tony appeared out of nowhere. He was with some big black dude. My heart sunk. He was like Freddy Kruger, just poppin' up when you least expected, puttin' the fear of God in you.

"Wassup pops? You came to get turned up with us," Tony said all hyped as he snorted a line of coke.

"No, son. I just need to talk to Juan for a second. Then, I'll let you young guys get back to having your fun. Juan, come with me."

What the hell did he need to talk to me about? I thought to myself.

"Juan let's take a walk."

"Cool," I said, gettin' up as we made our way over to the other side of the balcony, closer to where the orgy was goin' on. As we made our way through, there was so much moanin' and snortin' going on. It was time for me to go as soon as I could get away.

"So Juan, do you have any idea why I wanted to talk to you?" he asked as he leaned against the rail.

"No, wassup?"

"Take a look out into the world Juan. Cali is a beautiful city, isn't it?"

"It's cool."

"Take it in, son. It's a lot of money out there," he said, takin' a deep breath, as he gazed out into the city. As I overlooked the view of downtown, from the rooftop, suddenly the big black dude grabbed me forcefully, and lifted me up off my feet. Instantly I lost my breath, as I was abruptly turned upside down, danglin' from the balcony.

"Oh my God! What are you doin'? I gave you your money. What the fuck is this about?" I asked, as the overweight Black guy, barely held on while danglin' my body over the rail.

"Juan, you have a choice to live or die tonight. What will it be? The choice is yours."

Chapter 22
Denie

What the hell was Raymond doing with Juan? Why did he dismiss me as if he'd never met me? Maybe he didn't want my brother to know what he did to me, I thought to myself, as I sat in the windowsill of my boutique. As I watched the snowfall, all sorts of thoughts bounced around in my head.

Cornell thought I needed to get out of the house and that the boutique would help. But how I felt, there was no way I could make it through the day. My heart felt so broken. With Christmas approaching in less than two weeks, I couldn't imagine Christmas without my son. We had already not celebrated Thanksgiving. There was nothing to be thankful for, without BJ. I had been so stressed out, with no desire to care for myself. The wet and go look was easiest for me, at this point, with my hair. I had lost ten pounds, so my Victoria Secret Pink size small sweat suit, hung off my body, as if I was wearing Cornell's clothes. I just wasn't myself. It didn't help that I couldn't keep anything down. There was nothing that ginger ale, or crackers could do for me. Just as I felt my stomach about to erupt again, I ran to the bathroom and exploded in the hallway, not making it quite to the toilet. I called Cornell immediately.

"Hey babe, you okay?"

"Cornell, please come get me. I feel horrible. I just threw up all over the back hallway. I don't even have the energy to clean it up."

"Where are your employees?"

"Kiara should be here soon. Chaz left a little while ago."

"Cool, I'm on my way, babe. I love you, alright."

"I love you, too."

After trying to clean myself up as much as I could, I made my way back to my office, and laid down in my oversized white gold trimmed chaise lounge. As soon as I tried to take a quick nap, my phone rang.

"Hello, Cheri."

"Hey boo. How are you feeling?"

"Like 24 karat shit. I just threw up everywhere."

"Girl, it's your nerves. Denie, you gotta stop worrying. BJ is gonna be back home soon."

"It's hard, Cheri. It's so hard. I miss BJ, I feel so sick," I said as I burst into tears. I missed my son and as hard as I tried, I couldn't be strong. With the way I felt, I prayed it was only my nerves, like Cheri said. Since I was having a hard time keeping my pills down, my meds were the furthest from my mind. Deep down inside, I was praying that I wasn't having HIV complications.

"Awe Denie, don't cry. We just have to keep praying, that's all. Stay strong Denie."

"Where's Juan? Did he get back yet?"

"I talked to him last night. He should be home soon."

"Okay. Has my dad been by?"

"Earlier. He is a trip, girl. Flirting and shit."

"That's my dad."

"Well, do you need me to come up there and help you with anything?"

"No, Cornell is on his way to come get me. Actually, I just heard someone come in the door. I'll see you in a little bit."

"Okay sweetheart, see you soon."

I was really happy that Cheri was back in town. I needed her now, more than ever. She had really proven her friendship, during this difficult time and I felt bad for always treating her so badly.

"Cornell, I'm back here," I called out.

As I got some of my paper work together and put it in my Never Full Louis Vuitton bag, I looked up and saw that Kiara, my employee, was standing in the doorway of my office. She just stood there mean-mugging me for what felt like hours.

"What the hell is wrong with you, Kiara? Look, I need you to clean up the hallway. I'm sick and I…"

"You pathetic bitch! Clean up your own shit. Matter of fact, hang up your own over priced clothes, stack your own fucking shoes on the shelves, because I quit!"

"Okay, well I don't have time for your attitude today. I don't feel well, so if you quit, then get the fuck out. Bitch, my son is missing. Do you think I have time to babysit some stupid ass college student?"

"Yeah, I was stupid, for trusting you."

"Get the fuck out," I yelled with what energy I had left, as I held my head in the palms of my hands.

"Bitch, not before I finish. How could you?"

Before she could say another word, Cornell walked in.

"Um, babe, you alright? What's going on? I could hear yelling all the way outside," Cornell said being protective, making his way past Kiara, who was damn near blocking the door.

"Denie, how would you feel if I fucked Cornell? Would you like that?"

"Now Kiara, you're fucking crossing the line now. What the hell is your problem? You about to get your ass beat," I said as I stood up, and then fell back down in the chair. Between the sweating and hot flashes, it seemed as if I would eventually faint.

"Kiara, you are out of order the way you are disrespecting my woman. I think it's best that you leave. She's not feeling well and this is not okay. Denie, do you need some water?" Cornell asked me. "Sweat is pouring from your face."

I didn't answer him because Kiara folded her arms and gave me the look of death.

"Well Denie, does Cornell know that you were fucking Raymond behind my back? The same guy you hooked me up with. You were pimping me out like I was your whore. By the way, where's my fucking money you charged him?"

"What the hell are you talking about?" I asked Kiara, before realizing letting her continue to talk, was a bad idea.

"Denie, Raymond told me everything! Cut the fake shit."

"Who is Raymond, Denie?" Cornell's face tightened followed by a frown.

"This dude I know from Philly. We're just friends. Why would I sleep with him, Kiara, if I hooked y'all up?" I lied, glancing at Cornell, who looked like he was starting to believe her shit.

"Well, he said he didn't want to see me anymore because of you. He said he loved you! Raymond told me the only reason he was messing with me, was to have a reason to talk to you. Now you weren't answering his calls and…"

"Kiara, get the fuck out my boutique, before I beat your ass! I've let you talk way too much."

"Denie, fuck you and this stupid ass boutique. I'll make it my business that nobody at Howard University will shop here. Believe that," she said as she stormed out of my office.

"Babe, make sure that bitch don't steal anything. That girl is delusional."

As Cornell followed her out, I could hear Kiara carrying on. "Cornell, you so pussy whipped! You just don't know what type of chick you got…"

By the time Cornell made it back to my office, I started to feel even worse.

"Babe, what's this all about, with this Raymond dude?"

"I know you are not falling for all that bullshit Kiara was selling. She just put on a performance, and you fell for it. She was mad because I approached her about stealing from me. Chaz let me in on what she had been up to this afternoon before he left."

"You've got to be kidding. All you do for these Howard students, that's messed up."

"I know, right? I did hook her up with Raymond, but he told me the real reason why he wasn't fucking with her like that. One of his watches turned up missing…"

Cornell's sudden outburst made me instantly stop talking.

"Oh shit, babe! Your lips are turning dark, like they're blue or something."

"What do you mean, Cornell?" His worried expression made me panic even more. "I think I need to go to the hospital," I said as I held my face with hesitation.

All of a sudden the room went dark.

Everything was a blur. As I faded in and out, all I could see was Cornell's face. No sounds.

Nothing.

Eventually darkness.

By the time I woke up, I was in the ER at Washington Hospital Center, hooked up to an I.V. Cornell was right by my side, when I opened my eyes.

"Cornell, what's going on?" I asked wanting answers. There was an oxygen tube in my nose that felt way too uncomfortable.

"You okay, babe?"

"What happened?"

"You fainted. The doctors have been running tests and they should be in shortly. I had to call an ambulance. You scared me, girl," he said before he kissed me on my forehead.

"Oh my goodness, my king saved me. I do feel a little better. Just weak."

While Cornell rubbed my hair, I slipped back into a quick slumber, before the doctor came back in the room.

"Hi Denie, I'm Dr. Patel, how are you feeling?"

"I'm just tired."

"I was briefed a little about what's going on with you, by the triage nurse."

"What are you talking about?" I said nervously.

"About your son and all. I'm sorry to hear about everything you and your family are going through. It explains part of why you are not feeling well."

"How did you guys find out about my son?"

"Babe, I'm sorry. I didn't know much about your medical history, so I told the nurse that you had been stressed. I guess you have been here before, so she was able to pull up your info."

"You have to make sure that you are still taking care of yourself. Your body is very dehydrated, so the I.V. should definitely help with that. There is something else going on…" she said before I stopped her. There was no way Cornell was finding out my deepest secret. Not like this.

"I'm already feeling better," I said, interrupting the doctor, afraid of what she might've said.

"Well, I have some news for you. Is it okay to talk in front of your…"

"I'm her fiancé, Cornell. We're getting married soon, so we don't have any secrets, right Denie?"

"Right," I said hesitantly.

"Congratulations, how long have you guys been engaged?" she asked as my heart continued to sink into my stomach.

"Just a month," I said as I started to feel sick all over again.

"Well, hopefully, my news doesn't change anything with your engagement. Denie, you're pregnant."

"I'm what?"

"Holy shit. I'm so fucking happy," Cornell yelled, overjoyed.

"Well Denie, with your condition, we need to discuss if…"

"Hold on. Wait a minute," I said, stopping the doctor once I saw there was a news flash that came across the television. Grabbing the remote for the TV, I turned it up. There was no way the doctor was going to out me, to Cornell. I didn't expect the newsflash to be the news I had been waiting for. Grabbing my pillow tight, I sat back and listened closely once the image of my son appeared on the screen.

There has been an ongoing search for Juan Sanchez, son of the Washington Wizards, Cornell Willis, and nine year old, Carmen Sanchez. The children were kidnapped from their home, almost three weeks ago, by their nanny Maria Santiago. We regret to inform you, that two bodies were found, in Philadelphia, PA. in connection with this case. Police are waiting for the family to identify the bodies, before we announce…"

"Cornell, it can't be. Where's my phone, Cornell? My son can't be dead! Where's my phone?" I yelled hysterically as I cried and cried. There was no way I could live without my baby boy.

Chapter 23
Juan

I was really startin' to really think I had nine lives. As I watched my life flash before my eyes, while Big Tony's man dangled me over the railin' of that rooftop, it was clear. I could never fuck over Big Tony, or I wouldn't be that lucky next time.

Finally back in the DMV, I thought to myself as I navigated through the airport. As soon as Big Tony let me down, I knew I needed to get the hell home. There was no way that I was stayin' at the club with them niggas. Deep down, I felt like they knew that shit was about to go down, and said nothin'. So, I bounced on their asses. I stayed at the Westin at LAX, and caught the first flight back to BWI. Julio had been callin' me all night, but I sent him a text to say I wasn't feelin' good, and that I went back to the hotel. He was keepin' something from me, and I was determined to get to the bottom of what was goin' on with him, but first thing was first, I needed to let my father know I was safe. I briefed him last night on everything that happened.

"Hello."

"Man, I just touched down, what's good?"

"Glad to know you're safe. Your next meetin' with them niggas, I'm there. They ain't gonna keep shittin' on the Sanchez name like that."

"Man, I'm just glad to be the fuck out of L.A."

"You still comin' to scoop me up later?"

"Yeah. I need to run past my house and then I'll be back out to get you. Any word on who smoked Honey?"

"Naw man, I got my ears to the street though. Oh, and call your sister. She needs to hear from you ASAP. Some shit happened. I'd rather let her tell you."

"Is it BJ?"

"Just call her, man."

"Bet, I'm on it. See you later on."

Once I got back in the car, I pulled out of the parking garage of the airport and called Denie, to see what was so important. Maybe she had some info on Julio.

"Hello."

"Denie, what's up?"

"Juan, we're on our way back from Philly. Carmen and Maria are dead. Some sick fuck, shot them both in the back of the head," she said with her voice starting to crack. "Who would kill a little girl," she said as she burst into tears. This was no time to discuss the Julio situation. This was way more important.

"What the fuck? Where's BJ?" I asked anxiously.

"I don't know. Who is doing this, Juan? It can't be about money, because they haven't tried to contact me for a ransom."

"Why didn't Cheri tell me any of this last night when I talked to her?"

"She didn't know. She stayed at the house just in case any clues to where BJ was surfaced. I've been calling you all fucking morning! I've been in the hospital due to dehydration. There is so much going on. Juan, I don't know if I'm coming or going."

"I've been on the plane. Is Cornell with you?"

"Yes. He came with me. Who the hell has my son, Juan?"

"Denie, calm down. The good thing is that he hasn't been found dead," I said, tryin' to reassure her.

"You don't know that."

"If he were dead, then he would've been there with Carmen and Maria. Damn, I'm sorry about Carmen, Denie."

"I need my son. That's all I care about right now."

"Well, how far away are you guys? We left like a half hour ago, so we should be home in less than two hours."

"Okay, you going wit' Cornell or will I see you at the house?"

"I'm not going to my other house until I know my son is okay."

"Alright. I'll see you soon."

"Okay."

Throwin' on my Louis Vuitton aviator sunglasses, I hid the pain in my eyes. I missed my nephew and there was no amount of money, or gift I could buy to erase my sister's pain. Turnin' on my XM radio, I turned up the volume. This Christmas, by Chris Brown was on. I couldn't believe it was almost Christmas, and my nephew wasn't home yet. My family was all I had, and I needed this Christmas to be a happy time. To share the holidays with my father was a blessin'. Now, all we needed was my nephew to come home.

As I entered the gate to my house my mind wandered. There were so many movin' parts in my life, and I just didn't know how to handle it all. After parkin' my car and goin' in the house, I was greeted by Cheri as soon as I walked in. My mouth dropped as soon as we made eye contact.

"Hey," she said as she dropped her head and looked toward the floor.

"Hold your head up," I said, grabbin' her chin. "What the fuck happened to your face?"

"Allen happened."

"What do you mean? He blacked your eye. Man, I'll fuck that nigga up."

"Yes. Juan, I had to leave. He has been actin' so crazy lately and when I am here with you guys it's such a great escape," she started to cry, as she laid her head on my chest. Takin' her by the hand, we left the foyer and sat on the couch in the living room.

"This ain't the first time, is it?"

"No, it's been more frequent for the past year. Enough about Allen, Juan, I need to talk to you about somethin' very important."

"What is it?"

Before Cheri could say another word, in came runnin', a beautiful brown-skinned little girl. She was dressed in a little pink girlie nightgown with long coal black ponytails. She reminded me so much of Denie when she was a little girl. More importantly, she looked like the spittin' image of me.

"Mommy, Mommy, can you read me a story?" she asked, hoppin' up on the couch.

"Ariel, when you enter a room what are you supposed to say?" Cheri asked, as she wiped her eyes to hide her tears from her daughter.

"Hi, how are you?" she asked lookin' at me with eyes that were too familiar, as she reached out to shake my hand. There was no doubt, that those eyes were mine.

"Hello, pretty girl. You must be Ariel."

"My daddy calls me pretty girl. What's your name?" she giggled, with a shy look.

"I'm um…"

"Ariel, remember I was telling you about there was a really nice man I want you to meet that is going to love you just like Allen? This is him and his name is Juan. He's your daddy, Ariel. This is Juan, your real father," Cheri interrupted, with no hesitation. Her face softened as if a heavy bolder had been lifted from her shoulders.

"I have two daddies?" Ariel looked puzzled, as she cocked her head to the side.

"Yes baby, right now you have two, but eventually Juan will be your only daddy, so I wanted you guys to meet and get to know each other," Cheri said, as she rubbed Ariel's head.

I was in a state of shock. When I first laid eyes on Ariel, I knew she was mine, but to hear it was a different story.

"Why mommy? Do you want me to have a new daddy because Daddy keeps being mean to you?"

"Baby, no, that's not why. I love you and Juan is going to love you just as much as I do. We are going to live here now, right Juan?"

"Um, yes, Ariel. I'm going to love you, and buy you pretty dresses, and dolls. I'll give you whatever you need, okay? You don't have to go anywhere. This is your new house, okay?"

"All those toys upstairs are going to be mine?" she asked with her eyes open wide.

"Even better, tomorrow we'll go to the toy store and get all new toys. For now, I need to talk to your mommy, so go ahead upstairs and play for a little while, now come give me a hug."

Jumpin' off the couch, Ariel ran in my arms, and gave me a big hug. She held me so tight as if there was an instant connection. I didn't want to let her go. She was what I needed right now.

"See you later Mommy and Juan."

"Call me Daddy."

"Okay Daddy," she said with a big smile exposin' that infamous left deep Sanchez dimple, as she ran off. Instantly, Cheri and I made eye contact.

"Why the fuck would you tell her that shit? She's a child! And why didn't you tell me?"

"Juan, I can't lie to my baby any longer, and I'm sorry. I didn't know how. It wasn't like you wanted to be with me anyway. All you care about is Mecca. I wanted a family for my child, I wanted…"

"No, you wanted money! Now that you know I'm not a broke nigga, it's okay for my daughter to know me. What type of mother are you?"

"A bad one. A really bad one, for depriving both you and my daughter of a relationship," she said as tears streamed down her face.

"I should black your other fuckin' eye. How could you do this to me, Cheri? Fuck! That's why that nigga beat your ass, ain't it? He knows, don't he?"

"Yes."

"That's why you're here, bitch? That's why," I said as I got off the couch and paced the floor. I didn't want to be anywhere near Cheri.

"That's not the only reason. I'm here because of my godson."

"You're so full of shit! How you know she's mine?"

"When I was in town last time, Allen took Ariel and did a paternity test. His mother always questioned Ariel being Allen's child, but he didn't care, because he loved her so much. With Allen being light-skinned and me being white, his mom didn't understand how Ariel was brown. She took a swab test on my baby and I didn't know. Allen, then took a blood test while I was away."

"But, you always knew. Now, that nigga money fucked up, now it's okay for me to know my daughter?"

"No, Juan, I didn't always know. When I was pregnant, I thought I was carrying Allen's child. After she was a few months old, was when I realized she wasn't Allen's. Her features started to change. Then I thought back to you, Juan. It must've happened that time…"

"When you made love to me for the last time, before you ran off with that nigga? I remember it clear as day."

"Juan, I love you. I always have. If you don't want me here I'll leave, but Ariel needs you. Shit, I need you," she said as she cried.

The truth was, I needed her, too. I needed them both, but I was afraid to go back down that road with Cheri. Mecca was gone, and I felt alone. With not knowin' who I could trust, I was afraid of Cheri hurtin' me again, even if her tears did seem real.

"Look, I just need some time to think about all this. I know Denie needs you right now, so you don't have to leave, but just give me my space. I'm really pissed off at you, man. I gotta go. Just let Ariel, I mean, my daughter, know I had to make a run, and I'll be back before she goes to bed."

"Okay. Juan, again, I am so sorry. I hope you find a way in your heart to forgive me, so we can move forward."

Not givin' Cheri any eye contact, I walked away and ran down to my wing of the house. I changed my clothes really quick, grabbed my gun, and left my house to go pick up my father. We planned to have dinner and discuss business. Even though that nigga was foul, I needed him right now.

The entire time I drove to B-More to pick up my dad, Peaches was callin' my phone again wit' her bullshit. With everything that was goin' on, I definitely didn't feel like hearin' her annoyin' ass voice. Pushin' ignore once again, I took the exit to my father's house.

As I took a left I approached my father's buildin'. I got a text from Julio that fucked my head up.

Big Issue. Shipment no go. Hit me on my throw away.

I shot my dad a text and let him know I was in front of his building and called Julio immediately.

"Wassup my nigga?"

"Them folks got hemmed up in El Paso. Big Tony will be in town tomorrow. He's pissed."

As my father got in the car, I put my finger up to let him know not to say anything, as I put Julio on speaker.

"Fuck you tellin' me that for? That was your man, you let him drive," I said in defense mode. They wasn't puttin' that shit on me.

"Well, Big Tony looks at us as we all together. So, we all up the damn creek."

"That's some bullshit! When y'all pressed me out about that counterfeit, it was all me. You ain't take no heat for that shit."

"Like hell I didn't!"

"Nigga, you ain't hang from a balcony and have your life flash before you! I did. Man, I'm tired of this shit. I'll see y'all tomorrow."

"I'll text you where he want you to come."

"Me to come, or us?"

"You know what I meant."

"A'ight."

As soon as I hung up on his ass, my father went ham.

"Man, who the fuck this nigga Big Tony think he is? How the fuck he gonna get mad cuz somebody got caught up with some shit? He betta hope that nigga that got hemmed up in El Paso don't snitch. That's what he needs to be worried about. Man, I can't wait to see dem niggas tomorrow. I'm goin' with you son."

"No doubt, man I need you," I said with sincerity. As much as I knew my father was a fucked up nigga, times like this was what he was good for.

"Shit, you my son. If these niggas knowin' I'm alive will make them respect you, then I'm all in."

"Man, I just don't get why he wanna talk to me, like it's my fault."

"I tell you one thing. We gotta go in that motherfucker strapped," my father said, gettin' excited. He started to shake and that made me a little nervous. I don't think I could ever get used to him doin' that.

"You a'ight?"

"I'm good. I'm just tired of motherfuckers takin' you for a joke."

"Karma ain't no joke. When you fuck people over, it comes back. It's all good," I said sendin' a subliminal message straight at my father.

"That's your problem. It ain't all good. You got too much of your mother in you. Fuck that. You betta make examples out dem niggas so they know betta."

"You bein' disrespectful now. Anyway I…" before I could say another word my phone rang. It was that whore Peaches again.

I sighed heavily. "And this bitch keep on callin' my phone. I'm sick and tired of this shit. Man, I can't catch a break."

"Answer the fuckin' phone, Juan. Don't duck that whore. Put her in her place."

"What?" I answered thru my Bluetooth.

"Why the fuck you ain't been answering the phone?"

"Bitch, stop callin' my phone! What do you want?"

"I need some money from your ass. I ain't been able to dance because of you. It's your fault I got shot, and I got bills, bitch."

"Ain't your lil' punk ass son Lil' Man on the block. Betta yet, ask your fake gangsta rapper, baby daddy. You not my girl."

"It's all your fault. Do you even understand the distress you've caused my son? He has turned to the streets because of you. He can't deal with the fact that he shot me. You made him do that. Nigga, you owe me!"

"Fuck you, and that lil' nigga. I don't owe you shit. Matter fact, the only thing I owe you, is a bullet in yo' head."

"You threatening me?"

"Look whore, what's it gonna take to make your ass disappear?"

"That almighty dolla. Lot's of 'em. Look, I got real woman bills, and kids to feed. That's the least you can do. All this shit is your fault, all your fault. Man up, nigga."

"Bitch, I ain't givin' you shit. Fuck you and your fake wanna-be a gangster-ass son."

"Okay. Guess I'll send my goons after that bitch Mecca then. They'll love to take that red pussy. I know where that bitch live at, too."

"I don't give a fuck. She's not my bitch no more. Fuck both of y'all," I said, lyin'. I did care about Mecca, but I couldn't let her know that.

"Call my bluff, nigga."

"Hey look, this is Juan's partner. How much is it gonna cost to make you, and your baby father to go away? We got real live shit goin' on over here, and I am sick of you ringin' his phone the way you do," my father said, no longer able to contain himself.

"See, your man talking my language. Well it's gonna cost you. I need twenty g's."

"A'ight. How about I give you thirty? Where you want us to meet you at?"

"Around the corner from my house at the liquor store."

"Cool, we'll be there in like fifteen minutes, and don't play no games callin' your baby father and shit," I said, goin' in blind to my father's bullshit once again.

"I don't fuck with him. I'll be there in a minute," she said overly excited as if she'd hit the lottery.

As soon as I hung up the phone I looked at my father in disbelief.

"Man, why you tell that bitch you was gonna give her some money? I only got ten stacks on me."

"Son, do you trust me?"

"Yea," I lied.

"Well then sit back and watch me make this bitch disappear."

"Speakin' of trust, or should I say distrust, man I got something to tell you," I said as I made a right on Charles Street.

"Wassup son," he said with a worried look on his face.

"I got a daughter."

"What? By who," he said wit' a sigh of relief and a slight laugh.

"You know Denie's friend, Cheri?"

"The white bitch, with the black body."

"Yea, well I just found out her three-year old daughter is mine."

As I filled my father in on everything that had happened in my life, in the past two hours, we were gettin' closer to the store. After makin' a couple of turns we were at the liquor store in less than ten minutes. Just like clockwork, that money hungry trick was pullin' up.

"Pull around back, you gonna have to work for this paper," my father said as he motioned Peaches to the back of the store, where it was secluded. Her thirsty ass followed right behind us.

She hopped out the car limpin', with some gold Uggs on, skin-tight leather leggings, and a brown and cream fur bomber coat. Of course she was wearing bright pink lipstick, with red hair down to her ass.

"What's your name, OG?" she asked, tryin' to flirt with my father, thinkin' he was the highest bidder.

"That is my name, OG. Now, before I give you this money, you gotta suck my dick."

"Juan, you aight with me sucking OG dick? You don't care?"

"Why would I give a fuck? You want this money don't you?"

"You hate me that much? Why can't I suck yours?"

"Well suck his first."

Waistin' no time, my father opened the passenger car door and whipped his pole out. Just like the whore that Peaches was, she went to work in 20-degree weather, suckin', and slurpin', as if her life depended on it.

"Damn, Juan, this bitch got some good head, shit," he said as he groaned.

"That's right daddy, come for me," Peaches said as she gave my father the only thing I loved about her ass, that good head.

"I don't want to come like this, I want to fuck you from the back."

"Now, you tripping. It's cold as shit," she said, lickin' what was left of her pink lipstick.

"You want this money?"

"You gonna let your man just slut me out like that, Juan?"

"Peaches, you ain't nothin' but a thot. You slutted yourself out. Bitch, I'll give you all the money in my pocket, plus his, if you let me watch him fuck you. Show me a little longer, how much you were the biggest mistake I ever made."

"Ditto," she said, pullin' her pants down and got on her knees. The gravel on the ground seemed to not bother her. It was scary how desperate she was. All I could think about was fuckin her bare. What was I thinking?

"Look slut, don't lean in my car. Man, fuck her that way. I don't want to look at that trick."

"Awwwe. Juan's jealous," she said laughin', as she arched her back.

As my father shot me a devious look, I knew what time it was.

"Prop your butt up a little more. I can't hit it like that."

"Like this?" she purred, ready for action.

"Yea, just like that."

Once he reached in his coat, it was on. As I watched him put the silencer on his 9mm, I knew it was curtains for Peaches. As she kept her ass in the air, she complained about it bein' so cold.

"Bye-bye, bitch," I heard my father say.

Just like that my father shot Peaches in the back of the head. My worries with her had ended.

Peaches was dead.

Chapter 24
Rich

My work was still cut out for me with Juan. He still needed that grit, that fire in him, that killer instinct. He was born with it cuz he had my blood. I just had to make it come alive. Juan must've cared about that slut Peaches a lil' bit, cuz he looked a little hurt when I popped her. I hoped he ain't think I was payin' that trick.

Killin' Peaches sent her dumb-ass baby daddy the clear message, 'don't fuck with a Sanchez'. Shit, she reminded me of Trixie so much; One of those anything goes type of chicks. Head was off the chain, just like Trixie. I kind of missed that whore, but not like I missed Honey. It seemed so quiet around the house with Honey bein' gone. It made my mind drift off to that question that haunted me over and over again. Who would've wanted her dead? What did she know, and what was she into, that would make someone want to kill her? My gut was tellin' me it was more than someone wantin' to rob Juan's stash. Shit, all this time, I was the one doin' that. So who else was tryin' to get at my son?

"Babe, you ok?"

"Naw. I miss Honey," I said gettin' out of bed with Nicole. As much as I talked shit about how I fucked with Nicole, there was a void in my life, without Honey. As I walked in the bathroom to turn on the shower, Nicole followed closely behind.

"Rich, don't shut me out. She was my friend and I miss her, too."

"I'm not shuttin' you out. I just feel like I need a little space, that's all. I hate a thirsty bitch."

"You want me to leave?"

"Naw, nothin' like that. I just don't need you all up on me and shit, like that lovey dovey shit."

"You just want me on you when you want to fuck, huh?"

"Exactly," I fired. "I didn't know if I was explainin' it right."

"You're such an asshole and you don't even know it," Nicole said, walkin' away before I got in the shower. I had to get myself together to go to this meeting with Juan. I couldn't wait to sink my teeth into that Big Tony nigga. He was gonna learn today, not to fuck with a Sanchez. As I let the water run over my face, there was so much on my mind. Someone was targetin' my kids, and I wasn't connected enough to the streets to help them. Even though I was rippin' my son off, I had his back when it came to an outsider. Shit, I had a legacy to protect.

As I got out of the shower, I dried my body and looked at all my wounds in the mirror. I was one scarred up nigga, and every scar had a hell of a story. My life was a movie. Shit, I was like Jason. A nigga try to kill me and I just kept comin' back.

Gettin' in guerilla mode, I put on a black hoodie, some black Levi's, and my black Tims. I was ready for war. But, just before I put my phone in my pocket, it rung.

"Hello."

"You ready?"

"Son, I was born ready. I can't wait to see what these niggas talkin' bout. I'll meet you there. We need to have two vehicles though. You never know. I don't want them to see me comin'. More than likely, them type of bastards got eyes everywhere."

"Damn, Dad. How do you know?"

"It's not much I don't know. Where we meetin' them niggas at?"

"In some Pool Hall spot by Live Casino at Arundel Mills."

"What time?"

"Seven."

"Cool, I got a couple of hours to stake the spot out."

"Bet."

"Son, we all we got," I told him sincerely. "Make sure you come suited up with those two glock 18c's I gave you. Now let's go handle our biz."

"No doubt. I'm ready. I got my bulletproof vest on like you said but this joint feel light as shit. Man, I think you're overreacting but I guess it's better to be safe than sorry," he laughed.

"Nigga, stop bein' so trustin' of these niggas. They don't fuck with you. You gotta be prepared at all times. You never know."

"I guess you're right. See you soon."

"Cool."

After gettin' in a quick sex session, I got in my blacked out Suburban and headed over to the pool hall spot, where Juan and Julio planned to meet with Big Tony. As I took my exit off of BW Parkway, I followed my navigation to the address Juan texted me. As I circled around the buildin' I realized, that I had been to this spot before.

Back in the day, Uncle Renzo would have meetings here when he was in town. The pool hall was owned by a well-known mobster who was well connected from New York. He always made the Pool Hall available for head haunchos in the business. This was a definite plus for me, because I knew the buildin' like the back of my hand. Quickly, I shot Juan a text.

Gotta turn my phone off but I'm in position. I got u son.

Fully armed, I had my Mac 10 at my waist, while my holster held my two 40 Glocks with extended clips. You never knew what to expect at meetings like this, and I had to be prepared. While one of the workers took out the trash, I slipped in through the back, unnoticed. The pool hall was just as I remembered it, dark and smoky. It seemed as though there were a few upgrades, but still a hole in a wall. There was hardly anyone in the spot, which wasn't a good sign. Clearly somethin' was about to go down. Employees would clear out, right before the meetings took place. That wasn't good for Juan and Julio.

Just like old times, I slipped into the backroom where everything usually went down, and posted up. The room had a long black table with chairs. Pool tables surrounded the room and a bar was in the front right by the door. The DJ booth in the backroom was tented which was perfect. I set up shop there so I had a clear view of the entire room. This hidin' spot was usually unknown, and was where me, and Carlos used to hide before we took out people for my Uncle. It felt like old times, minus my right hand man.

After sittin' for what felt like eons, my nerves started to fuck with me a little as my head rocked from side to side. I had to stay focused. No one could know I was in the room. Suddenly, I heard voices get closer as I got in position.

Two guys came in armed and posted up in opposite corners of the room. Next, a familiar voice rang through the room. I knew that voice from somewhere. I just couldn't place it. Once I got a good look at the voice, I realized that the voice must've been Big Tony, because this oversized, bald, Italian man strutted into the room. Once he sat down at the head of the table, some mixed lookin' tall guy walked in as I listened closely.

"Hey Dad, Julio and Juan just pulled up."

"Okay son, thanks for the heads up," Big Tony said as he took another pull from his cigar, and pulled his gun from his waist. After placin' the gun on the table, he let out a huge sigh. From where I was standin', I had a clear shot of both him, and his two armed guys, just in case. Finally, Julio and some fat Hispanic dude, lookin' like Big Pun, walked in. Juan followed in, soon after.

"Hello, gentleman," Big Tony roared.

"Wassup, Big Tony," they all said in unison, as they all took a seat around the long table. That shit pissed me off, to watch another man have that much power over my son.

"So, Juan, tell me, do you know what happened with our driver, being arrested, transporting my shit?"

"Well, I don't know the driver. He was a relative of Julio's. Maybe your questions should be directed to him," Juan said with nervous energy.

"Wrong answer. Just when I thought you had changed, you're still a snitch," the heavy-set guy chimed in.

"Blow, what the fuck you mean, I'm still a snitch?"

"Juan, you were responsible for taking down one of the most lucrative drug businesses ever, and you thought we didn't know?" Big Tony laughed.

I didn't like where this conversation was goin' but I knew for sure how it was gonna end. Julio and Juan started to go back and forth passin' blame. The more Julio talked down to my son, I could see the anger build up inside of him. It was definitely personal. Julio was clearly out to get Juan. Julio's shit talkin' made me want to start bustin' off straight through the glass. He went on and on about how Juan was a snitch, and betrayed his own family, which had nothing to do with the driver bein' arrested.

"All I gotta say is, it's not my fault the dude got locked up," Juan said, standin' his ground.

"Enough, that's enough," Big Tony said, as his son walked back into the room, and took the empty seat next to his father.

"What's goin' on? What did I miss?" the son said.

"Well Tony, your friends just had a big blow out, on whose fault it is that my shipment is now with the FBI. There's no telling what the driver is now telling the…you know what Juan, I'm gonna cut straight to the chase. I can no longer go any further with this charade."

"What charade?" Juan asked confused.

"Julio, you want to tell him, or should I?"

"Juan, the truth is, there was never really a driver. We punked yo' hot ass. And now we see you still a snitchin' bitch."

"Yo, what type of shit y'all niggas on? Julio, I trusted your bitch ass. If it wasn't for me you wouldn't be eatin'. I made you, bitch."

"Nigga, I already started takin' over your territory. That was my plan. Juan, you made it easy for me to connect with all your folks, it was like takin' candy from a baby," he laughed.

"Man nigga, who the fuck you think you are? You fuckin' betrayed me!" Juan yelled.

"Betray you? Nigga, you want to really know who I am? I'm Armondo's son, your Uncle Lorenzo's right hand man. Blow here, is Pablo's son, the man that took your ass," Julio laughed, then got serious. "You're the reason my father is dead. You thought you were gonna get away wit' being hot? You thought you were gonna just be out here in these streets makin' money and not have to pay for the shit you've done? Killin' you off wouldv'e been too easy. I wanted to shame your ass in these streets."

Waitin' for the right time to strike I paid attention closely to the armed guys and Big Tony's gun on the table.

"Fuck you, Julio," Juan yelled, jumpin' up out his chair, ready to fight, right before Julio pulled out his 9mm from his waist, and aimed straight at my son.

"Naw, Juan, I ain't into boys. Fuck me, huh? Like Pablo, fucked you? Or, how I fucked your sister? Man, when I found out Denie was pimpin' bitches I made my move. She was so hell bent on gettin' from under your thumb, that she was actually pimpin'."

"Nigga, you lyin'. My sister ain't no fuckin' pimp, you don't even know my damn sister…hold up…"

"Yeah, see Denie knew me as Raymond. I would hit her off with a couple of stacks to fuck her little pussy friends. The last time the bitch came to get her money, I took that pussy. She was fakin' like she ain't want it, but I pinned her down and got in that shit. That pussy was so good, nice and wet."

"Nice and wet, huh. You fucked my sister raw, nigga?"

"Yea, I pulled out after I came in her a little bit. Shit, I might give her a baby like that nigga Javier did. The bitch makes pretty ass kids. How's the search for nephew comin'?" he laughed as the others followed in with laughter.

Pullin' out my gun from my waist, I knew I was gonna kill everything in the room. My nerves had gotten the best of me, and I couldn't control it. Focus or die, focus or die, I said to myself, as I gained control.

"Nigga, you fucked with my nephew? You killed Marisol's daughter?"

"Juan, let's be real, why would he kill Carlos' daughter?" Blow chimed in with broken English.

"Where's my fuckin' nephew?"

"Look, I ain't got your nephew, but I hope I put a new nephew up in your sister."

"I guess Denie failed to mention to you that she was HIV positive. So whatever happens to me, don't matter. It seems as though, my sister killed you, or should I say, you committed suicide."

"Man nigga, whatever. Why the fuck you defendin' that slut anyway. She the reason your uncle knew you was hot. Renzo always said Denie had more heart than you."

"What the fuck you mean?"

"Juan, no one told you. Denie sent Renzo the text that let him know you were hot. Damn, I'm a bearer of a lot of bad news today."

The hurt in my son's eyes pained me. Waitin' for the right moment, I laid low and let them continue to go back and forth as everyone around the table did. Julio continued to point the gun at my son as they argued back and forth. The next bit of news made me no longer be able to contain myself.

"Yeah, and once I'm done wit' you, I'mma kill your sister, the same way I killed that bitch that own the club out B-more."

"You killed Honey, and robbed my stash spot."

"Oh that was your spot. Shit, the bitch told me she needed someone to help her move some shit for her father that was in the game that was sick. So, I went back up there and hollered at the bitch a few times, to see if she would be any use to me. I finally killed her."

"Julio, nigga, you really fucked up," Juan said as soon as he saw me appear from out of the DJ booth.

"You heard my son, you really fucked up," I said pointin' one gun at Big Tony and the other at Blow. I had that raw, rugged tone in my voice ready to let them know I wasn't playin'. "Now, nigga get that fuckin' gun off my son before I kill them both. Big Tony, have your men put down the fuckin' guns," I roared.

"Put your fuckin' guns down," Big Tony demanded quicker than I expected. The two armed men in the corner of the room did as they were told, but that fuckin' Julio still wouldn't listen. He was determined to keep Juan as his trump card.

"You heard the man, put your gun down, Julio," I said. I kept my gun aimed right at Pablo's head, but had a clear shot at Big Tony.

"Holy shit. Mr. Rich Sanchez, is in the mo-ther-fu-ckin' buil-din'... it's really about to pop off," Julio said jokingly, right before he pulled another gun from his waist and fired it straight at Big Tony, shootin' him right in the head. The niggas aim skills was sick.

A loud, piercing scream sounded throughout the room. It was Tony hollering like a bitch for his father.

"What the fuck have you done, Julio? You killed my father!" Tony yelled, jumpin' up right before Julio shot him dead, twice in the chest. His dumb ass ain't realize that takin' those two out, increased the odds of me and Juan gettin' out of here that much easier.

"Put your gun down, Julio, or your cousin dies," I yelled.

"I'm callin' the shots here Rich. I just got rid of two people I been waitin' to smoke. Now you next. Damn, I used to look up to you. And always wanted to be like you. I know your son is a big disappointment though. Who would've thought he'd be the one to fuck up all the money we had comin' in."

"It's over now, Julio you got one more chance to make shit right, before…"

"Nigga, I thought you were dead," Julio yelled right before Blow's big ass ducked down throwin' his weight, pushin' me back as Julio started bustin' off at me tryin' to take me out. As I fell to the ground my first shots I fired were straight at the guards, takin' them both out at the same damn time. Once I looked up, makin' my way off the ground, Juan and Julio were tusslin', while Blow made his way to a gun and started firin' at me. As bullets flew past my ears, just missin' my head, suddenly Blow fell to the ground. While I was fightin' for my life, my son now held the cards. While Julio was tryin' to get at me, Juan took the right opportunity to get the upper hand on Julio.

"Nigga, get on your knees," Juan yelled at Julio.

"Juan, I ain't doin' shit. You a bitch. I don't take orders from faggots, Nig…"

Before Julio could say another word, Juan shot him in his foot.

"Aiggh," Julio screamed before fallin' to the ground.

"I'm tired of motherfuckas takin' me for a joke!" Juan taunted. He was fired up, angry and beating at his chest as he spoke. "I'm nobody's punk! I'm nobody's faggot! Every time I let somebody in, they cross me. I'm a good nigga. I don't deserve this shit! Nigga, I trusted you."

"That's your problem, you shouldn't trust nobody, nigga. That's your biggest downfall, and everybody can see straight thru your dumb ass. Juan, everybody is not like you."

"Shut up!"

"Son, kill that nigga," I said as I walked closer to them.

"Rich, let me ask you somethin', did you rob me? Were you workin' with Honey?" he asked, shakin' with anger and eyeing me down like an enemy in the streets.

I had never seen my son that enraged.

"Juan, are you kiddin' me? Don't ask me no shit like that! Bust that nigga, Julio. Stay focused on what we're here to do."

"Rich! I need to know! Yes or no!"

"Juan, handle your business, kill that nigga!"

"Did you? Did you rob me?" he asked me again, with the gun aimed at Julio's head while blood poured from his foot.

"Fuck no! Do what you gotta do? Pop that nigga," I ordered.

"I just needed to know that you got my back. Everybody around me, fucks over me. I'm tired. Now Julio, you gotta go."

"Juan, as soon as I get to hell, I'm gonna fuck the shit out your whore ass mother…"

Those were Julio's last words, because before he could say another word, Juan emptied his clip all through Julio's body. That grit I wanted to see in my son came through.

All he heard tonight officially made him damaged goods. The glimmer of hope in his eyes he always had was gone. For a minute, I thought he was gonna kill me. Now, he had joined the dark side. Now, he was just like me.

Chapter 25
Denie

"Cornell Willis should just take a leave of absence. His fiancé's son being missing is really taking a toll on him on the court. All this week he hasn't played well, but his game tonight, stunk up the arena like never before..."

No longer being able to listen to the commentators talk about Cornell's bad games, I turned off the television in the family room. I was glad Cornell would be over soon. I was sure since his game was over because I was starting to feel a bit lonely. Cheri and Ariel had gone out to do some Christmas shopping and Juan was out and about as usual. Cornell was what I needed right now, and I couldn't wait for him to come home and just hold me. I felt so bad for him, and for the past couple of days, he had been very distant. I prayed that he wasn't giving up on us. He was starting to make me feel like I was more of a burden. From my situation with BJ, and me being sick, I felt like he was getting tired. Feeling overwhelmed with bad thoughts, I made my way to the kitchen. My health hadn't been the best lately, and my nausea called for a warm ginger ale.

Turning on the Bose system in the kitchen for a few tunes before I went upstairs to lie down, the soulful voice of Regina Belle, rang through the speakers. But I would if I could, if I could I would try to shield your innocence from time. Instantly, I thought of Lisa, and how she would bolt the lyrics to this song to Juan, dancing around the kitchen when we were young. Now, I understood. That mother-son bond they had. It made me yearn for my son that much more. As I burst into tears, I sat on the barstool, at the marble island in heavy thought. Just as I popped open my Seagram's ginger ale and tried to take a swig, it was smacked out of my hand and went flying across the kitchen.

"You fuckin' connivin' snake! You just like your father," Juan said as he open hand smacked me straight across my face. I didn't even hear him come in.

"Juan, stop it, what are you talking about?" I asked, covering my face as he placed his hands around my neck and started to choke me. The sad thing was, I had betrayed Juan so much that I didn't know what he was talking about. As his grasp got tighter around my neck, I coughed and felt like I was about to lose consciousness.

"Bitch, I should kill you right now," he said before throwing me to the floor and pulling his gun from his waist.

"Juan, what are you doing?" I was scared to death wondering what had him so outraged.

"It was all your fault. Mecca warned me about you, shit, my mother warned me about you, but I was so blind. You supposed to be my sister, man. How could you? I protected you when no one else would. I fuckin' took care of BJ like he was my own. You fuckin' turn against me and told Renzo I was hot! All the shit that's wrong in my life is your fault. You did this to me. You're no different from Rich," he said as he got closer to me as if he was making sure he got a good aim. I had never seen my brother in this state. He was so mad he was shaking.

"Juan, please don't kill me. BJ needs me," I said laid out on the floor with no energy.

"Stop usin' my nephew to keep me off your ass. Bitch, he don't need a mother like you. Man Denie, you so fucked up, you just need to go."

"Juan, I'm sorry. I was a fucked up person, but I've changed. Yes, I was always jealous of you growing up. Lisa loved you, while Daddy was out in the streets. I always felt alone. After Lisa took me to that warehouse and tortured me, I had no more good in my bones. She started this, Juan. She did this to me. She made me hate you. I'm sorry for hating you, Juan. You have been so good to me and my son and I need you."

"Shiesty ass bitch! I always had your back. When the fuck is somebody gonna have my back? I was raped by a nigga and shot in the head, all because of you. I couldn't see my mother during her last days, and it's all your fault."

"I'm sorry," I said as I wiped blood from my nose onto the sleeve of my sweatshirt.

"Denie, I almost died tonight, all because of a vendetta Renzo's people had against me, for some shit you started."

"Give me another chance, Juan. Let me prove to you I have changed," I said as I looked up at Juan with tears in my eyes. He looked so cold. I didn't know who the man standing before me was. I knew he had the heart to kill. He had killed before. The question that raced through my mind was, could he kill me?

"Look at you. All fuckin' sick, karma's a motherfucka, ain't it. All the shit you did to me and you sittin' there with HIV. Maybe I should let your miserable ass live. You gonna die anyway."

"That hurt, Juan, that really hurt."

"Do you think I give a fuck? Bitch you're dead to me. Don't ever breathe my name again! I hope you rot in hell, you stupid bitch. Your life ain't ever gonna be good. You just like Rich. Man Denie, I hate you," he said as he lowered his gun and left the kitchen. His words cut like a blade.

Barely being able to pick myself off the floor, I got up and made it upstairs to my room. No matter how much I always had a vendetta against Juan, my subconscious mind knew, he would always be there for me no matter what. For the past couple of years I had been out to hurt him, and now that I had succeeded, it wasn't fulfilling. It made me feel more weighed down. As I sat at the vanity in my room, I looked at my face, and wondered who the girl was in front of me. My nose bloody, above my right eye was swollen, and my heart wounded. All I could do was cry. As I cried with my hands over my face, I could feel someone's presence in my room. As I turned around, I saw Cornell standing in the doorway.

"Cornell, I'm so glad you're here. Look what Juan did to me," I said, as I got up and ran to him, collapsing into his arms.

"Denie, get off me," he replied, pushing me away. I rushed over to sit on the edge of my bed, heartbroken.

"What, what do you mean, Cornell? I'm sorry about the game tonight. You can't let the critics get to you. If I'm causing you to be off your game, then…"

"Then what, Denie? What are you going to do, to make it all better? Give me some Reyataz? Would that make me feel better, huh Denie?" he asked, as his eyes narrowed in on me like he was my father.

"Cornell…"

"Cornell, what? You thought I wasn't gonna find out? You let me love you and believe that you were the woman I was gonna spend the rest of my life with…"

"Why are you listening to what people are saying? I do love you, Cornell."

"Denie, do you see this?" he asked, waving a piece of paper in my face, "Read this shit, and you explain to me what I am supposed to believe. This shit was in my locker the other night," as I grabbed the papers from his hand I read the first one.

Dear Cornell,

Do you really know your fiancé? It's so painful to watch you throw your life away with this little girl. Your life is over now that you have decided to be with someone with so many demons. It's just a matter of time that you will fall down that small tunnel that she is spiraling down. You are a good person and deserve so much better. I just hope it's not too late.

Too sum it up, your fiancé is HIV+… And if you are sleeping with her unprotected so are you.

No need to know who this is from,

Just thank me later!

As my heart stopped, I turned to the next page. It was a copy of one of my HIV test results.

"With all that I am going through right now, who would lie like this? Who would do this to me? To us?" I asked, with the little energy I had left. I felt so hopeless and alone.

"You're such a liar, Denie. Admit it! You are HIV positive. Just say it! Tell me the truth."

"I don't know what you are talking about," I lied.

"Who are you? What type of low-life chick are you?"

"It's a lie!"

"I swabbed your mouth, last night when you were sleep. You know how easy it is to know if somebody is HIV+ or not? It was that easy, to get a sample of your saliva to verify that everything in this letter is true," he said with so much pain in his face. As a tear escaped his eye, I broke down.

"Okay, Cornell. It's true. I'm HIV+. That doesn't mean you are, too."

"Denie, I am. You've ruined my life, and I never want to see you again."

"You can't leave me, Cornell. I need you. My son needs you. You said you would be the father he doesn't have."

"That would mean I would have to look at the woman that ruined my life everyday and I don't have anything left in me for you. I'm done," he said, turning to walk out.

"Cornell, wait. You said you would love me forever. Flaws and all, you promised me. Javier, my son's father let his friend rape me and they had their way with me and infected me with this deadly disease. I never thought I would trust another man. I never thought that anyone would accept me for who I was. But you did. You accepted me and my son."

"And Denie, It's sad you fucked it up. You fuck up everything good in your life. I don't have kids, there's no hope for my future, and I have you to thank for that. You're the devil, so evil. It's over, don't ever contact me again," he said as he walked out of my room with his head down. He looked powerless, but his words were so powerful. Now that Juan and Cornell hated me, I felt more alone than ever.

As I laid across my bed and cried like a baby, my phone rang from a blocked number.

"Hello," I answered barely able to control my sobs.

"Denie, it's me Kim, Lamar's girlfriend. I know where your son is."

Chapter 26
Juan

These niggas is haters, and I made myself so easy to love…The story of my life, I thought to myself while I turned up my Jay-Z and Kanye West song. It was me against the world, and no matter how people thought in the past they could take me for a joke, it was a new day. Fuck everybody. I had taken a 'L' because of Julio tryin' to fuck wit' my money. With him gone, now I knew it was time to take back what's mine; what I worked hard to build. It was grind time.

As I drove down Georgia Avenue, in my blacked out Escalade, I had to go around Morton St. to holler at my man Sadique. Over the past week, I had lost three of my main soldiers, all killed the same way, a bullet to the back of the head. Sadique was a bit nervous, and had some info he needed to tell me, so we thought it was best to meet in person. I definitely wasn't tryin' to talk over the phone. As I drove around the circle, Sadique was comin' out of building 611, where his grandmother still lived. I could spot his tall ass anywhere, especially wit' his long beard, lookin' like he was from Philly. As he walked to the car, his facial expression said alot, he had bad news.

"Wassup my nigga, get in."

"Man, the streets is fucked up man," Sadique said, as he got in my car.

"Don't I know it? What you had to talk to me about?"

"Man, brace yourself. You know Tay got killed last night, right after I gave him his shit. Somebody robbed him and popped him."

"Stop playin', my nigga."

"Naw, man. Somebody is fuckin' wit us. Over the past two weeks, everytime I hit somebody off with their dope, they get robbed and popped. I think somebody tryin' to send a message, Juan. Shit, Tay had like 300 g's worth of shit. I lost 650 g's in three weeks."

"Fuck! I know one nigga that was tryna fuck my money up, the nigga Julio I was fuckin' with. But shit, that nigga gone now, so who the fuck would be tryin' to get at me now?"

"Juan, this shit gotta get handled. Fuck that, I ain't out here riskin' my freedom for a motherfucka to just keep takin' from me like I'm some type of sucka. Whoever the fuck these niggas are, need to die," Sadique said, as he took a pull from his jay. I didn't allow anybody to smoke weed or cigarettes in my car, but times like this made me want to take a pull myself.

"Man, has anybody been tryna cut into you or anybody workin' for you?"

"Look my nigga, I ain't tryin' to start no shit, but your sister Denie, man she was tryin' to get me to fuck wit' some dude she had a connect thru. She was tryin' to have me not fuck wit' you. I don't know who the dude was, but she kept pressin' me to stop fuckin' wit' you."

"You know what, man that's it. That bitch, man, I'll handle her. What about our dudes on 14th St? Who they be fuckin' with?"

"Some nigga named Rich. Shit, he tried to come around here wit some niggas I know and get me to fuck wit' him, but I'm loyal man, I fuck wit' you homie."

"Man Sadique, thanks. I gotta go. I think I know what's up. Trust me, I'm puttin' a stop to this shit tonight." My blood boiled.

"You need me to roll wit' you, my nigga?"

"Naw. This some shit I got to handle. I'mma hit you in the mornin'."

"Aight, bet."

Sadique couldn't get out of my car fast enough. As I screeched up the block I called that nigga Rich immediately.

"Wassup son?"

"Hey, Rich, where you at?"

"Oh, now I'm Rich? Fuck you mad about now?" he replied with a chuckle.

"Where you at man?"

"I'm uptown hollerin' at one of my ole' timers around 1-4."

"Meet me at Society up on Georgia Avenue. I gotta holler at you about some real shit," I replied. I was so angry I could barely see straight.

"The spot on the Silver Spring side?"

"Yea."

"Cool, I'll be up there in like 20-30 minutes."

I just hung the fuckin' phone up. I was pissed. All of a sudden the phone rang. As I picked up my throwaway phone, and saw that it was blank, I checked my iPhone and saw it was blank as well. Finally, it dawned on me. It was Grady's phone that was ringin'. I had been meanin' to go through his phone, but I had so much goin' on. As I fumbled through my Versace leather coat, I found the phone. It was a missed call from a 202 number. I waited to see if they were gonna leave a message, and like clockwork, they did.

As I parked in front of Society, I decided to listen to Grady's messages.

Message #1

Grady, it's your mama. Call me son. We worried sick about you.

Message #2

Yo, Grady this Rich. Man, let me know if Honey left yet wit dat bread. Nigga, I need that. Good lookin' out. Remember, keep this shit between me, you, and Honey. No pillow talk. Aight my nigga, hit me back.

Message #3

Man, nigga hit me back. Honey made it home, but I ain't heard from you. Let me know if you got the shit out the house. Call me.

Message #4

Grady, it's Denie. I've called your phone a million times! I've left you four messages. Nigga, I need my money. No more favors!

"Fuck!" I yelled as I threw Grady's phone on the floor of my truck, crackin' the screen. My heart sunk. How could my family hate me this much? My soul was hurt to the core. I couldn't take anymore of this shit. Rich was gonna pay. Tonight. I needed a drink.

Gettin' out of my car a few minutes later, I went into Society, and hit the bar. A thin brown skinned girl greeted me.

"You look like you need a drink, what can I get you?"

"Give me a triple shot of Patron."

After drownin' two triple shots, Rich finally walked in.

"What's good, son," he asked as he pat my back before takin' the seat beside me.

"Don't fuckin' touch me, nigga. You are worse than I thought you were, you are really fucked up man," I said, starin' him straight in the eyes.

"Juan, come on now. What's the deal? Aye babe, give me whatever he's drinkin' cuz this nigga's nice and…"

Smack, smack, smack.

Before he could say another word, I don't know if it was the drinks, or the rage inside of me, but I opened hand smacked the shit out of Rich repeatedly, and I just couldn't stop. There was no security guard that could hold me back from whoopin' his ass.

"Nigga, what the fuck is your problem," Rich said, holdin' the side of his face, as one of the security guards helped him up off the floor. He started to shake a little bit, but I didn't give a fuck, I hated that nigga. If he dropped dead to the ground, I didn't give a fuck.

"Get these guys out of here now," the owner yelled to security, as we both ignored him.

"You was workin' wit' that nigga Grady the whole time! You fuckin' snake!"

"Juan, fuck you! If it wasn't for me your ass would be six feet deep," he yelled back as security threw us out of the restaurant, and we were still at it.

"How could you do this shit to me? Your own fuckin' son, man. Why are you and Denie so fucked up? What did I ever do to you," I asked Rich as I leaned against my truck.

"You never loved me. Not like you loved her. You always looked down on me. I wanted to teach you how to be a man. Nigga, I took your shit, cuz your ass was so fuckin' sloppy. You have been gettin' money yea, but the way you carry yourself in these streets is a disgrace to my family name," he said, gettin' closer to me. As soon as he got close to my face, I couldn't help myself, I pulled my gun from my waist, and shoved it straight in his stomach.

"You right. I loved my mother, and I hated you. I don't know what possessed me to think that we could have a father son relationship. That we could take over these streets together. But, no. You had to try and take what was mine. Los trusted you and you killed him. Why would I think, I would be different."

"Go ahead Mister Messy, kill me in front of all these people out here. Go right ahead. How'd you find out about Grady anyway, son?"

"Nigga, I'm messy? You and your dumb ass daughter are the messiest of us all. You should've never let me get hold of Grady's phone. Who would've thought? Grady's phone held all I needed to prove that you were a piece of shit."

"Nigga, I don't give a fuck what you do to me now. Do what you do. Nigga, that's right, you tough. I'm callin' your bluff. Shoot me," he taunted as I felt his spit hit my cheek as he talked.

"Naw, killin' you would be too easy. Now, I know what I gotta do. Nigga, you are dead to me, this time forever."

"Son, you know how many times I've heard that shit."

"Once I'm done wit' you, nigga you gonna wished you pulled out, the night I was created. Trust me. You gonna get exactly what's comin' to you."

"Was that a threat? Juan, wait. You can't survive in these streets without me. I'm Rich Sanchez," he yelled as I backed up, and pulled off. I so badly wanted to run over him, but the way I'd get him back would destroy his life forever. He was gonna pay, and it had to happen tonight.

Chapter 27
Denie

"Charlie, thank you for helping me. You are all I have right now."

"We should be at the Gaylord Hotel in less than five minutes. Remember what I told you. I already have my men set up in the room next door to where Kim Bucksley's suite is."

"I owe you big time. I will forever be indebted to you. Anything you need…"

"Anything? I'm gonna remind you that you said that tomorrow, for now let's stay focused and get your son back."

As we drove down I-295 I thought of happy times with BJ. His smile. His deep dimples. His curly hair, but most of all, his silly laugh. I missed my son and couldn't wait to hold him in my arms. Breaking me from my daze, Charlie's phone rang. As he answered the familiar voice that rang through the speaker, made my skin crawl.

"What's up, Mecca?"

"Charlie, are we still meeting with the…"

"Um, let me talk to you about this later. I have Denie with me, and we are in the middle of something important," he said, cutting her off, as if she was about to expose something.

"You know what Charlie, some things never change. All this talk about how much you love me and how Juan wasn't good for me. The entire time, it was fake. What's this about? The baby. Is that why…"

"Mecca, calm down, it's not what you think!"

"Well, whatever else you need for your case, get it from that bitch," she yelled before hanging up the phone.

"Really though? Mecca is working with you to take down my brother?"

"Denie, you can't breathe a word of this to anyone, especially Juan. If he found out this could ruin my career. I can't risk…"

"Charlie, you and Mecca's little secret should make you work that much harder to help me get my son back, safely," I said, interrupting him as he dropped me off at the corner. We had a plan that had to work, and it was important he stayed focused.

As I walked up the hill to the hotel, I was glad that I was bundled up. My Chanel snow boots kept me nice and warm against the snow below my feet. Visions of BJ and me entered my mind as I walked through the glass doors to the hotel with butterflies in my stomach.

"You good?" Charlie asked through the wire.

"Holy shit, you scared me. I'm so not used to this. I'm good. I just walked through the door."

"Okay, do you remember what the code word is?"

"Yes Charlie, for the umpteenth time, it's cash."

"Cool, see you in a sec."

"Charlie, thanks."

"We're gonna get your son back, don't worry."

Who would've ever thought I would be working with the police? Me fucking with Charlie was just to piss Mecca off, but now it's all paying off. Right about now, I would do anything to get BJ back. If only I could have my son back for Christmas, that's all I wanted, I thought to myself as I admired the well lit Christmas trees in the lobby. As I got on the elevator I watched families laugh and look happy. Something I never experienced in life. I never had a happy family, but I was determined to make things different for my son. Without Juan or Cornell, BJ was all I had.

Getting off on the 10th floor, I made my way to the end of the hallway where Kim said they were, Room 1024. Taking a deep breath, I knocked on the door. As my stomach did somersaults, I listened and couldn't hear anything. As I knocked repeatedly, still no answer. My heart sunk. What kind of games was Kim playing? She seemed so sincere on the phone. I promised her no police, I wondered if someone saw me get out of Charlie's car. As I started to get upset my eyes swelled. Just as I turned away from the door, it opened.

"Can I help you with something?"

"Oh my God, what are you doing here?"

"The question is, what are you doing here, Denie?"

"Lamar, where's my son?" I demanded as I pushed my way through the door.

"Wow, you're so upset, Denie, calm down before you have a heart attack, or something. Then again, you probably don't give a fuck. You gonna die anyway, right?"

"Where is he, Lamar? Where's my son? BeeeJaaaayyy," I yelled constantly through the penthouse. Suddenly, Lamar grabbed me by my hair, and pulled me close.

"Shut the fuck up! With all you've done to me, you're gonna pay."

"Get off of me! Where's my son?"

"He's right here," Kim came down the steps with a gun to my son's head, from the room upstairs in the penthouse suite. He had duct tape across his eyes, and his arms were taped together, too. BJ was wearing a dingy t-shirt and sweatpants. Kim was already skinny, but she looked even thinner. Her fake butt implants in her sweatpants looked like it was gonna make her body tilt over.

"Kim, what are you doing? You said Lamar was gonna be at the game. Why is my baby taped up like this? Why didn't you warn me that he was gonna be here?"

"Mommy, is that you? Kim, you said my mommy was with the angels with Carmen and Maria."

"Yes, baby it's me, come to mommy," I said reaching out for my son, before Kim cocked her gun back.

"She a ride or die, ain't she," Lamar laughed.

"Bitch, you wouldn't dare," I said as I walked a little closer to the bottom of the stairs where they stood.

"Try me. If I put a bullet in your little irritating little sister and nanny, what makes you think I won't pop his head off?"

"Fuck them, let my son go, Kim. Lamar, who have you turned into? I thought you loved me and my son," I asked trying to guilt him.

"Denie, you gave me HIV! You fucked not only my life up, but my daughter, and Kim. We are ticking time bombs because of you. You're gonna have to pay."

"Mommy, I'm scared," BJ said as he started to pee on himself. I was afraid for Charlie to come in because I was afraid they would kill my son, and I thought I could possibly talk Lamar into letting him go.

"Denie, you are the reason my baby is HIV positive and you expect me to help you. You're dumber than I thought."

"Lamar, you better get your bitch in line." I reached out for BJ.

"Kim, this is my son, he's innocent in all this, kill me. Just let him go."

"I think I want to be the one to make you suffer, Denie. Kim, give me the gun," as Kim handed over the gun, Lamar grabbed BJ as he screamed and kicked. As he sat on the couch, he held BJ close.

"No, please Lamar, what do you want CASH? Is that what you want, some CASH?" I asked, alerting Charlie that I needed him. Suddenly, the door burst open and police rushed the penthouse suite.

"Put the gun down, Lamar. Put it down, it's over," Charlie yelled, as the other four officers pointed their guns at Lamar, while a female officer grabbed Kim. As Lamar put the gun to BJ's head, my heart sunk to my ankles.

"Lamar, please don't kill my baby, please. He's all I have."

"Denie, I loved you and me making a mistake caused you to give me HIV. All I did for you…"

"I was a mistake, Lamar!" Kim yelled.

"I just need time to think," Lamar replied. He was starting to scare me as he sat on the couch with BJ across his lap with the gun to his head. As he rocked back and forth, Charlie tried to reason with him, but his words fell on deaf ears.

"I'mma die. She gave me HIV."

"Is he serious, Denie?" Charlie asked, as if our last encounter together flashed through his mind. There was no way I was gonna admit to that, when Charlie was all I had to save my son.

"He's lying."

"No, he's not!" Kim screamed.

"Shut up! My life is over. All the years I worked hard to become this big time football player to take care of my family, and now it's over. It's all over," Lamar said as tears poured from his eyes. As he raised the gun off of BJ, I knew what he was about to do.

"Come here BJ, come here sweetheart," I said in a calm tone.

"Mommy, I can't see," he cried.

"I'm sorry, BJ…"

Pow!

"Oh, my God!"

Chapter 28
Juan

"Okay, so what you're reporting, Supa Ken is, Washington Wizards star Cornell Willis' fiancé, Denie Sanchez is the reason why the Philadelphia Eagles running back, Lamar Bucksley committed suicide yesterday. This is some messy stuff here."

"Yea Russ, it's reported that Lamar was distraught and ended his own life because Denie infected not only him with HIV, but his wife and daughter also has it, because of Denie," Supa Ken reported.

"Damn, so that means Cornell Willis got it, too. That makes me wanna whoop her ass. That fine piece of caramel got HIV, too now, all because of her. Damn, that's messed up," Shaqwana added.

"So, Lamar Bucksley was the one that kidnapped her son, all this time. All that Cornell Willis did to help that chick. Real talk, that girl needs to move away somewhere in Idaho somewhere, because so many people are going to want to get at her. Well, the good thing is, her son was rescued," Alfredas added.

Karma's a bitch, I laughed as I listened to the Russ Parr Morning Show. I was happy that my nephew was okay, but Denie was gettin' all she deserved. As I drove from makin' my last run, I was tired as shit and ready to go lay it down. I hadn't been asleep in over twenty-four hours. After I left that fuckin' Rich, I was even more motivated to go get back what's mine. Startin' up Philly, makin' my way back down to Maryland, I got a lot accomplished. It was important that I took care of the streets. There was no room for distractions, before I delivered the best Christmas present Rich could ever ask for. I knew exactly how to be his Grinch. He really had fucked up crossin' me and I knew what I had to do. I was prepared, no more messy shit.

As I entered the gate I noticed a slender frame walkin' up to the door, what the hell was she doin' here? As I parked the car and got out, wearin' the mink coat I bought her ass, Mecca started to walk towards me.

"Juan, we need to talk," she said with sincerity.

"About what? I don't have the energy for any drama today. I want to enjoy my Christmas Eve," I said, tryin' to brush her off.

"It's important," she said, followin' me to the door, "Can I come in?" Not sayin' a word, I opened the door, and she followed. Stoppin' in the foyer I turned around to Mecca to hear her out.

"Wassup?"

"Look, Juan, I know things have been horrible between us, but I really fucked up. I just want to say now, that I am so sorry, I had been so angry at you for hurting me, and…" Before she could finish, Ariel ran in, still dressed in her pajamas.

"Daddy, Daddy, BJ is home. He's in the playroom. Come see him, Daddy!"

"Hey baby girl, I'll be in there in a little bit. Go ahead and finish playin', okay."

"Okay, Daddy," she said, smilin', exposin' her dimples, as she ran off.

"Daddy? Juan, who the fuck was that?"

"My daughter. Look, I just found out about her, and it was before I was…"

"You get to have a daughter, while I mourn mine? You know what, I don't know what I was thinking coming over here to try and help you. Juan, I wish I never met you," she said as she started out the door.

"Mecca, you walk around here as if you are Mother Teresa. Every five minutes your ass is sneakin' out the house as soon as I leave, jumpin' when I walk in the room while you on the phone, man who knows, that baby probably wasn't even mines," I was tired of bein' taken advantage of and was no longer takin' shit from anybody, not even Mecca.

"Juan, you're right. That baby wasn't yours. It was Charlie's. Nigga, I loved you and you constantly drug my heart through fire. Charlie caught me while I was vulnerable, yes, when I saw the text message you sent Shana. Yea, y'all didn't think I didn't know that y'all fucked! The night I was with Charlie, or should I say Detective Charles Santiago, I was weak with hurt."

"You were fuckin' the agent who was questionin' me about the murders in Baltimore, and when you came in this house, you didn't even give me a heads up! You ain't no different from the rest of these bitches out here. Get yo' whore ass out my house!" A part of me almost grabbed my hammer from my waist and popped her right there. Deep down inside, I felt she was tryin' to hurt me and was talkin' shit.

"I'm completely different from anyone you ever been with. I'm the only one that had the balls to take your ass down. I can't believe I was starting to feel sorry for you. Trust me, I hope fucking my best friend Shana, that skank Peaches, and all the other hoes you cheated on me with, were well worth it. Once upon a time you were a good man, now I don't know who you are," she said as she ran to her car.

"Bitch, you better hope you bluffin' cuz if I find out you workin' wit' those peoples, you won't make it to court. Bitch, I will bury your whole family. Fuckin' red whore!"

As her car screeched out of the gates, I slammed the door. As soon as I got closer to the steps I heard a lot of commotion upstairs and could hear glass breakin'. Runnin' up the steps I could hear all the noise comin' from Denie's room.

"You fuckin' whore, you were supposed to be my friend," Cheri yelled at Denie. There were red scratches all over her face and neck.

"What the hell is goin' on in here, man?" I asked annoyed.

"That bitch had been fuckin' Allen the entire time y'all were in Florida. He called this morning, saying how stupid I was for befriending such a whore. He called because of all the shit in the media. Juan, I don't know if you've heard, she's fucking HIV positive," Cheri cried with rage.

"So, what? I'm HIV positive. All y'all looking down on me like I'm some type of outcast or something! Javier did this to me. He ruined my life. Cheri, you think I give a fuck about what you or Allen have to say about me? Cheri, you was always jealous of me, always a hater and..."

"Did you fuck him, Denie? Did you fuck him without a condom?" I needed to know.

"You damn right I fucked him raw. Let him bust all up in me, guess that sucks for both of you, huh? Welcome to my world, motherfuckas, the big world of the disease with the little name, HIV. Guess I won't be that lonely after all, hahaha," Denie laughed uncontrollably, rollin' all around on her bed, as if she was just told a funny joke or somethin'.

"Bitch, I'm so fuckin' tired of you. First, you betray me wit' Grady..."

"What the fuck are you talkin' about?"

"Bitch, you was workin' wit' that nigga when he robbed me."

"Nigga, I wish I would've known he was robbing you because then I would've got in on all the action. That nigga owed me money from the bitches I let him fuck," she said with arrogance, wit' that matter-of-fact same face Rich made. No longer able to take another moment of that bitch's mouth, I pulled my .45 caliber from my waist.

"All I did for you bitch, you gonna fuckin' betray me wit' Sadique, and worst of all you deliberately tried to infect me with HIV through Cheri…"

"Don't forget Mecca, too. Charlie was up in this shit, too," she said, as she laid back on her bed with her hands behind her neck, as if she didn't have a care in the world. Her lack of respect for the fact that I had a gun in my hand, showed me that I had to handle my business. Not only for me, but for all she did to my mother. Raisin' the gun up, aimin' straight at her head, I knew what I had to do.

"Juan, what are you doing? Don't do it, she's not worth it," Cheri pleaded.

"Bye Denie, Merry Christmas, Rich," I said as I let off one shot, straight between her eyes. Strangely, I felt no remorse.

"Oh my God, Juan, you killed her. Denie is dead," Cheri sobbed. She stood over her body in disbelief. As I stared at my sister, blood started to drip down her nose, and out of her mouth, I was paralyzed. A weight was lifted. She was finally out of my life.

"Juan, you have to get out of here. I can't risk you going to jail. Juan are you listening to me?" Cheri yelled as she shook me, "Juan, Ariel needs you. You have to leave. Get out of here!"

"No one ever helps me, Cheri. No one ever has my back. You're gonna turn on me too," I said as I raised the gun and put it right under her chin. I couldn't take any chances.

"Juan Sanchez, you listen to me right now. You're my daughter's father, and I love you. We need you. Ariel needs you, and so do I. We are going to be a family. I'm going to love you and treat you like you're supposed to be treated. I swear on my daughter's life. Now, give me the gun, so I can wipe it off, and get rid of it. Juan, you can trust me," Cheri said, lookin' at me with tear filled eyes. Finally, I felt like somebody had my back, and meant it. Handing her over the gun. I grabbed her by the head, and gave her a long seductive, passionate kiss.

"Cheri, I never stopped lovin' you. Thanks."

"Juan, I know."

Comin' to my senses I knew Cheri was right, I had to get outta dodge. As I ran down the spiral stairs, and opened the door I was stopped in my tracks.

"Nigga, you thought you was gonna kill my mother and get away wit' it," Lil' Man said wit a .45 pointed straight at me. Slice was right behind him, muggin'.

"Pop his ass, son, just like I taught you. Do it for your mama," Slice said right before the gun went off.

"Mommy, come quick, Daddy's bleeding!"

Suddenly, my daughter's voice and Cheri's screams faded.

Chapter 29
Rich

"How far away are you, Rich?" Cheri yelled into the phone.

"I'm pullin' up in the ER parkin' lot right now," I said, hangin' up the phone. I was in a state of shock. I couldn't dare lose my son. No matter how much Juan felt like I betrayed him, I still loved him. He was my firstborn.

As I ran through the parkin' lot of Suburban Hospital, frantically I didn't know what to expect. Racin' into the ER waitin' room, I spotted Cheri sittin' over in the corner rockin' back and forth, with BJ and Ariel. I went straight to the nurse's station.

"I need to see my son. He's been shot. His name is Juan Sanchez. Where is he? I need to see him," I demanded.

"Sir, he's in surgery right now. Once the doctors notify us, we will let you know when it's okay to see him," the white nurse said as she continued to answer the phones as if I wasn't important.

Turnin' my attention to Cheri, she spotted me, and made her way towards me.

"Rich, I can't lose Juan, I just can't. I love him," she said as she ran into my arms in tears. As her breast rested on my chest, I knew it was wrong for my dick to be hard, especially at a time like this.

"What the fuck happened? Where's Denie?"

"Rich, Denie is dead," she whispered so that BJ didn't hear her.

"What do you mean my daughter is dead? What do you mean? You just said Juan got shot! My daughter can't be dead. She can't be!"

"I didn't want to tell you about Denie over the phone. They killed her Rich, and then they shot Juan."

"So, how the fuck are you livin'? Huh? You workin' wit' those motherfuckas!"

"How dare you question my love for Juan after all you and Denie did to him? I love him. Me and my daughter need him."

"Bitch, you just now tellin' my son he got a daughter, and I'm supposed to believe you love him!" I yelled, just before a security guard came over, and asked me to lower my voice.

"Look Rich, there's no reason why we should be at each other's throats when we are on the same team...."

"Yea, yea, yea, tell me what the fuck happened!" I demanded from Cheri, the entire story from start to finish, leavin' out no details.

"Some little teenage boy and that rapper dude from Baltimore, Slice, came up in the house looking for Juan. I was in the bathroom and I could hear Denie arguing with somebody. All of a sudden I heard a lot of glass and shit break, and then I heard a gunshot. I got into the tub and called Juan and told him what I heard, and told him to get the kids. All of a sudden I heard Ariel calling my name. I didn't know what to expect. When I came out of the bathroom, I looked down from the top of the stairs and saw Juan laying on the ground bleeding with both of the kids over top of him."

"So, how the fuck you knew that Slice and them shot my kids if you were in the bathroom the whole time?"

"When I came to the bottom of the steps, the guy Charlie was right out front."

"Who is Charlie?"

"The detective that helped Denie get BJ back. Him and some other police officers caught the dudes trying to leave off the property..."

"Hold up. What the hell were they doin' there anyway?" I asked, confused.

"You are not gonna believe this, but that bitch, Mecca was an informant."

"What?"

"She was fucking Charlie the whole time, and Charlie said he was there to lock Juan up for murder. He had a warrant for Juan's arrest. It seemed like it killed him to call an ambulance, to get Juan to the hospital."

"Oh shit. Did they say anythin' about me? Were they lookin' for me? I wonder what that bitch told them."

"No. They just were looking for Juan. I can't lose him. He told me he still loved me," she said as she started crying again.

"Where did they take my daughter? Is she here?"

"No. She died right there. Her body was still at the house when I left."

My heart sunk. Denie was the one thing in my life that I couldn't live without. I loved that girl with every ounce of my body. Tryin' to hold it all together I put on a brave face for her son, even though I was dying inside.

As we walked back over to where the kids were, Ariel and BJ ran by Cheri's side. I hated that this was the first time I had to see my grandkids. They looked just alike, just like me. Ariel reminded me of Denie so much at her age, and BJ looked just like Juan. My eyes started to tear up as I watched them both.

"Mommy, what's wrong?" Ariel questioned as Cheri tried her best to stop cryin' and wipe away her tears.

"I'm okay."

"Hi Ariel and BJ, I'm your grandfather, Rich."

"Our grandfather," BJ asked.

"Yes, you can call me Pop-Pop. Ariel, I'm your Daddy's father…"

"Who, Juan or Allen," she asked, catchin' me off guard.

"Juan is your only Daddy, baby. BJ, I'm your mommy's daddy."

"I thought you were dead. That's what Mommy said. She used to always cry. Yup, I remember you from the pictures," BJ said like he was way beyond his years.

"Naw, BJ, your Pop-Pop ain't goin' nowhere. Your Mommy would want me to always make sure you were good."

"Where is my mommy? She said she wasn't gonna leave me no more. I want my mommy," BJ said as he started to cry. With all he had been through, I knew it was gonna be tough tellin' him his mother was dead. As he held onto my knee I just picked him up, and cried, too. There was nothing that could prevent me from holdin' back my tears. After fighting for my life to get back to my daughter, I couldn't believe she was gone.

"BJ, you gonna be alright. Lil' Man I'm gonna take good care of you," I said as he held me around my neck real tight.

"Did Lamar get my mommy?"

"No BJ, he can never hurt you again, okay. I will make sure nobody ever hurts you again."

"That's what Mommy said."

After a couple of hours of waitin', my patience was wearin' thin. The kids had taken naps and Ariel was up first talkin' about Juan.

"Pop-pop, my daddy said he was Santa Claus and he was gonna buy me a whole bunch of toys," Ariel said full of happiness. She had no clue of what was going on around her.

"I know baby," I said with a smile, hidin' my pain.

"My mommy bought me a whole bunch of toys, too. She said Santa Claus was fake," BJ chimed in.

"That's right, my man. Now let me go and check on your Uncle Juan," I said, walkin' back up to the nurse's station. There was a different nurse on duty.

"Excuse me, ma'am. Do you have an update on Juan Sanchez?"

"Um, sir. He is currently under police surveillance and we aren't able to give any information on this patient," the young white girl said all chipper, with a smile.

"Look, I've been sittin' here patient, waitin' to find out the status of my son's surgery..."

"Oh, I'm sorry I didn't know you were his father. Only parents and if he's married, his wife. What's your name, sir?"

"Juan Sanchez, Sr. Here's my license," I answered, throwin' it at her on the counter.

"Okay thanks. Wait right here and I will get the doctor, so that he can tell you what's going on."

When Cheri walked up and joined me at the nurse's station, we waited together. After a few minutes a young white male doctor approached us, still in scrubs.

"Hello, Mr. Sanchez. I'm Dr. Saltzman."

"Hey, what's goin' on with my boy?"

"We have moved Juan to ICU. His condition is very delicate and the next couple of hours are crucial. He was shot twice in the chest. One of the bullets punctured his lung, ripped his intestines, and crushed his spinal cord. At one point of the surgery his heart stopped and we had to open the breastplate and massage the heart to get it to start beating again. His upper lobe in his lung..."

"Excuse me, I don't understand all that doctor talk. Can you just tell me, is my son gonna die," I interrupted.

"To be honest Mr. Sanchez, it's too early to tell. Right now he is hooked up to a ventilator and an ET tube."

"Is he conscious? Can we see him," Cheri asked anxiously.

"He is conscious, however he cannot talk. Please do not put any stress on him. He's still not out of the woods. I will let you see him for only a few minutes before he is moved, however there can only be two visitors at a time."

"Okay, can we go in now," I asked.

"He has one visitor right now, that means only one of you can come in."

"I know that bitch Mecca didn't weasel her way into his room. When that snitching ass whore comes out here, I'mma fuck her ass up. How did she sneak pass us," Cheri said with rage.

"Look, I'mma go in, and let her know she has to leave. For now, go sit with the kids, and we'll trade off, just so they are supervised."

As Dr. Saltzman led the way to Juan's room, I started to get a little anxious. My nerves started to fuck with me a little, as my head started to rock back and forth.

"Are you okay, sir," the doctor asked.

"Yes, I'm just a little nervous, that's all. I got a lil' condition."

"Oh, okay. Please again sir, not a lot of questions and no stress."

"No problem, I just want to see my son, I'll be quick."

As I walked in, I saw a small frame by Juan's bedside. It was some woman holdin' his hand, with a short edgy haircut, and a long black mink coat. As I got closer I was paralyzed, with disbelief.

"Holy fuck! What are you doin' here?"

Chapter 30
Rich

"Lisa, is it really you? You're alive?" I asked in a state of shock. I couldn't believe what I was seein'.

"Oh, yeah, it's really me," she said as she turned around and looked at me crossing her arms across her chest.

"It can't be," I said, as I got closer.

"Don't come near me or my son."

"I just need to know that you are real. I'll stand back, but I just need to know I'm not trippin'."

"You know what Rich, all this time, who would've thought that we would both cheat death, and find ourselves by our son's bedside praying that he pulls through."

"Lisa, I can't believe..."

"Believe it, Rich. You and my dumb ass mother, God rest her evil soul, thought y'all was going to lock me up in a mental facility, and think I was gonna just go away, out of your hair. I wasn't going out like that."

"You needed help, Lisa. You let Los get you caught up on drugs and ruin you. Man, you fuckin' killed my baby daughter! You smothered an innocent baby."

"God has forgiven me for that. Yes, I was sick, but you still haven't taken responsibility for all you did to me. Rich, you are to blame for my son lying here fighting for his life, and why your daughter's life is fucked up the way it is. It's sad, but that little bitch is just like you."

"Denie's dead, Lisa."

"Damn, that pisses me off. I wanted to be able to look that bitch in the face and let her know all I had done to ruin her miserable, pathetic life."

"What the fuck did you do to my daughter?" I asked, gettin' a little closer as I glanced at Juan. He was wide-awake not takin' his eyes off of Lisa.

"Just some light shit. I just needed her to know, that I was the one haunting her with letters. Shit, the last one to Cornell, really fucked her up, I'm sure," she laughed. Lisa was so different, so emotionless, and unsympathetic.

"Lisa, I just told you my daughter was killed and you…"

"Rich, fuck your daughter! She got what she deserved. Look at my son. Look at my boy. All I wanted was to be a mother again to him. I was waiting for the right time to come back. I was so fixated on fucking Denie's life up, that I lost focus on who needed me most. I might have waited too long. That stupid ass mother of mine knew he was alive for three years and didn't tell me. I could've been back in my son's life a long time ago."

"I don't get it. We had a funeral for you. I saw you in the casket," I said still confused.

"My mother had connections in all the right places; with my father being a pastor and all. Dumb ass, that wasn't really me," she laughed.

"Well, who was it then?"

"Do you think I really give a fuck who it was? All I know is that I made it through it all. Yes, I was once a weak woman that needed a strong man to get me through. Now, I know better. I now realize that I never needed a man to get me through anything. I'm good now, and I will forever be thankful to the woman that saved my life."

"Who?"

"My nurse at the mental institution. Once I attempted to take my life, she came in and was able to save me. My mother thought it was best to move me to St. Louis. Especially since you acted like you didn't give a fuck once she told you I was dead. Yeah, she told me all about the way you acted about the life insurance, that you didn't get. To top it all off, I couldn't believe how you carried on at the repast."

"Lisa, you know I loved you. I was just angry."

"Anyway, so I was moved to St. Louis, where my mother did nothing but try to tear me down. Her and my aunt thought I was gonna just be some type of vegetable or something. They were just concerned about collecting a social security check off of me. The more they tried to tear me down and pump me with meds, the stronger I got."

"I thought your mother had moved down there cuz she was sick."

"Well, now you know, but karma's a bitch, because God always makes a way."

"Lisa, I just can't believe this. How did you know Juan was here? How did you know he got shot?"

"I was about to come and bless him for Christmas. I was looking forward to seeing my son for Christmas Eve. I thought that would be perfect. My waiting period had ended. All I wanted to do was to get back to my son, and destroy your daughter."

"Stop disrespectin' my fuckin' daughter or…"

"What you gonna do Rich, hit me? Haha."

"Say another word, and I just might."

"You're so pathetic, defending that little sick whore. You know what, I can't take no more. I think it's time I let you in on my latest discovery. It's sad, but that little bitch ain't even yours and acts just like you."

"Rich, she's not your daughter. See I did the math. You know being in the crazy house gave me lots of time to think. Once I…"

"What the hell are you talkin' about Lisa?" I interrupted.

"Rich, once upon a time, Marisol and I were friends, best friends. She confided in me and told me Uncle Renzo took her virginity. That was the reason why she went to Puerto Rico. He sent her there. I remember it like it was yesterday."

My blood boiled to the point where I wanted to hit Lisa. "You don't know what you're talkin' about. She looks just like me."

"I thought you would say that. So I did a little digging, and found this diary of Marisol's hidden in Los' old Porsche in the backyard. She told me a long time ago, that's where to go anytime I needed the spare key. As soon as I opened the glove box, the diary was right there, as if someone had placed it there, just for me."

"Denie is my daughter! I don't believe you!"

"Rich, my instinct was right. I couldn't wait to get in town to see if I was right. I just had to be sure." Lisa laughed as she pulled out this blinged out notebook out of her Louis Vuitton oversized bag, and threw it at me across the room. Pickin' the book up from the floor, I opened it. There was a velvet ribbon laid between the pages. As I started readin' my heart dropped to my ankles.

Lorenzo died today. A part of me was sad, but then I felt relieved. Was it normal to feel sad for the man that raped me as a teenager and took my virginity? Afterall, he was my daughter

Denie's biological father. There was no way I could let my husband Los know, so Rich was the one that I had to pin the baby on. Now that Renzo was dead, my deepest, darkest secret died with him. No longer was that dark cloud following me. Rich would be devastated and kill me if he ever knew Denie wasn't really his. It was so ironic how much she looked like him, but I guess those Sanchez genes were strong...

What the fuck? This can't be. Denie looks just like me, I whispered to myself as I fell to the floor in shock. The little girl that I raised and loved, it couldn't be. How could that bitch Marisol do that shit to me? After 21 years. How could this happen? As I started to shake, my head pounded, as tears filled my eyes. That conivin' ass Marisol, was hauntin' me from her grave. My blood boiled and rage filled my soul. Extreme anger came over me, as I envisioned digging up Marisol's body and breakin' up whatever was left of her corpse. I wanted to hunt her mother down in Puerto Rico and kill that slut for not swallowin' that trick Marisol. The pain I felt in my heart burned deep. Denie was my world, all that I lived for. She was my life. I didn't know what hurt more, her being gone, or me findin' out my love for her, was all built on a lie.

"Now I bet your ass wished you would've taken a blood test, but you ain't wanna listen. You kept going off looks. "*She looks just like me*," she taunted.

"Bitch, I should kill you!" I said jumpin' up ready to attack, until she pulled out a .25 little pistol, and aimed it straight at me.

"You know what? I don't think you are in the position to talk shit to me."

"Why not? Because you on some new, strong, black woman shit. Bitch, fuck you. A part of me was just happy to see you, and then I stopped feelin' with my dick. You ain't shit, and ain't never gonna be shit, you dope snortin', baby killin'..."

"What else, Rich?" she asked, pointin' the gun at me.

"Lisa, slow down. Be easy. Don't pull no gun on me, unless you gonna use it."

"Some things never change. You still that arrogant nigga you've always been. It's funny because when I found out you were dead, I was hurt. Now look at you, your nerves all fucked up, making noises and shit, rocking that empty ass head of yours from side to side. I know now that was me feeling with my heart. Now I use my brain."

"I never thought you had one."

"Oh, I gotta hell of a brain. My brain was what made the last month of your worthless daughter, haha I mean Denie's life a living hell. Now my brain is gonna be what helps me put together my story on why I had to kill you."

"Lisa, what are you doin'? Come on man, that ain't for us. Look at Juan, you want to kill him, the doctor said no stress. He's still not out of the woods yet."

"Don't bitch out now Rich, it doesn't look good on you."

"I ain't never a bitch. I just don't want you to put no stress on my son while he fights for his life."

"Rich, I'm positive that Juan would be happy to see me blow your fucking head off your shoulders. I mean damn, I think this shit was meant to be, it was supposed to happen just like this. Let's see here, if I kill you, I could plead insanity, or maybe self-defense. Either way, the world would be a better place without you. Don't you want to join Denie in hell? Now that you know she's not your daughter, maybe you can fuck her…"

"Man Lisa, who the fuck are you?" I asked, tryin' to stall her, hopin' someone would walk in and catch her holdin' me at gun point.

"Not the same dumb ass Lisa, that I used to be. Look Rich, you're gonna die tonight, so it's really no need for us to keep going back and forth. I've been yearning to put a bullet in you, ever since I saw your face the other night."

"You wouldn't. Not while…" before I could say another word, Lisa emptied three shots into my body, and the last one in my head. I thought about all the people I loved; Juan, Denie, Honey, and strangely, Lisa. In deep pain, I knew it was my time to go. Along with the Sanchez name, the room went dark.

Epilogue

Damn Ma, if only you could hear my thoughts. I was tryin' to stop you. Now look what you've done. That nigga Rich wasn't worth it. He was gonna kill himself eventually. A nigga like Rich, would die, just when he least expected. Shit, I guess that's what just happened. As I watched the police run into my hospital room, I started to feel my body tremble a little. The female officer grabbed my mother and threw her to the ground, as if she was some type of criminal, as Rich's body was rushed out of the room.

"He was tryin' to kill me. I had to protect myself. My son will tell you. He saw everything," she said right before she was carried out of my room. My mother was alive the whole time. My grandmother was right. When she first came into my room, I thought I'd died, until I felt her touch my face. But, deep down I knew it was true, I felt her spirit all along.

Damn, I had to beat this. I cheated death before, I could do it again. I promised my daughter, Ariel a Christmas filled with lots of toys and presents. Cheri needed me. We were gonna be a family. I was gonna take care of BJ, too. Shit, it was sad that God gave him the parents that he had. He was a good kid. Now that I know Denie was never my sister, just a cousin, I don't feel as bad for killin' her ass.

As I tried to keep my eyes open, I started to feel a tremendous amount of pressure fill my chest. All of a sudden it felt as though the air was bein' sucked out of my lungs. Damn, I felt this feelin' before. It was too familiar and more than ever, I wasn't ready to go. Finally, I had way too much to live for. I was gonna have a family and my mother was alive. I couldn't leave now. Not when the women in my life needed me. Wait a minute, what's that long loud beepin' noise. Shit, it's so fuckin' loud, and I can't open my eyes. This can't be happenin'. Not now. What the fuck? Flatline?

Also by Miss Kp:

Paparazzi

Other HOT LCB Titles:

Game Over by Winter Ramos
Mistress Loose by Kendall Banks
Welfare Grind by Kendall Banks
My Counterfeit Husband by Carla Pennington
Kiss of Death by Chris Renee

CHECK OUT THESE LCB SEQUELS

053631074

ORDER FORM

MAIL TO:
PO Box 423
Brandywine, MD 20613
301-362-6508

Date:	Phone:
Email:	

Ship to:	
Address:	
City & State:	Zip:

Make all money orders and cashiers checks payable to: **Life Changing Books**

Qty.	ISBN	Title	Release Date	Price
	0-9741394-2-4	Bruised by Azarel	Jul-05	$ 15.00
	0-9741394-7-5	Bruised 2: The Ultimate Revenge by Azarel	Oct-06	$ 15.00
	0-9741394-3-2	Secrets of a Housewife by J. Tremble	Feb-06	$ 15.00
	0-9741394-6-7	The Millionaire Mistress by Tiphani	Nov-06	$ 15.00
	1-934230-99-5	More Secrets More Lies by J. Tremble	Feb-07	$ 15.00
	1-934230-95-2	A Private Affair by Mike Warren	May-07	$ 15.00
	1-934230-96-0	Flexin & Sexin Volume 1	Jun-07	$ 15.00
	1-934230-89-8	Still a Mistress by Tiphani	Nov-07	$ 15.00
	1-934230-91-X	Daddy's House by Azarel	Nov-07	$ 15.00
	1-934230-88-X	Naughty Little Angel by J. Tremble	Feb-08	$ 15.00
	1-934230820	Rich Girls by Kendall Banks	Oct-08	$ 15.00
	1-934230839	Expensive Taste by Tiphani	Nov-08	$ 15.00
	1-934230782	Brooklyn Brothel by C. Stecko	Jan-09	$ 15.00
	1-934230669	Good Girl Gone bad by Danette Majette	Mar-09	$ 15.00
	1-934230804	From Hood to Hollywood by Sasha Raye	Mar-09	$ 15.00
	1-934230707	Sweet Swagger by Mike Warren	Jun-09	$ 15.00
	1-934230677	Carbon Copy by Azarel	Jul-09	$ 15.00
	1-934230723	Millionaire Mistress 3 by Tiphani	Nov-09	$ 15.00
	1-934230715	A Woman Scorned by Ericka Williams	Nov-09	$ 15.00
	1-934230685	My Man Her Son by J. Tremble	Feb-10	$ 15.00
	1-924230731	Love Heist by Jackie D.	Mar-10	$ 15.00
	1-934230812	Flexin & Sexin Volume 2	Apr-10	$ 15.00
	1-934230748	The Dirty Divorce by Miss KP	May-10	$ 15.00
	1-934230758	Chedda Boyz by CJ Hudson	Jul-10	$ 15.00
	1-934230766	Snitch by VegasClarke	Oct-10	$ 15.00
	1-934230693	Money Maker by Tonya Ridley	Oct-10	$ 15.00
	1-934230774	The Dirty Divorce Part 2 by Miss KP	Nov-10	$ 15.00
	1-934230170	The Available Wife by Carla Pennington	Jan-11	$ 15.00
	1-934230774	One Night Stand by Kendall Banks	Feb-11	$ 15.00
	1-934230278	Bitter by Danette Majette	Feb-11	$ 15.00
	1-934230299	Married to a Balla by Jackie D.	May-11	$ 15.00
	1-934230308	The Dirty Divorce Part 3 by Miss KP	Jun-11	$ 15.00
	1-934230316	Next Door Nympho By CJ Hudson	Jun-11	$ 15.00
	1-934230286	Bedroom Gangsta by J. Tremble	Sep-11	$ 15.00
	1-934230340	Another One Night Stand by Kendall Banks	Oct-11	$ 15.00
	1-934230359	The Available Wife Part 2 by Carla Pennington	Nov-11	$ 15.00
	1-934230332	Wealthy & Wicked by Chris Renee	Jan-12	$ 15.00
	1-934230375	Life After a Balla by Jackie D.	Mar-12	$ 15.00
	1-934230251	V.I.P. by Azarel	Apr-12	$ 15.00
	1-934230383	Welfare Grind by Kendall Banks	May-12	$ 15.00
	1-934230413	Still Grindin' by Kendall Banks	Sep-12	$ 15.00
	1-934230391	Paparazzi by Miss KP	Oct-13	$ 15.00
	1-93423043X	Cashin' Out by Jai Nicole	Nov-12	$ 15.00
	1-934230634	Welfare Grind Part 3 by Kendall Banks	Mar-13	$15.00
	1-934230642	Game Over by Winter Ramos	Apr-13	$15.99
			Total for Books	$
			Shipping Charges (add $4.95 for 1-4 books*)	$
			Total Enclosed (add lines)	$

*** Prison Orders- Please allow up to three (3) weeks for delivery.**

Please Note: We are not held responsible for returned prison orders. Make sure the facility will receive books before ordering.

***Shipping and Handling of 5-10 books is $6.95, please contact us if your order is more than 10 books. (301)362-6508**